THE MANHATTAN RED RIBBON KILLER

A JOEY MANCUSO, FATHER O'BRIAN CRIME MYSTERY BOOK 3

By Owen Parr

COPYRIGHT

A Joey Mancuso and Father O'Brian Crime Mystery Published by Owen Parr

ISBN: 9781979273800

Published in United States

DEDICATION

To New York's First Responders &
The spirit of New Yorker's "New York Strong"

QUOTE

"Murder is not about lust and it's not a about violence. It's about possession."

Theodore Roberts Bundy—Convicted and executed serial killer, kidnapper, rapist, burglar, and necrophile.

PROLOGUE

Ten days passed, and the NYPD still had found no clues to what they quietly tagged as "The Case of the Manhattan Red Ribbon Killer." They racked their brains over the small amount of evidence, hoping to find something that would bring them closer to a breakthrough in the mysterious and brutal deaths of three young professional ladies. The MO, or modus operandi, was the same. They were killed in their Manhattan apartments. At first, it appeared like a case of extreme sex gone wrong. Choking during sex led to the accidental death of the first victim, followed by the partner vanishing. Ditto for the second and third victims. While the form of sex and the choking seemed consensual with the first victim, the last two were entirely different. Strangulation and breasts sliced in the shape of a cross.

My brother, Father Dominic O'Brian, Associate Pastor at Saint Helens' Church in Brooklyn and a part-time private investigator like and me. I had was just hired as consultants to the NYPD's Homicide Division—my old precinct in New York City.

I'm Giuseppe Mancuso, but everyone knows me as Joey. After sixteen years in the NYPD, I had reached the status of First Grade Detective. During my last year at the force, I pissed off some politicos with juice. In response to my supposed "lack of proper police procedures," the IAD, or Internal Affairs Division concocted some charges against me to an end style of bringing the perps to justice. Admittedly, I'm not without sin. Regardless, every one of my cases led to a clean conviction and for me, justice for the victims. As an NYPD detective, I had the best ratio of solved cases in all of New York City, and even better, I took pride in having earned the moniker "The Last Advocate" for the victim.

Captain Alex Johnson had asked my brother, Dom, and me to consult for the NYPD after getting the go-ahead from Police Commissioner O'Malley and, I'm sure, the New York Mayor himself. It was like a -we owe you kind of gesture after our PI investigations solved three homicides that the NYPD had overlooked last year.

My brother, Dom, and I were paired off with First Grade Detective, Mrs. Lucy Roberts, my former partner whom I lovingly called Lucifer. Lucy had one more year to put in before she could call it quits. I was excited to be working with her again. When I was a rookie detective, she had been my mentor. Grooming me to be relentless in pursuing perps and to in bringing justice to the vics.

CHAPTER 1

As promised, I made it into my old precinct, Midtown Precinct South, by eight in the morning. This was a coveted post to work from. Many of the officers who served here ended up being top brass. Known as 'a union house,' they heavily influenced the precinct. Or should I say controlled by the Police Benevolent Association. Right now, that was neither here nor there. I was back, and I loved it.

'Never enough layers, Joey,' my mom used to say. Her words still ring through just as they did back then. I was happy to be indoors in the precinct's warmth. The thirty-degree city temperature made me shiver like a swimmer whose body smacks into the cold air after basking in a heated pool.

It was Monday, and the phones were ringing off the hook. I immediately felt at home. A steady stream of energy was constant in the station—people coming and going, perps being interrogated, others filing complaints, the colorful lady pros always insisting it was merely consensual and all. The lingering scent—the smell of burnt coffee, left- over food, and other usual mystery odors that hung heavy in the detective squad was still there, just as I remembered it. Nothing much had changed since my year's absence. After some handshakes and well wishes from the old gang, I sat in a stark conference room waiting for Lucy.

Usually, the SVD, or Special Victims Division, would handle a sex crime. Since this was a hushed investigation, it got handed over to 'Homicide'. They assigned me to work with Detectives Farnsworth and Charles. In my world, I had specific terms of endearment for these two macho dicks, Cagney and Lacey—like from the television series about two lady detectives back in the 1980s. Farnsworth and Charles were neither excited to see me nor appreciative of my sense of humor. Detective Farnsworth is an old-timer with a thick, rough Brooklyn accent. In his late fifties, he's tall—maybe six two, broad shoulders, thinning blonde hair. While he stays in shape, his girth was sprouting. Perhaps from too many beers at the Hudson Station Bar and Grill across from the precinct. He was, also, an asshole, in my respectful opinion.

Detective Charles had been a partner of mine for a time. At forty, just a few years older than me, he comes in at about five feet ten inches. Aside from the short cropped black hair and large ears that stick out like two cable TV reception dishes on either side of his head, he was developing a beer belly like Farns. When not with Farns, Charles could be a nice guy. But for some reason, when they paired up, he'd turn into asshole numero dos.

Farnsworth walked into the meagerly decorated conference room. The only embellishments were two pictures hanging on the wall—the Mayor and one of Police Commissioner, O'Malley. I was reviewing the murder book when Farns welcomed me back to the precinct... "So, Mancuso, here you are, again. Isn't that... special?" His raspy smoker's voice couldn't mask his plastic excitement. It was a question that he didn't want me to answer.

"Happy to see you, too, Detective," I replied, returning the gesture without looking up.

"Have you solved the case yet?" His question was laced with sarcasm.

I could see this headed in the wrong direction, and I had only been here thirty minutes.

"Listen, we can do this in two ways. Either we collide at every turn and fuck each other up. Or, we work together and try to solve this case before any of us get killed. Have it your way. Just let me know which way to go."

Farnsworth moved closer to me; too close, unfortunately. Close enough that I could tell he had inhaled an onion bagel before walking into the conference room. My dad had a phrase for breath like that, 'alito puzzolente', bad breath."

"As long as you know who is lead in this investigation and who calls the shots. Then, we should not quote, unquote, collide as you say, Mancuso."

Yep. Good ole asshole Farns. I let that go. I didn't want to battle with this guy now. "Tell me about the case," I said, as I ignored his little tirade and I turned my face to locate and inhale fresh air.

Farns panned the room as if he was looking for someone. He was. "So, ... is your brother, the priest, joining us today?"

I didn't know if he was mocking Dom or not. "My brother, Father Dominic, works with me as much as he can. His church duties are a priority. I'll fill him in later."

"Very well. I suppose you want to start with victim number one. Hand me the book," It must have felt good to command me about as he pointed to the murder book. He promptly sat down. "You mind if I smoke?"

What an idiot! Smoking is not allowed inside these buildings. "You mind if I fart?" I replied.

"What's with the attitude? Just tell me if it bothers you," he retorted.

"Knock yourself out, sport. Can you start with victim one?"
"Odette Romano. Italian, like yourself. Twenty-nine years old.

Associate attorney at Mars and Samson—a law firm in Midtown. Single. No record of any kind."

"What did she look like?"

"Like shit when we first saw her," He was trying to be funny as he lit a filtered cigarette. He's trying, all right. Like trying my patience.

Seeing my deadpan expression, he frowned and looked down at the book again. "Cute young lady, about five six, long brown hair, hazel eyes, perfect figure. You can see for yourself here. What else can I tell you about her?"

"How was she found?" They loaded me with questions.

"Her neighbor, another lady attorney, knocked on her door in the morning ten days ago. It seems they ride the subway together. Hearing no response, she called her on the cell. After many attempts, she called the police."

Notice, I had asked Farnsworth 'how' not 'who.' The biggest problem we have in the world today is poor communication. We might avoid wars if we could only understand each other. I, inconspicuously, rolled my eyes before I went on, "Then, what?"

He let out an enormous cloud of gray smoke that just hung there in front of his face. "The uniforms on the scene called the building super, and he opened the door. She was dead on her bed, naked and faced down. Her legs extended over and down at the end of the bed. You get the picture?"

I ignored his question, but yes, I got the picture. "What caused death?"

"The medical examiner determined COD as strangulation with a satin ribbon, like the ones used to wrap a gift package. No ribbon found, though, but there were small threads of red satin material detected around her neck."

"Was the ME Doctor Frankie?"

"Yeah, Doctor Death."

"What else did he conclude?"

"The rape kit showed only anal sex. No semen found. Doctor Frankie assumes the killer was standing behind her. She was facing down—" Farns paused, "when he entered her from behind, and,"

I interrupted, "You said he. Do we know that to be a fact?"

Farnsworth gave me a hard stare and let out one of those hesitated sighs—the kind that comes with the 'how dare you question my abilities' type of look. "No, that was my conclusion."

Incredibly, he's reaching conclusions now. "Go on."

"Okay, so, she's faced down, the killer is behind her, like this," he says, standing in front of the conference table mimicking the act.

I interrupted his demonstration, "You don't have to act it out. Save that for show and tell later when the rest of the class shows up. Go on."

Taking the cigarette out of his mouth, he added, "Okay. So, then the killer takes the ribbon, about half an inch thick according to the contusions found on her neck and begins the choking process." He stopped to look at me. "You know, they say that many do this."

"What? Using a ribbon?" I knew where he was going with this. I played along but refused to make eye contact.

"No, choking the female partner during sex with a ribbon, or a belt, whatever he or she can find. Supposedly, the lack of oxygen makes the female reach orgasm quicker. Did you know that Mancuso?"

"Yes, it's called erotic asphyxiation. It, also, works for men. You should try it next time, Farnsworth." Maybe his wife might pull too tight and rid me of this guy.

"Don't want anyone squeezing my neck during sex. Fuck no, thank you. Do you do this shit?"

Another one of his asinine questions I ignored. "Go on.

"This ratchet lady, probably, thought this was just part of the sex. However, the perp strangles her while still inside her."

"Any defensive wounds?" I inquired.

"None. That's why we think the sex was consensual. Until the end, of course."

"So what? The killer leaves?"

"It seems that way. The apartment cleaned, nothing found," he said, putting out the cigarette in a paper coffee cup he brought with him.

"Did you say clean or cleaned?"

"You love little f-en details. Don't you, Mancuso?"

"I find them important. So?"

"Frankly, it looked as if a maid had gone through the place, except for the signature triangle on the toilet paper, maids' leave to make sure, you know they were there. You know what I'm talking about, Mancuso?"

"Yes, I've stayed in hotels. Do we know if the killer rapes them post-mortem?"

"No, but maybe, ask the ME that question." "What about prints? DNA? Anything?"

"Nothing. The killer was meticulous not to leave anything behind. He wiped everything clean."

"No hairs on the bed? Saliva? Anything?"

"Nothing, man. This guy must be suffering from an obsessive-compulsive personality disorder," Farnsworth added. "He cleaned everything. Nothing seemed touched or moved."

Seriously, Farns? I didn't know you could handle big words like that.

I bit my lip hard before asking my next question, "Let me see the photo of her." I wanted to see the position they left her in. Farnsworth slid the book over.

I glanced at the picture of Odette, victim number one. The first picture was from behind. She was facing down on the bed, her legs spread and dangling from the end of the bed, totally naked. With no ligature marks on her ankles or wrists, I assumed they were not tied to the corners of the bed. Then I looked at the side view photos. She faced to her right with eyes wide opened. If I ignored her bug-eyed expression, I could see that she had been a very nice-looking young lady.

"So, there is no trace of the killer anywhere. What about her anal cavity?"

"Some jell and feces, which we know is hers," Farns replied. "Anything in the bathrooms?"

"Like I said, nothing. Wiped clean."

"Then, he's done this before. To be so meticulous and leave nothing behind, he takes his time after he kills them. Very deliberate."

"I agree." Farnsworth turned toward, nodding affirmatively.

I had his attention. "Did you canvas the other apartments? Anybody see or hear anything?"

"We did, Mancuso. It's all there in the murder book. Her neighbor and friend, the one who called it in, was out that night. One older lady says she knocked on our vic's door at around nine in the evening, but no one answered."

"What did she want?"

"She was bringing her a homemade apple pie."

"And?"

"And, nothing. She knocked. No one responded. So, she left."
"Did she leave the pie by the door?"

"No, she took it back to her place. But she says she came back at eleven that night and knocked again. No one was home."

"What was the TOD?"

"The ME estimated time of death to be between ten in the evening and one in the morning. Since they did not find her until the next day, estimation was difficult."

"Was the apartment cold? I mean, was the air conditioner turned on?"

"I don't remember that detail. It's winter outside, Mancuso. Why would anyone want to have the air on? That makes no sense."

I didn't reply. These details set me apart from other dingbat detectives. Reading stories from Sir Arthur Conan Doyle's Sherlock Holmes taught me to be creative and look beyond the obvious. I decided I would pose my question to the ME since a cold apartment would keep the body from decomposing with little or no detection of smell until many hours later. This tactic would delay the police from finding out about the murder. That said, it was a good thing the neighbor called it in. Detectives Charles and my old partner, detective, Lucy Roberts, walked into the conference room.

Charles sniffed the room as he walked in. He glanced at Farns and shook his head. I don't know if he was showing disapproval for the scent of cigarette smoke. Or, if he had detected the aroma of the onion bagel his partner smelled like.

"Well, good morning, ladies. Glad you could join us," I said, smiling and moving into hug Lucy.

"Welcome back, Mancuso," Charles said in a modulated singsong fashion, as was his custom.

"Thank you," I replied, letting go of Lucy and extending a hand to Charles. Lucy, who was in her late fifties, never looks her age. She has a fresh face. Not to mention, her beautiful smile and sparkling white teeth. She must have been a real hottie in her earlier years. African American and born in the South, she was very proud of her ancestry. I always got a smile from her every time I said, "I love Lucy." She was like my second mom. I have always had the highest respect for her.

"How is Mr. Roberts?" I asked, glancing back at Lucy.

"Sweetie, he is just fine. Said to give you his best," Lucy replied with her silvery sound. "How about Marcy? How is she doing?"

This was not the time to talk about Marcy. I kept it short and to the point. "She's fine. Just fine."

Lucy got the message and probed no further.

Captain Johnson walked in, raised his nose in the air, and pulled in a few sniffs. Then, he said in his crotchety fashion, "No time for a reunion party, we have another body. Same MO. Get going."

CHAPTER 2

We walked out of the precinct, and I jumped in the car with Lucy. She was still driving a brown Crown Victoria. The same one we had shared back when we were partners. Since parking was limited, I couldn't believe where she had parked her vehicle. Right in front of the precinct on the side- walk next to the fire hydrant—a spot reserved for police cars. Like it was her usual routine, she backed up and off the walkway. Making a left turn on West 9th Avenue, we made our way to the crime scene.

I was itching to research the murder book for information on the other two ladies. But since there was a fresh murder scene waiting for us, I had to hold off.

"Just like old times, Joey."

"Yeah, other than we have three dead ladies, it feels good, Lucy. How are your three boys?"

"Growing fast. Soon, they will all be on their own. No more allowances, baby, no more college tuitions. After that, Harry and I can relax. I'll hang my shield in one year and become a pensioner."

"Moving to Florida?" I added.

"Flo-ri-da? No way, honey! We want to be close to the guys. Plus, we're too young to be snowbirds. We'll see where the boys end up. That's when we'll decide."

"If you stay in the area, you're welcome to join us." I couldn't pass up on the invitation. "We could always use a dedicated detective."

"Hmm ... that actually could be fun, Joey. I'll keep that in mind. She paused for a moment. I had a feeling I knew what was coming up next.

"So, you going to tell me what's up with Marcy? I noticed you didn't want to go into details before."

"Marcy, Marcy. My very special FBI Special Agent. We've been together for two years. Twice we talked about marriage. Then, I got shot, as you know."

"Oh, I won't forget that. We answered the call on that one. Go on."

"Well, the whole situation made her think twice about marriage, kind of like the same way I look at dessert with whipped cream."

Lucy gave me a strange look. Okay, it wasn't the best analogy; I admit. It was the only thing I could come up with now. "Anyway, you know she lost her dad in Nam. At that time, they deployed her brother in Iraq. Marcy and her mom worried non-stop until he came back. Long story short, she has this fear of me not coming home one day."

Lucy was listening, quietly. I could tell that she was processing all the information. I continued. "Well, there's more. Marcy got shot in the arm last month while on a plane at Newark. Even though she's recovering nicely, the chances of her losing significant movement in her right arm are high. That means when she comes back from medical leave, she may not pass the FBI's required firearms curriculum. That has her pissed, not to mention, depressed, too."

"Not to change the subject, but that was one hell of a heroic act she pulled on that plane. I mean, two terrorists inside a closed airplane with long firearms. Shit, man, that could have been a massacre if she and the deceased US Federal Marshal hadn't prevented it."

"Yes, it was," I let out a long sigh, replaying the horrific scene that could have ended her life. "Right now, she's working on her physical rehabilitation. I just wish she would visit the shrink to help her deal with shooting a man to death. I think there are deeper implications, if a person doesn't deal with something like that."

"Give her time, give her time. Tell me, are you working with her on the FBI firearms qualifications?"

"Marcy went into a mild depression while at the hospital. I think the idea of losing her ability to work in the field, coupled with my new opportunities—you know, the consulting gig with the NYPD, and the work with the attorneys at Bevans and Associates made her a little resentful." I paused. "So, Marcy asked that we take some time apart from each other."

"She did?" Lucy asked, surprised.

"I'm giving her space as requested. Just calling once a week for now."

"Baby, that's your skinny ass soul mate. You told me that before. Don't give up on her."

Marcy did not have a skinny ass by any means. I know, for a fact. But Lucy always called her that. "I don't plan to, but it takes two to tango, right? And by the way, for the record, I never called her my skinny ass soul mate. Just my soul mate."

Lucy laughed hard, flashing those brilliant white teeth of hers. "She'll be fine. Just wait and see. She'll come back to you."

I nodded in the affirmative, and added, "In the meantime, do you remember Marcy's new partner, Special Agent Tony Belford? He's been around here for about three weeks. Well, I think he is trying to move in on her."

"What a stiff-necked asshole! What's up with him?"

"GQ Tony. That's what I call him. Perfect body, perfect shape, not one blonde hair out of place, a flawless fashioned pencil mustache. He might even wear a blue cape with red FBI emblazoned on it underneath his tailored Armani suits. Yeah, he's an asshole all right—right out of FBI central casting. He's taken over her cases, and he's the one helping her at the range."

"The hell with him. He's no Joey Mancuso," she said, smiling and glancing over at me again.

"We'll see. In the meantime, Cagney and Lacey don't look thrilled with me on this case." I looked out the window at the apartment in front of us.

"Farnsworth and Charles have their issues. But honey, they'll just have to get over them 'cause we're on the case, too. By the way, Joey," Lucy said, as she pulled into a parking spot, "no one in the precinct's homicide division has come close to your ratio of solving cases. Every- one's still trying."

"And this is one reason why I love you, Lucy." She lightly smacked me on the backside of my head before we got out of the car.

There was a slight mist in New York City. It was cold and down to the mid-twenties. You'd think by now I'd know to wear enough layers, but I didn't. Again. I could hear my mother's words niggling at the back of my head. As I got out of the car, I felt I was walking in the Alaskan tundra. Lucy and I headed over to where the two detectives were standing. The four of us walked to the scene of the murder. Two uniforms had secured the scene. CSU had not arrived yet but were expected any minute. We put on latex gloves and booties, registered with the uniform by the front door, and entered the well- appointed apartment unit in Midtown.

"Who discovered the body?" I asked a very tall and gangly uniformed officer whose name tag read 'Sanchez'.

"The building manager did, sir. The victim's office called when she didn't show up for work. They said she had never been late for work in two years. After trying to call her to no avail, they called the manager of the apartments."

Lucy asked Sanchez, "Did the manager disturb the scene?"

"No, detective. He says he stopped at the door to the bedroom when he saw the body," Sanchez replied, eyeing her detective shield.

"Did anyone hear anything?" I asked.

Sanchez turned to me, trying to find my shield, "My partner, Edwards, is knocking on doors. So far, we have nothing."

"She's as cold and stiff as Alaskan King crab on ice," Farnsworth said, after gently examining the body.

"We'll wait for the coroner to verify, but this probably took place last night. She's already gone into rigor mortis," added Detective Charles.

I walked around the apartment. I detected a strong cologne scent. I doubted anyone else picked up on that. Just to make sure, I asked to meet the manager who had opened the door. I could confirm that he was not wearing any cologne. As he approached me, I deduced that Mr. Bullard, the manager, had eaten corned beef hash and eggs for breakfast. Not sure on the type of toast or how the eggs were prepared. The temperature in the apartment was cold, maybe in the low sixties. As I looked around, I noticed nothing was out of place. No drinking glasses. Zero disturbed. All her clothes were in the closet and mail was neatly stacked on the kitchen counter.

"Her name is Margaret Tobias," I called out. "She works for Knell and Slovak, Attorneys at Law."

Farnsworth asked, "How did you get that?"

I replied from the living room, "Her mail and pay stub are on the kitchen counter."

Farnsworth added, "Same MO. Naked, facing down. Her legs extended over the end of the bed. I can see blood pooling under her chest. Same as the last two."

Sanchez looked surprised and asked, "The other two?"

Lucy looked at Sanchez, "Keep that to yourself, Officer Sanchez."

"There's a serial killer?" Sanchez asked me in a hushed manner.

I nodded and put my index finger to my lips. Glancing at Farnsworth, I said, "You said blood pooling under her breasts like the last two. Explain."

"Yeah," Farns replied, "you haven't seen the murder book on the second and third victims. The same MO. Except the first one didn't have her breasts cut as a cross."

"Shit, it's freaking cold in here. Turn the AC off, would you? And close that window. Where the hell is the coroner?" Charles asked, annoyed.

"Please, don't touch the air conditioning switch. Take a picture. Dust for prints around and on the air conditioner switch. Also, on the window that's opened," I said, quickly.

Lucy turned to me, "What do you think?"

"I haven't looked at the other scenes. Just the photos of the first murder. But from what you guys are saying, do you think this fits in with the others?"

"Yes," replied Lucy.

I looked at our newest victim. Young and good-looking Margaret Tobias lay there naked, face down, and very dead. Indeed, there was blood pooling from under her breasts. She, probably, went to a bar after work, planned on having a few drinks and maybe dinner, but not this. "So, the couple came in. She undressed and put her clothes away. Or maybe the perp did that for her. They must have gone directly into the bedroom because there's nothing in the living room or kitchen. Nothing in the dishwasher, either. They disturbed no cushions on the sofa. Nada. It's like no one had been here."

"There're signs of strangulation on her neck. No question. This is number four," Farnsworth added, wanting to be part of the discovery.

"No one heard a thing, and no one saw anything." Officer Edwards, the second officer on the scene who was a little too hefty for the tapered uniform shirt he was wearing, walked in and put in his two cents' worth. He was, also, not wearing any cologne.

"Any cameras at the entrance of the building?" Charles asked, glancing at Sanchez.

Sanchez had just opened his mouth when I replied, "None anywhere."

Charles turned to me with an inquisitive 'what the fuck?' look.

I gave Charles a hard stare in return. "I checked that as we walked in. No cameras anywhere."

Charles nodded and quickly glanced at Farnsworth. In my peripheral vision, I could see a smile growing on Lucy's face.

"Anything in the bathroom?" Charles asked to no one in particular. I waited for someone to reply, but seeing that no one did, I said, "Clean as if the maid had been here. Towels are dry. Same with the shower. No condoms. Toilet and trash cans are both clean."

Farnsworth asked, "So, this couple walk in, go directly to the bedroom, undress, and start having sex? No drinks or foreplay anywhere? No Sinatra or wine?"

Charles asked, "Could our perp be drugging our victims before they get here?"

"Did they do a toxicology report on the other three?" I asked.
"They did," Lucy replied. "They found no drugs in their system."
"Right. I forgot about that," Charles replied, slightly
embarrassed.

There are days I wonder how he ever got into detective work. I
swear he sits on his brains more than he uses them.

"What did they find?" I inquired while restraining myself from
bopping Charles hard on the backside of his head.

Farnsworth responded, "All three victims had been drinking
alcoholic beverages. Victim one, sōchū. Number two, white wine
and vic three, saké. All had Chinese type food in their stomachs."

"What kind of Chinese food?" I asked.

"That raw fish stuff. Sushi," replied Farnsworth. "That's
Japanese.

Sushi is Japanese," I said.

"Same shit. Japanese. Chinese. They're all slant-eyed,"
Farnsworth retorted.

Lucy asked me in a hushed tone, "What's that tell you?"

That Farnsworth is a racist asshole. Instead, I replied, "The perp
takes them to the same place. A place he, or she knows."

"Exactly," Lucy said, as her eyes widened.

I asked Lucy, "Does the ME's report show stomach contents?"

"It does, but I don't remember exactly what it says," she replied.
"Perfect," I replied, "I'll examine that once we are back."

The coroner finally arrived with the CSU crew, and they began
doing their thing.

"Lucy, please, ask the coroner to estimate TOD," I said.

Lucy went over to the coroner. "Hon give us an approximate
time of death. Would you, Ed?"

After a few minutes, tinted blue-haired and right earring wearing
Ed came over to Lucy. He was whistling a tune like he didn't
have a care in the world. "Detective, I estimate TOD to be
between eleven last night and two in the morning. You want a
COD?"

"Eddy, baby, I think we know the cause of death. Unless you think it's different than strangulation."

"We'll know better after I perform an autopsy, but strangulation seems the right call. This is victim four, right?" Ed asked.

"Seems that way," Lucy replied.

I had seen enough. I wanted to get back and finish reviewing the murder book for the first three victims. "Lucy, let's go back to the precinct. I need to research this better."

We left the scene, bidding farewell to the other detectives and wishing them luck.

Entering her car, Lucy said, "I'm so glad you're back working with me. I'm going to enjoy my last year. You have such a knack for this work."

"Everything I learned, I learned from you," I replied.

"Honey, maybe you learned the relentless pursuit of the perps and the need to bring justice to the vics from me. But let me tell you, your style and ability to see what no one else sees is uncanny. Uncanny. That's all yours, baby."

"Those who apply themselves can learn to observe versus just look- ing. I don't look. I scrutinize."

"You've got some enormous eyes, Mancuso. Big ones, honey."

CHAPTER 3

I wanted to catch up on the investigations. The murder book, which contained all the reports, forensics, autopsies, interviews, photos of the crime scenes, et cetera, was at the precinct.

However, I needed a quiet environment, not only to do my review, but to brainstorm with my team like we usually would do.

As we were getting close to the precinct, I asked Lucy, "Can you do me a favor?"

"Sure, hon. What do you need?"

"Go in and get the murder book. I want to do my review at the pub, not here. After that, can you drive me back?"

"They will not like that," she said.

"Who? Cagney and Lacey? I don't care. Captain Johnson will back me up."

We arrived at the precinct and Lucy had no place to park. I got it. Having retrieved the murder book, we were on the way back to Captain O'Brian's Pub and Cigar Bar in the Financial District in Lower Manhattan. I called brother Dominic, Mr. Pat, and Agnes Smith. I wanted to have them meet me at the pub.

Lucy was driving and inquired about the recent addition to the pub. "It's exciting. Especially if you consider that the pub has been around in the O'Brian family since 1948. Father Dom's granddad was the one who opened it after World War II. Anyway, we're not changing that. Instead, what we did is take over the space next door. The old Dino's Deli. That's going to be the cigar club," I paused, looking out the window, as two uniforms were hand cuffing a man near the intersection of FDR Drive and East 20th Street. "Plus," I went on, "we converted into our investigative offices to the back of the club."

"Nice added touch with the cigar club idea. That should be successful, considering your locale."

"Right? We have a built-in customer base from Wall Street so close, NYPD Police Headquarters, and FBI offices a few blocks away. Not to mention our regulars. Both, Father Dom and I are excited at the prospects."

"I heard Agnes Smith is joining you full-time?"

"It's already happening. Agnes was bored to death at the insurance company she worked for. She's been a key player in the investigations we've done recently. Her computer skills and ability to get into files and backdoors, if you know what I mean, is eerie."

"Honey, you need to be careful with that. You're now consulting with the NYPD. Make sure you don't break any laws or come up with stuff that's not admissible. You get my drift?" She asked, turning to face me.

I smiled but didn't reply.

She mentioned, "Father Dom told me Patrick is also becoming a private detective."

"Good ole Patrick Sullivan, or as we call him, Mr. Pat. Yes, the sneaky guy had been studying to get his license. He wanted to surprise me. It turns out he was a Naval Crime Scene Investigator while in the Marines. He's been with the family since Dom's brother, Brandon, took over for Dom's grandfather, Captain O'Brian."

She asked, "We're talking late '60s. Correct?"

"You're right. 1969, to be exact, when they both came back from Nam. Brandon, Dom's Dad, saved Patrick's life in '68 during an operation called *'Rolling Thunder'*. I know little more than that. Since they were not open about sharing any stories."

I paused briefly before shifting gears. Nam was not a cheerful topic to discuss. "Getting back to Patrick, I like he wants to become a private detective. Even though his red hair and beard, plus his Irish brogue, give the pub authenticity, I'm happy to announce that Mr. Pat has found the perfect replacement. A guy named Riley MacClenny. You'll get to see him soon."

"You know what else I'm thinking?" I was on a roll, "Imagine for a moment, you come on board after you retire, and Marcy joins the team. Put us all together, and what have we got?"

"Baby, you got yourself an eclectic dream team," Lucy replied. "We would be more diverse than the undercover cops from *'Fast & Furious.'* "Hey, speaking of movies, our first case was made into a novel called *'.'*

Now it's being considered for a television series. How about that?

Maybe we'll become famous. At least, on the small screen."

Lucy gave another one of her bright, beautiful smiles as she headed toward the pub on Beaver and Hanover Streets.

Opening at two in the afternoon, well before patrons would make their way in, Mr. Pat was grooming Riley. His new Mr. Pat look-alike was to become the fresh face of Captain O'Brian's Pub. A forty something year old who had experienced bar tending and managing, Riley looked authentic with his red hair and full red beard.

"Mr. Pat, join us when you can in our office. Is Agnes in there already?" I asked.

"She is, and I will be there in a minute, lad." Mr. Pat replied and turned to see Lucy. "Mrs. Roberts, good to see you."

Lucy smiled and waved at Pat as we walked into our unfinished new office. It was a big squad room with desks facing each other and a round conference table off to one side. There was a nice electronic white-screen and television monitor at the front of the table. The office was almost complete. The only missing item was the flooring. A mixture of deli food scents still lingered in the air. A reminder of when Dino's Deli was in business. "I think I'm going to be hungry," Lucy said.

"I know, right?" I said, "We have more paint and carpeting coming in. Also, once we install the new exhaust system for the cigar smoke, I think we'll solve the lingering scents."

Agnes was behind a computer screen, intensely looking through her big black rim glasses. She was a good-looking lady in her mid-forties. She likes to wear her long blonde hair in a ponytail. For the sake of our burgeoning little enterprise, it was very fortunate that she had found a partner, a parishioner at Dom's church. For the longest time, she had, or maybe still has, a crush on Father Dom. To where, for over a year, she attended Father Dom's Mass daily.

A few minutes after we made ourselves comfortable, Father Dom walked in followed by Mr. Pat. We gathered around our new conference table. Large and round, it included eight plush executive type swivel chairs and a stand-alone big ass Arturo Fuente ashtray for my cigars.

I began, "Okay, team. This investigation is still very hush-hush. The police have released no details to the press yet. So, we need to keep this amongst ourselves, for the moment."

Everyone nodded in understanding.

We re-examined the information on victim number one, Odette Romano. In her late twenties, brunette, employed at a law firm, no defensive wounds, lived alone. These all seemed like reasonably identifiable markers.

I said, "Look at the toxicology report, and stomach contents."

Lucy read from the report, "Her blood alcohol level showed she had been drinking, but not drunk. They found traces of sōchū in her system."

Father Dom asked, "What is that?"

I pointed my finger at Mr. Pat who came back with, "It's a Japanese alcoholic beverage containing rice, barley, sweet potatoes, and brown sugar. It's stronger than saké and wine, but not as strong as whiskey."

"Do we serve that here, Mr. Pat?" Dom asked.

"No, Father. It's usually served at Japanese restaurants and sushi bars. Rarely at an Irish pub."

Getting back to the report, I said, "Lucy, go on with the stomach contents."

"Speaking of sushi, she had consumed some. The report shows raw tuna, rice, seaweed, wasabi, ginger, avocado."

Agnes chimed in smiling, "A tuna roll."

Father Dom raised his eyebrows. "A tuna roll? Never heard of it."

"What Lucy read off," Agnes replied, "well, those are the ingredients of a tuna roll, an entrée that you'd find at a sushi restaurant."

"Okay, Father Dom continued, "What about the sex, Lucy?"

My brother is all about facts. He might not care about minutia, but he certainly gave me a perfect opening, and I had to take it.

Without missing a beat, I quipped, "Tuna rolls don't have a sex, they're genderless, brother."

Dom looked at me. I could tell that my brother had to work hard to suppress his *'if looks could kill stare'*, being a priest and all. Regardless, annoyed since his otherwise extreme white facial features had now turned to a deep crimson. Ignoring my immature comment,

he replied, "Lucy knows what I meant."

Lucy looked at me. I could tell she was a little embarrassed to discuss this topic in front of Dom.

"El Padre has heard it all before, plus he asked. Go on," I said to Lucy, while glaring at Dom.

Looking at the murder book, Lucy added, "Okay, no signs of rape.

Thus, we're assuming consensual. The only sex seems to be anal sex."

I broke the momentary silence. "The sex, or erotic asphyxiation, includes choking. Which is done to enhance the—," I paused, "the experience," I said, instead of orgasm. I went on, "So, our unsub, or, the unknown subject goes beyond choking at this point and strangles the victim with a satin ribbon as he stands behind the victim. I assume that he, or she, does this to enhance the experience."

Patrick asked, "The gender of the unsub is still undetermined?"

"Officially, that's correct. Although, I suspect it is a male."

Dom turned to me and asked, "What makes you say that?"

I replied, "This morning, at the latest victim's apartment, I picked up a scent of cologne. It was not perfume. It was a bit strong. I smelled that before. Can't think of where, though."

Dom asked, "How do you know the cologne was not from anyone already there."

Prepared to answer another question, I said, "The only men there were the two uniforms. They had no cologne smell on them. I know that for a fact."

Patrick asked, "Could the cologne be from the building manager who found the victim, Joey?"

I glanced at Mr. Pat, "It could have been, Mr. Pat. Except he, the manager that is, smelled like corned beef hash. I am positive that our unsub wears cologne."

Lucy smiled. "There's nothing in the murder book about that. No mention of an odor in any of the victim's apartments."

I smiled back at Lucy. "Did you expect Cagney and Lacey to pick up on that?"

"Touché, Joey," she replied, and added, "Farnsworth has over ten years of experience in the homicide division. He should have picked up on the scent."

I added, "There's a difference between having ten years of experience and having one year of experience while sitting around for the next nine. You understand, right? Let's look at victim numero dos," I said, glancing at Lucy.

Paying attention to the book once again, Lucy added, "Mary Ellen Vickers. Twenty-seven years old. Brunette—an attractive lady. Single. Worked as a court stenographer. Has a roommate, Sally Anders, who was away on a trip during the murder."

Dom asked, "What about stomach contents?"

"Getting there," Lucy replied, "she consumed white wine, not enough to be drunk, same as Odette. She, also, had sushi. Crab meat, rice, avocado, cucumber, and soy sauce found in her stomach. Along with wasabi and ginger."

We all turned to Agnes and waited for her comment.

Agnes smiled, "That would be a California roll."

"Amazing! You are our sushi expert," Patrick said, laughing. Dom asked, "No defensive wounds on Mary Ellen either?"

Lucy replied, "No, Father, and everything else is consistent with the other victims. Sex and strangulation. The only difference is that she is the first victim whose breasts they have sliced as a cross. Also, all her clothes are neatly put away in her closet. Nothing is out of place."

Dom added, "We need a profiler. Too bad Marcy is not here to help with this."

"Marcy is FBI. Not a profiler," I replied, sternly.

"But they have trained her in this kind of stuff," Dom replied. "Yeah, well, we'll find someone else to help," I retorted.

Everyone looked at me, probably wondering what the hell was up with my response. "Maybe I'll run it past her when I call her."

"What about her partner, agent Tony Belford?" Dom asked.

Lucy and I looked at each other before I answered, "Special Agent Belford. He's probably an expert at profiling, as well. Maybe I'll ask him," I said.

Dom asked, "Is it a cross, or the letter T."

Lucy turned to Dominic, "Father, it's a cross. I mean, maybe, the unsub intended to do the letter T. But clearly, the cuts are a cross."

I asked, "Why Dom? You think it's religious related?"

"I'm hoping not," Dom replied, "Although, if a cross, then there's a reason for it. A reason I can't figure out yet."

"Changing subjects," Lucy began, "Let's look at our third victim," she said, glancing around the table.

"Please, go on," I said.

"Margarita Espinosa. Divorced, no children. Thirty-two. Brunette. Lived alone in the city. She was a civilian employee of the NYPD at One Police Plaza. She was, also, a paralegal before joining the police. Law student on a part-time basis."

"Agnes, are you taking notes on all this?" I asked.

"I'm creating a spreadsheet. Listing all similarities side by side. Is that okay?" Agnes asked.

"*Bene, va bene*," I said, nodding. "Go on, Lucy."

"Margarita drank saké in moderation. Also, she ate sushi." Patrick chimed in, "Here we go, Ms. Agnes."

Lucy read on, "Besides the saké, her stomach contents showed only fried tofu and rice. Nothing else."

Everyone looked at Agnes.

Agnes smiled, and added, "Now, that's a rare sushi. Not served in many places. Although, it's simple to make."

"So, what's it called, Ms. Sushi Expert?" asked Pat.

"It's called Inari sushi, or roll. They cut thin layers of tofu in a triangular fashion and made into a pocket, which is stuffed with rice before it is fried."

"Very interesting, Agnes," I said.

"I assume the rest of the MO is consistent with the others? I mean, the sex, the cuts on the breasts, et cetera?" Dom asked, missing the importance of what Agnes had just said.

"Yes, Father," replied Lucy, "all the same."

I added, "I'm afraid we may have more victims pretty soon unless we find the unsub. We've had four dead ladies in just over ten days. Weneed to get on this quickly. Whoever this is, he seems to be on a mission. Something is triggering his killings."

"Joey, why do you think this first victim's breasts were not sliced with a sign of the cross like the last three?" Lucy asked.

I thought for a second, and replied, "Maybe our killer was spooked by the pie lady knocking on the door at eleven that night. Or, since there was no mentioned of the murder on the news, he added a signature to the other victims to let us know it is him. He wants recognition."

Lucy added, "This type of killer doesn't just start killing like this. These are not his first victims. Nor his last, I fear. He has various traits, one of which is OCD, or obsessive-compulsive disorder."

I said, "The compulsive part is the one that worries me the most." I got up and started pacing around the office. My mind was engaged, with all the pistons firing.

CHAPTER 4

The room went suddenly quiet, except for me. I was on a roll. Pacing back and forth, I thought about these horrific murders. There was a killer—some maniac—stalking young professional women in our city. Even for New York City, four killings in less than two weeks were four too many. The authorities had been reticent about releasing the information, so as not to create a panic. On the one hand, I understood what the authorities were trying to do. However, someone had to say something so that single females fitting these profiles could be alerted and take precautions. Otherwise, this serial killer was going to continue. Unabated.

I broke the silence. "Let's review what we have so we can begin forming a profile of this killer. Agnes, please, read from your spreadsheet"

Agnes read from her computer screen. "The victims have the following as commonalities. All single, brunettes, early thirties or late twenties, and professionals."

Dom broke in, "Before you go on, let me ask this. Are there no cameras in any of these apartment units where these ladies lived?"

I could tell that Dom needed to play catch up since this was the second time. He had interrupted Agnes from reading the compiled list.

I jumped in. "Great question, Dom. The apartment buildings from the murder scene photos indicate that they are older and smaller. We still need to visit them to confirm this. However, none of them look like they have cameras outside, or in the lobby area. So, I'll ask the rest of you, what does that tell us?"

Everyone thought for a minute. Then, Lucy replied, "To me, that tells us the unsub stalks the victims before he, or she, makes contact."

I added, "Go with him, for now."

Lucy sat back and added, "Okay. He, the perp, probably selects a victim, or maybe over one. Then, he follows them to establish where they live, and if they live alone. This way he can look out for security issues."

Patrick, looking at his notes, asked, "What about the second victim, Mary Ellen Vickers? She had a roommate, a Ms. Sally Anders." Do you suppose the unsub knew Ms. Anders would be away?"

"Excellent point, Mr. Pat," I replied, "You need to follow up with Ms. Anders and find out what she knows."

"I'm on it," Mr. Pat added, making a note on his pad.

"What else is like our four victims? Anything else stands out?" I asked the group.

For a moment, I felt like I was in a classroom. With me being the teacher asking a question and my crew, the students, burying their heads in their books hoping to look studious even though they were clueless. "Come on? There's something obvious no one has picked up on. And, don't tell me the victims are all females."

Patrick cracked a smile and began answering, "All the victims are employed in a job related to law enforcement. Look at the lineup. A court stenographer, two attorneys, and a civilian employee of the NYPD.," he continued, glancing at me, "they are all sexually permissive since they don't seem to have a problem taking in a complete stranger to their apartment on their first date."

I pointed at Pat with a big grin on my face. "Patrick, you get an A plus for noticing the law enforcement angle, an extra credit point for the sexually permissive angle. The latter is something we can't quantify now. If anyone has any ideas on that, please let me know ASAP.

Father Dom chimed in, "So, do you think it's likely that it involved our unsub in law enforcement?"

Lucy replied, "It sure seems to lean that way, yes."

"Getting back to similarities," Agnes said, "all victims ate a sushi, one drank saké, or sōchū, a Japanese alcoholic beverage, and one had white wine. The last victim we don't know yet."

I added, "I'm willing to bet our last victim ate sushi, as well. This guy probably takes all of them to the same place—a place that he knows has no cameras and where he might go unnoticed."

Dom asked, "What if we took photos of the victims to sushi restaurants to see if anyone recognizes any of them?"

Agnes replied, "Father, not only are there hundreds of sushi restaurants but also, many other places that serve sushi. It has become quite trendy."

"Good point," I said, "we need to narrow down the location of where these ladies lived. I have a feeling our unsub is working within a certain geographic location. Probably, within walking distance from where he works, or where these victims lived. Perhaps, both. Agnes, please, develop a correlation along those parameters. Let's get a map and post pins on these locations."

"Yes, boss," Agnes replied, smiling.

Pointing to Agnes, I added, "You said that the Inari roll was not a common sushi offered in too many places, right?"

"Like I said," Agnes replied, "while it is simple to prepare, many places don't offer it."

"That's fine. Once we narrow the location down, we'll search for places offering Inari sushi, or rolls."

Lucy turned to me and asked, "Are you going to share this information with Farnsworth and Charles?"

"Yes, of course. But we'll continue our research and brainstorming here, as well. I have little faith in those two. You know what I mean?"

"Okay, just asking," Lucy responded.

Father Dom said, "We know a lot about the victims, but we know little about our unsub. We're not even sure he, is a he. I still think you should ask Marcy if she can help with this. Or, perhaps, she can recommend someone at her office that can help profile this serial killer."

"I hear you, Father. I'll talk to Marcy," I replied, glancing at Lucy. Lucy said, "When I get back to the precinct, I'm going to search ViCAP, the Violent Criminal Apprehension Program's database. Maybe, our killer has done this before in another location besides New York. If so, we might get more clues there."

I said, "Good. In the meantime, Lucy, how about you and I visit the murder scenes of the other victims tomorrow? Patrick, you are going to locate Sally Anders, the roommate, to see what she knows. Agnes, you'll get our map going with the location of the murders and sushi restaurants in the area."

"What do you want me to do?" Brother Dominic asked.

"Father, I want you to pray that we have no more victims," I said, smiling. "Also, help Agnes here with the map, or, if you like, go with Patrick. Your choice."

"I'll do all three. How's that? I'll pray tonight, go with Mr. Pat in the morning, and come back to help Agnes."

"Perfect, Dom."

Lucy needed to get back to the precinct. She brought up my brother as we walked alone to the parking lot. "I noticed Dom was not as hesitant in working with Agnes."

"Well, that's an interesting turn of events. Sometime back, I had a conversation with her. She had inquired about Dom's commitment to the church. I came right to the point and suggested that she look for Mr. Right elsewhere."

Lucy said. "So, how did she take that?"

"At the moment, she's currently dating a parishioner who, coincidentally, attends early Mass daily."

CHAPTER 5

Our brainstorm session was very productive. Except because what we needed was to build a profile on our likely murderer. Narrowing down our perpetrator was a crucial element in the investigation.

Marcy, although not a profiler with the FBI, could be very helpful with this since she went through the behavioral analysis training—a requirement for all agents. At the very least, she could point us to a profiler within the New York FBI offices. Even though I'm sure Captain Johnson was already doing this officially. I wanted to remain independent and do things my way.

I wanted to call Marcy, but I was suffering from fear of rejection. In the last few weeks, she had been aloof with me. That we'd lived together on and off for nearly two years and we had been close to marriage not once, but twice, didn't seem to affect her desire to be apart for a while. I chucked it all to her current condition of mild depression. I will wait for her to get over it for as long as it took.

Back in the conference room, I glanced at my watch and saw that it was a little after four in the afternoon. I made the call, waiting a few moments before the medical examiner picked up.

"Doctor Death, how you are doing? This is Mancuso."

"Mancuso, welcome back! I heard you're consulting for your old precinct. What's up?" Doctor Frankie replied.

"Happy to be back, Doc. Say, listen, I'm on the case about the four ladies who were murdered a few days ago. I wanted to ask you a couple of things. You have a moment?"

"Sure. Let me head over to the files. Ask away. With as many bodies as I get in here, I don't trust my memory on all of them. What do you need?"

"The MO seems the same on all four. But from your report, you don't nail down, no pun intended. The gender of the killer. Or whether they did before the anal sex, or, after killing the victims. Any thoughts?"

"Aha, good questions, Mancuso. Let me say this. From the penetration marks, the offender was a male. Any other—" he paused, "any other item that would have been used to penetrate would have left different abrasions. You follow?"

"Yes, I do. So, you're thinking a male partner. That confirms my initial clue."

"Yeah, based on what?" Doctor Frankie asked.

"Not on forensics," I laughed, "The one scene I observed had a distinct smell of a male cologne. I've picked up that scent before, but I can't place it."

"Funny you should mention that because I picked up a scent on the back of all the victims. Must be a transfer of the cologne. But since I did not visit any of the murder scenes, I didn't experience that scent in the apartments. Good pick up Mancuso."

"Any chance you know what that cologne is?"

"No, not at all. It was almost unnoticeable. I mean, I received the bodies hours after they were killed."

"Let me ask you, Frankie. Did the cologne scent the same on all the victims?"

"What little I detected, I picked up the odor on all the victims.

And, yes, it is the same cologne every time."

"So, would you say that it's safe to say that the scent is common to our killer? It would be impossible for all our victims to have that scent on them otherwise. Agreed?"

"Joey, I would agree with that. Here is a little trivia for you. Supposedly, Napoleon Bonaparte wore his favorite cologne to every battle."

"Is there a point to this?" I asked.

Frankie ignored me and went on. "The scent made Napoleon feel refreshed. It was like it inspired him into battle. Possibly, our killer feels the same way before going out on a kill."

"That's a very interesting point. I wish we could tell what brand of cologne it is."

"It would just be one more circumstantial fact to be made."

"Moving on to another observation. See if you agree with me? This guy takes these ladies back to their place and goes directly to their bedroom. They undress, and he begins foreplay while standing naked behind them. I assume. Right?"

"So far, I'm with you. I don't know how much foreplay, or what kind. The ladies' lipstick is intact in all cases. There does not seem to be any kissing, or oral sex."

"Okay. So, I'm if wherever they met, they discussed the type of sex—extreme sex—they're planning on having. After that, it was just a matter of following through with their plans when they came into the apartment, undress, put away their clothes and get on with it. I mean, no romance, no caressing, no kissing, no Sinatra, no drinks. Nada. Just boom."

The doctor replied, "Sure seems that way. Lipstick intact, no signs of anything other than the sex."

"It seems this guy, our killer, has no emotion, or affection for his dates. On a mission. He's robotic in some ways. And, doesn't even want to look at them. They come into the room and undress. The killer bends them over in front of the bed and penetrates from behind using a condom. None of the ladies had any semen in them, right?"

Doctor Frankie replied, "Correct. Go on. I'm with you."

"Fine. As they're having sex, he takes the red satin ribbon, which appears to be consistent with a gift package type ribbon. I think you wrote it was a half-inch wide, correct? He chokes them while still from behind. The ladies would think this is just part of the extreme sex. But then, our perp goes beyond the extreme, and he strangles them."

"I would have to agree with all of that. One other thing," the doctor paused.

"What's that?"

"They, the ladies, all had orgasms. The rape kit analysis shows secretion on their part as a result of multiple orgasms. So, in fact, they must have thought they were having sex, or, extreme sex, as you called it. That is until the ribbon got tighter."

"No sign of fighting back from any of them?" I asked.

"They did not know they were about to die. As the ribbon got tighter, the sex got better. Perhaps, he timed his orgasm to the final tightening of the ribbon."

"You know what, Frankie, I can see it happening, man."

"I know. I can see it, as well."

"Did you find anything else?" I asked.

The doctor continued, "We found traces of lubrication. One with petroleum jelly. The other three had a silicone-based lubricant. I haven't been able to pinpoint the brand. But we also found traces of latex."

"What do you think happened there?"

"Our perp seems to know what he is doing. He probably brings his lubricant, the silicone based. The petroleum jelly can damage the latex in the condom, making it break–something the perp would want to avoid, of course. Except because it happened with the first vic. Petroleum jelly was used, and they found traces of latex from the condom."

"Another reason to suspect our unsub to be a man, right?" "That confirms it, yes."

As I was listening intently to Doctor Frankie's dissertation on the sex, one disturbing thought crossed my mind. So, I asked, "One thing I can't understand is that there's no trace of the perp. There are no hairs of any kind from him—pubic or otherwise. Is this true?"

"We found the victim's hair, but no other. Here are a few possibilities. The perp could be naturally bald, or even better, he could have a shaved head, chest, and pubic area."

"A shaved chest and pubes? Who does that?"

"Obviously, you haven't been to a gym lately. Many guys do that these days."

"Do you?" I shot back.

"Ah... no," he answered, laughing. "Seriously, the genital area?"

"From what I see here, some guys do."

"Fuck that shit," I said.

"Speaking of that, we found feces consistent with each victim on the bed, and on their rear ends."

"They had their shit … on their asses?"

"You figure things out fast, don't you? That would be consistent with the sex they had just had."

"I get it, of course. Can you tell if the perp had an orgasm before or after he killed them?"

"No, I couldn't tell you that. But with a psycho like that, I wouldn't doubt he stayed in the women for a while."

"You mean after he strangles them, he continues having sex?"
"Very possible. But I can't be sure. This guy is a sick puppy, Joey."

"We've got to catch this maniac. Tell me about the sliced breasts as a cross, or is it a T?"

"As you know, the first victim did not have that signature. On the last three, yes. He used either a small pocketknife or what they call a grip knife like a box cutter."

"I understand the cuts were not deep, just superficial. A signature, though. Is it a T, or a religious cross?"

Doctor Frankie replied, "With the tool, he was using, he could have easily fashioned a letter if he wanted to. The marks he left on each of these women's breasts are definitely in the shape of crosses."

"I see."

"Unfortunately, I expect more bodies in here. He's not done. Some- thing is driving him to these horrific acts. Anything else, Joey?"

"Have you examined the stomach contents of the latest victim?"

"Not yet. Let you know as soon as we do."

"Do you have anything? Anything that could identify this guy?" I asked, as I sat back and put my feet on top of the conference table.

"Other than the cologne, this guy is very meticulous. He leaves nothing behind, no pun intended there. And, even if you find someone with the same cologne, it could be very circumstantial, right? I mean, how many men could use the same cologne?"

"So you're no fucking help?"

Frankie laughed, "You have a way with words, Mancuso. I'm afraid we will not solve this case using forensics. Unless, he makes a mistake, it's all up to you detectives to find this guy."

"Thanks, buddy. I hope I don't have to call you again," I said, clicking off my phone. Now, I had to make the call I didn't want to make. Even though I knew Marcy could help with this case. I punched number one on my speed dial and hoped for the best.

"Hey, Joey, how are you?" Marcy asked as she answered the phone."

"I'm happy to see you haven't erased me from your phone contacts,"

I replied, with a quick, nervous chuckle, "how are you feeling?"

Marcy ignored my mild wisecrack about the contacts. "I'm feeling much better. Doing my physical therapy every day. I'm even writing your name with the little rubber ball on the wall."

"I don't understand," I said.

"There's an exercise in which I have to pretend I'm writing things on a wall with a rubber ball the size of a baseball. I must extend my arm out and write. It's boring, and I hate it."

"You hate it? Is that why you write my name?"

"No, silly. I just need to entertain myself. I write other nasty stuff, too. Lots of four-letter words."

"I got it. If you don't use my name in a sentence with the other four-letter words," I said with a chuckle.

"You just gave me a good idea. Are you working a case?"

"That's the reason I called. How are your profiling skills?"

"I'm not a profiler with the bureau, but I can help. Why?"

"Could you listen to what I have, possibly? Perhaps, start me out on a profile of my unsub?'

"Sure, I could," she replied. "Joey, hang on a second, would you?"

I heard her ask someone a question. Even though it seemed as if she had covered the phone with her hand.

"When do you want to do this?" Marcy asked.

"I was hoping today. The sooner the better, you know?"

Again, she spoke to someone else covering the phone. "Come over after six this evening. Tony Belford can help you, as well."

"Is he there now?" I asked, trying not to sound pissed.

"He was just leaving, but he'll come back to help us. Plus, he says he'll bring dinner," she replied.

Tell him to stick dinner up his ass, I said to myself. "Oh, that's great," I lied. "Tell him I eat meat. None of that vegan crap."

I could sense a smile from Marcy, as she said, "We'll see you at six."

I clicked off the phone. We'll see you at six? What's this we shit? I wanted to ask how her firearms training was going since this was the one issue that would keep her from rejoining the bureau and fieldwork. I knew GQ Tony was helping her with that. I avoided asking her because I didn't want to hear how great El Tony was doing with her.

CHAPTER 6

Marcy's Brooklyn apartment had been my second home for almost two years. A serene ambiance made up of pastel colors and pleasantly decorated with a lady's touch, of course. As I entered, I didn't feel at home anymore. Butterflies were flying every which way in my stomach as Marcy opened the front door. "Hi, Joey. Good to see you. Come on in," Marcy said in her husky, sexy voice that drove me crazy. She was wearing her lounging clothes. A loosely fit black sweatpants outfit with nothing underneath, typically. Her hair was pulled up in a fashionable style, like a rooster tail.

Her Jimmy Buffet parrot tattoo was visible on the back of her sensuous neck.

I moved in to kiss her on the cheek, and, fortunately; she reciprocated. I made a point of complimenting her before I asked about her GQ sidekick, "You're looking good. Happy to be here. Tony here yet?"

"Yes, he just got here. He's putting the food in the kitchen. Hope you like sushi. That's what he brought," she said.

"I love sushi. I use it for bait when I go fishing," I said, as my eyebrows narrowed.

"Hah, hah. It's all cooked. Nothing raw."

"Oh, great. I bought red wine. I hope it goes with sushi."

"I'm sure it will be fine," she replied.

I needed to clear something up for my benefit before I sat down with Marcy and GQ Tony. "Marcy, can I use your bathroom— the one off your bedroom, not the little one by the kitchen. I need a little privacy."

"Sure, help yourself. You know where it is."

"Thanks," I said, as I walked into her bedroom. My purpose was not to use the bathroom. Instead, I wanted to check the closet where my clothes used to be. I was hoping, even praying, that I would not find Tony's clothes in there. Quietly, I slid the closet door opened.

"Mancuso, where are you?" Tony called out from the living room.

There was a harsh tone to his voice.

My heart stopped, "I'll be right out, sport. Give me two minutes," I replied.

"Take all the time you need. Just make sure everything comes out alright," Tony added, laughing.

Hah, hah. Asshole. No male clothes had replaced mine. I glanced at the other side, which was usually Marcy's. I just wanted to be sure. Boom! Just Marcy's stuff. I felt better. Much better. Next step, the bathroom. I went in and found only Marcy's things. No other tooth- brush. No shaving cream. Nothing male related. I flushed the toilet, turned on the faucet, and walked out with a smile.

Tony got up from the dining room table and extended his hand, "Feel better, Mancuso?" He asked, smiling in return.

"I feel much better, Special Agent," I said, shaking hands with Belford. He looked like a Ken doll. Barbie would have been very pleased, dark blue polo shirt with the emblem of an actual guy on a horse playing polo, khaki pants perfectly ironed, his Gucci shoes with no socks of course. What an ass! That was my immediate impression.

I wear shoes without socks, too. Usually, because all my socks are dirty or hiding somewhere.

"Have a seat here," Tony said, pointing to a dining room chair between him and Marcy. "What are you working on?"

I didn't reply right away. I sat down and opened the murder book I had brought with me. "This is not out for public consumption yet. I'm working on a potential serial killer in Manhattan." I turned to Tony and asked, "How much training have you had on profiling techniques?"

"Joey, I'm being groomed for a leadership position," he said, looking beyond me at Marcy, and smiling.

I glanced at Marcy as she smiled back, and without turning to Tony, I asked him, "So, what does that mean?"

"I spent a year in DC at the BAU."

"Speak English, sport. Your feds use too much of that alphabet lingo," I said.

"The Behavioral Analysis Unit at the FBI's main offices in Washington, DC."

"I had the DC figured out. And, while there, I'm sure you became an expert at profiling."

"That's correct, Joey. Lay it out for us. We'll tell you who your unsub is," Tony said, full of confidence.

Oh, shit.

"Tony, I've meant to ask you something," I said.

He asked, "About what?"

"Do you wear that thing on your ear twenty-four seven?"

"You mean my cell phone wireless receiver?" He replied, touching the damn thing.

"What's up with that, man?"

Why have it, if you will not use it. I replied, "It's part of me, now."

Marcy cut off my silliness, "Joey, tell us about the case."

Over the next half hour, while we had dinner and drank wine, I described the four murder scenes and how the murders were committed. Considering that we were eating, I skipped the ME's report on stomach contents, and a few other details.

Tony asked, "Has the first murder, the one they said was a case of extreme sex gone bad, reported as an accidental homicide?"

I replied, "Yes, the suits in charge don't want to alarm the public, yet. But they won't be able to contain the news too much longer, now that there have been three other homicides with the same MO that immediately followed the first one."

Tony queried, "You said the killer left a signature?"

"With the last three young ladies. That would be the superficial slicing of the breasts with a sharp knife as a cross. Yes."

"In that case," Tony began, "that was a mistake. By leaving a signature, the killer is looking for recognition. Since the first murder was not reported widely, that probably gave the perpetrator just cause to do it again, and again."

"So, you think this person wants public recognition for what he did?" I asked.

Tony moved forward, and opening his arms said, "Obviously, I'll profile in a second. The sooner the news goes out, the better—not that he is going to stop. It may slow him down, knowing that he's being talked about."

"I agree with that," I replied. "They have deprived him of the credit his deranged mind seeks for his acts. I'll pass that up to the chain of command."

Tony added, "I think you should, or, someone is likely to leak the news. In which case, you won't be able to control how the facts are reported."

"I know. But you know how politicians worry about bad press Especially, in a city like New York."

Tony sat back, "That would be my first suggestion, Joey. They're going to have to come clean, at some point. Might as well be on our terms."

Marcy put things away, and said, "Why don't you guys sit in the living room, while I make three *cortaditos*."

"I love those *cortaditos*. Don't you, Joey?"

I smiled and ignored the question. "Here, Marcy, I'll help you put things away," I said, as I gathered the plates from the dining room table and took them to the kitchen.

GQ Tony didn't take my cue. Instead, he moved to the living room to work on the perp's profile.

Marcy and I worked quietly in the kitchen. I washed and dried dishes while Marcy made the drinks. At one point, we exchanged glances. More like an extended gaze. It seemed to last several seconds. I had a difficult time reading her thoughts, and I'm sure she was trying to read mine. I assumed GQ was getting ready to work on a profile for my unsub.

Fifteen minutes passed. I peeked into the living room, and there was Tony, fixing the crease of his perfectly fitting khaki pants before crossing his legs. If Barbie could see Ken now, I think she'd puke. I couldn't take the view anymore. Gladly, I went back to washing and drying.

As much as I didn't like the guy, I could tell that GQ took his job seriously. He had turned the coffee table into a miniature office with his laptop, and other related materials that had been, conveniently, set up for his profile presentation. I was just putting the last dish away when Tony called out my name. "Joey, I think I'm ready with a profile." Retrieving a notepad and a pen from my briefcase, I sat down on the sofa by myself. Marcy brought out the cortaditos, setting the tray of rich and steamy espressos on the other end of the coffee table. She made herself comfy and cozy in her recliner before picking up her drink and fixing her attention on GQ. "Okay. What'd you got?" I said, looking at Tony.

"Listen, before we start," Tony was pulling a large manila envelope from a briefcase while he talked. "When I first met you at your pub, I complimented you on all the photos you had with all the various celebrities. Do you remember?"

"I remember," wondering where he was going with this.

"Yes, well, if you also remember, I said that I had a picture of President Obama and me. I offered to give you one so that you could hang it on a wall in the pub."

"You brought the original?"

"Oh, no. That one is priceless. I brought you a glossy copy," he said, pulling it out of the envelope.

"Brother, you could probably get a couple of bucks for that on eBay. Count them. One. Two," I said.

"That's funny. I want you to have it and hang it up," he said, handing it to me.

"With all due respect, Tony. If you noticed when you were there, all the photos are with either Captain O'Brian, the original proprietor, or his son, Sergeant Brandon O'Brian, who took over the pub after the captain..." I glanced at Marcy, "... but I'll take it. Thank you," I said, not wanting to be rude. "Possibly, I can Photoshop it. Add myself in between the two of you," I said, looking at the picture.

"Hah, that would be good," Tony said, faking a laugh.

"Yeah... anyway, can we get back to the profile?" I asked, returning the photo in the envelope before tucking it away in my briefcase.

"Take notes, Joey. Because, I'm going to be very specific," Tony said, sitting back.

"I wouldn't expect anything less," I replied, biting my tongue. "Tell me this. How old do you think our unsub is?"

Tony replied, "I'd say he is anywhere between thirty and late forties. What's your theory?"

"I agree. This guy is enticing these ladies with extreme sex wherever it is they meet. They take him back to their place for immediate sex, from what it appears. So, he is older than his victims."

"Let me ask you, Joey. Why do you think this person is a male?"

I explained what Doctor Frankie had said about the penetration and the remains of some latex from the condom.

He thought for a second and said, "Hah, interesting. Well, that was an oopsie. Let me go on. Your unsub is a power junkie. The anal sex act puts him in total control from the get-go. You said it didn't seem like there was any kissing or foreplay. He probably entices them over a drink, or two, and sells them on the sex. I bet all, or most, of these ladies had never experienced anal sex before."

"Okay, so he likes to be in control," I repeated, as I wrote it down. "He is probably a charmer. Comes across suave and experienced.

He talks his way into their apartments. Ted Bundy was a manipulator, a charmer, and use those skills to bait his victims."

Marcy added, "So far, we have a control freak, a power-seeking person who is a manipulator and a charmer."

"Noted," I said.

Tony leaned forward and ticked on his laptop keyboard.

"Doctor Elizabeth Yardley is the notable Director of the Centre for Applied Criminology at Birmingham City University in England. She defines a serial killer as quote, '*A person who commits a series of murders, often with no apparent motive, and typically following a characteristic, predictable behavior pattern,*' unquote. She lists five behavior patterns of a serial killer. Four of which fit your unsub."

"Let me have them," I said.

"Right. Here are the four that fit. *'A power junkie, a manipulator, egotistical, a superficial charmer.'* The fifth that I don't think fits your guy, she calls, *'An average Joe.'"*

"Why do you think he is not an average Joe?" Marcy asked.

"To me," Tony began, "I think this person is an executive, a well- dressed, an elitist type. Not your average Joe."

"Very well, the only thing I'm adding here is an egotistical bragger," I said.

"Of course, this person is a psychopath, and Doctor Yardley describes five types of psychopaths. One of them fits your guy. She calls this type *'the unprincipled psychopath.'* So, what is the definition, you ask?"

"Do share," Marcy bantered.

"Thank you. I will. Yardley writes, *'Unprincipled psychopaths are highly narcissistic and take delight in wrecking vengeance through humiliation. They love to exploit and abuse other people, and they genuinely enjoy the anguish they create.'* I think the anal sex is a way for the unsub to show that."

I looked up from my notes, "Therefore, you equate anal sex with humiliation, abuse, and anguish? Who the hell wants that?"

Tony moved in my direction, and with unflinching determination in his eyes said, "Remember, you need to add the choking part of this sex act. Let me ask you, Joey, have you ever had anal sex?"

From my peripheral vision, I saw a crooked smile growing on

Marcy's face. She crossed her legs and sat back, stiffly in her recliner. Tony waited for my reaction.

I responded in kind, keeping my eyes fixed on Tony, "I have neither been on the receiving end nor the driving end of anal sex. So, the answer to your question is plain and simple. No."

Momentarily, Tony became very pensive. After about a few seconds he said in a serious tone, "Perhaps, to research for your case, try it. At least, the driving end, as you call it. Once you do, you'll see what I mean."

"I'll let you know," I replied, and turned to Marcy. "Anything you want to add to this topic?"

She smiled, "No, thank you. I think you guys *'anal-lyzed'* that, sufficiently."

I turned to Tony and asked, "Let me ask you something before you go on? You agree there was no rape involved, right?"

He smiled, sat back, and asked, "You know the difference between rape and love?"

"I'm sure you're going to tell me," I replied.

"Salesmanship, Joey. Salesmanship," GQ Tony said, laughing. Marcy retorted, "I don't think that's very funny, Tony."

Ignoring Marcy's comment, Tony began, "So, let me get into the narcissistic behavior of the unsub."

I leaned back, crossed my legs, and put the notepad on my right leg. "Let's hear what you got."

Tony started his dissertation on narcissism. "We've all heard of Narcissus, a character in Greek mythology. When Narcissus first saw his reflection on a pool of water, they say that he fell in love with the reflection of himself. The story says that he died looking at himself in the pool of water, unable to look away from admiring his reflection."

Marcy quipped, "I know a few people like that."

"I'm sure you do, Marcy," Tony added, "Most of us have some traits of a narcissist. That's how we develop our egos, self-esteem, and self-respect. However, few have all the traits, and there are nine traits associated with NPD. Also, known as Narcissistic Personality Disorder."

"And you think our killer has these traits?" I asked.

Tony moved forward again in his chair. He seemed to enjoy being the center of attention and sharing his expertise on the subject. "I don't know if this person has all nine. Only Ted Bundy was said to have all nine of them. All other recorded and known serial killers have had many of them, but not all nine. Of course, that's based on recent history."

I asked, "So, what are they, professor?" I inquired somewhat sarcastically.

Tony smiled, "Right. Grandiosity is one. An exaggerated sense of self-worth," he answered, pausing. He went on, "Success. This person dreams and fantasizes with success. Are you writing these down?" He asked.

"Yes, please, go on," I replied.

"Number three. Uniqueness. They think they are different than everyone else. That they are one of a kind. Another one, the fourth, is a sense that they need to be admired."

I interrupted, "These aren't that bad. Having a healthy ego doesn't lead to be a serial killer. I mean, Presidents Obama and Trump have been called narcissists. It would seem you need these traits to be an achiever."

"That's correct," replied Tony, "it's when you add the rest and display all of them in one person who things can go awry. Let me go on."

"Please, do," said Marcy.

Tony glanced at Marcy and smiled, "Thank you. Entitlement is the next one. This person feels entitled and expects favorable treatment. Subsequently, we have exploitative as a trait. Wanting to manipulate and take advantage of others. Number seven is a person who lacks empathy. They have no feelings for others. Then there is number eight, envious. They believe that others are envious of them because of their own perceived superiority. Finally, number nine is domineering.

They want to control everything, often coming across as arrogant. That's it. Those are the nine traits."

I looked up from my notes, "You're saying our killer has all, or, most of these?"

"You'll know better if you catch him. I doubt this person has all nine. What happens is when true narcissists are challenged, they become unpredictable. Specifically, if they have NPD."

Marcy said, "This is all very significant, but I still don't know who Joey is looking for."

I closed my notepad, leaned forward, and replied, "I think I can put this together, Marcy."

Tony chimed in, "Let me hear it, brother. Tell me who your perp is.

I'm going to grade you."

I smiled as I glanced at Professor Tony. "I'll share once I'm done reviewing my notes. I want to have the team together as we do that," I said, not wanting to share all my findings now.

Marcy asked, "Is anyone searching on ViCAP, the Violent Criminal Apprehension Program's database?"

I replied, "Yes, Detective Lucy Roberts, is."

Tony said, "Excellent, you'll be able to find a match if this perp has done this before. ViCAP tracks serial killers involved in sexual assault, if they followed the same MO. It's, specifically, helpful if they have a signature."

"You've been a great help, Tony. Thank you very much," I said, wanting this guy to get out now. I wanted to have some time with Marcy. I sat back and got comfortable on the sofa.

Marcy got the message, and said, "Tony, we'll talk tomorrow. Thanks for sharing this with us."

"Oh, okay. I'll leave you guys to catch up," he said, getting up to kiss Marcy on the cheek and shaking hands with me before packing up his 'office'.

"Keep me posted, Mancuso. I'm very interested in this case."

"I'll do that, and thanks again. Keep your earbud on. I might call you soon."

"Anytime brother, anytime," he said, as he walked out the door.

I sat down again after checking my hands for fractures. "You have cold cervesas?"

Marcy replied, "Help yourself. I'm sure I do." "You want one?"

"No, thanks. I'm good. I'm tired and want to get some sleep."

This was Marcy-code for *'please, leave soon.'* So, I replied, "You kicking me out, already?"

"No, just don't get too comfortable."

I grabbed a Brooklyn Lager out of the fridge and returned to the sofa. "Can I ask you a question?"

"Can I stop you from asking?"

"No," I said, smiling. "How many of those traits you think Tony has?"

"What? I think that between the both of you, you have, maybe fifteen out of eighteen. That's what I think."

"Very funny. Are you and he—" I paused. I needed to ask about the elephant in the room. Although, I thought it was only me who saw the elephant.

"What, Joey?"

"Are you and he … dating?"

"I'm not dating or doing anything else with anyone, Joey. Is that what you want to talk about?"

"He looks very intense around you. Very comfortable is a better word."

"Truth be told, he's asked me out socially. I have no interest in going out with him or anyone else."

"So, why is he always here?"

"Remember, I'm on medical leave, and he's taken over my cases. So, he is keeping me in the loop."

"What about us?"

"What about us?" She asked back.

"You always do that—answer a question with a question. You and me. When can we get back to be a couple again?"

"It's only been, what? Three weeks since we spoke about taking a break from each other?"

"You wanted to take a break from me. Not I."

"It wasn't taking a break from you. I just asked for time to think about my future. And, that includes everything. You, my work, my therapy."

"How is your therapy coming along?"

"I feel great about that. So much so, I may want to take the FBI's firearms test in a couple of weeks. I'm working my way back."

"How often do you go to the range?"

"Three times a week. I'm almost back."

"Sounds great. Have you practiced with long arms, also?"

"Pistols and revolvers are no problem. Long arms are coming along.

The shotgun test is the hardest."

"I feel confident you'll pass the test. But do you want to rush it?"

"I've set my goals, and as soon as I can do it on the range, I'll want to take the test."

"Have you set goals for us?"

"Let me work on getting my job back first. Then, we can talk about us, fair enough?"

"I ain't going anywhere. Like the song says, *'I will wait for you.'*"

"Get your ass out of here, Mancuso. Call me in a few days."

I walked towards the front door. Turning around to look at Marcy, I asked, "Are you wearing your usual? Under the sweats?"

"Out, now," she joked with a smile.

CHAPTER 7

As I was getting ready to start the engine of my red '67 Ford Mustang GT, which is my second love and probably the most significant investment I have, my cell phone rang.

"Where are you, Mancuso?" Detective Farnsworth inquired in his rough tone.

"I'm in Brooklyn. Headed home. Why?"

"We have a suspect in the murders. They are taking him to the station. Join us, if you like. Charles and I are on our way."

"Who is he?"

"Join us. We'll find out more once we're all there." Farnsworth clicked off his phone.

I made my way to the station, hoping they had, in fact, found the perp. Even though I had my doubts. It just felt like it was too easy and too soon. Once there, I joined Detectives Farnsworth and Charles, who were getting ready to interrogate the suspect.

"What happened?" I asked them.

"We have the guy in the interrogating room. He's *'lawyered'* up. So, we are waiting for his attorney to begin the questioning," Farnsworth replied.

Charles cut to the chase. "His name is Richard Mathews. He's a salesclerk at a lady's jewelry store. Evidently, he made a proposition to a customer who then slapped him. He came around the counter as if he was going to hit her when this other guy nailed him with a punch to the face."

"What kind of proposition?"

"She's writing her statement in another room. She says this guy, Mathews, asked her if she liked extreme sex. He told her he was into choking, and that his partners found it very stimulating."

"That's it?" My immediate thought was that this guy didn't fit the profile.

I could tell a slight hesitancy in Charles's response. "We'll get more once we can talk to him."

"What does the lady do?" I asked.

"She's a server at some steakhouse in upper Manhattan."

"It doesn't fit the profile." I finally said it.

Farnsworth asked indignantly, "What profile?"

"A profile I've been putting together," I replied.

"Yeah, you a profiler now, Mancuso?" Farnsworth always must have a snarky comeback whenever I challenge him.

"No, but I've been talking to people who know about this."

"Like who?" Charles asked.

"That's not important. What is important is that we are looking for a professional type person who preys on other professional ladies who are in the law enforcement field?"

Farnsworth gave me his snobby look. "Yeah? Well… you stick to that. In the meantime, we have a live one here. And, we're under a lot of pressure to find the bastard doing this."

I exchanged glances with Detective Charles. He had a look of resignation on his face. He raised his shoulders as if to say, *'It is what it is. Nothing much I can do about it.'*

The suspect's lawyer arrived. He followed Farnsworth into the interrogation room where Mathews was waiting. The first thing Farnsworth did was handed the attorney a warrant to search Mathew's apartment in Queens. He made it clear to them that the search was going on as they spoke.

Detective Charles, Captain Alex, and I watched the bullshit scene from behind the double glass one-way mirror. The suspect, Mathews, was a scrawny guy. Conceivably, one hundred fifty pounds max. Wearing a cheap off-the-rack suit. He sat there, furious. He wanted to charge the guy that punched him with assault. Matthews just didn't have the look or the type to convince our vic's hooking up with him.

Captain Alex got a call on his cell phone. Clicking off the phone, he banged on the glass for Farnsworth to come out. The captain told him to get the password for the Matthews' computer.

"They found pornographic photos and magazines in this guy's apartment, all extreme sex type stuff. We're sure the laptop has a lot more," the captain barked to Farnsworth.

55

When Farnsworth went back in, I pulled the captain aside. "Captain, this is not our guy. You're wasting time on this."

"Joey," the captain began, "right now, this is the best lead we have. The type of sex in those photos is very similar to what our murderer has been doing to his victims."

I shook my head, "If you're going to arrest every person who is into extreme sex, we better open Alcatraz."

Farnsworth blurted out loud the password without coming out, "Chokemeplease. All one word. Capital C."

The captain called the detectives searching and gave them the pass- word. Moments later, they got back to the captain with the news that this guy had videos of him and his sex partners doing it. Choking and all.

I asked the captain, "Does it have anal sex and choking with a ribbon?"

The captain replied, "They weren't specific. They're bringing the laptop and the photos here. We're booking this guy."

"On what?" I challenged. "Possession of pornography is not illegal."

"No, but they said some of those girls looked like minors, and that is illegal. So, we're going with that until we have more," Captain Alex shot back.

Incredulously, I looked towards Detective Charles, shaking my head again. "I'm out of here. I have other things to do. By the way,

Captain, when are you going to let the public know that there is a serial killer out there?"

The captain looked at me, "Good timing on your part. The chief just called to tell me the mayor is holding a press conference in an hour. He is going to announce that we have a suspect in the four killings."

"Captain," I said, a bit too loud as everyone looked at me. "This guy is as much a suspect in this case as he is in the assassination of John Kennedy."

"Mancuso, look at me. We do the police work, others oversee the politics," the captain replied, staring into my eyes.

"So, we solve this case? Is that what you're saying here?"

"Not until we prove this guy is the killer. Keep digging on your end."

"I think it is a huge mistake to tell the public we have a suspect. Ladies out there are still in danger. And second, this is going to piss off the actual killer. Mark my words, he is going to kill again to prove everyone wrong."

The captain grabbed my arm and pulled me aside. "Or, the killer is going to stop hoping we can pin the murders on this guy. If that's the case, it will buy us time until we find the real perp."

"You should get help from the FBI and have them help you with a profile of our killer. From the profile we developed, this guy is a narcissist, and he will not be happy that someone else is getting credit for his killings. Trust me on that."

"Possibly, we will. In the meantime, continue working your leads," the captain stated.

I knew my crew was on the right path. I just hoped we could crack this case before we had another statistic.

CHAPTER 8

The night had gone by without any new incidents. It was now nine in the morning. Detective Lucy picked me up at the pub. She and I spent the better part of the day and afternoon visiting the other murder scenes. The only thing I confirmed was the lack of cameras or any security at the apartments. Lucy had to get back to the precinct. So, she dropped me off at the pub.

I was eager to meet with Mr. Pat, brother Dominic, and Agnes. From what I could see here at the precinct, they were going to go with this suspect until he proved otherwise. Precious time was going to be wasted in this political bullshit.

It was already five in the afternoon. The pub was packed and vibrant with the sound of laughter. There was a constant buzz as one walked in. Tony Bennett's, 'That Old Black Magic' was playing in the background. Riley O'Sullivan, our new pub manager, was handling the pub just fine. I waved at Riley, and he pointed to our new office, alerting me the group had already gathered. I said hello to a few patrons, shook a few hands, patted a few backs, and made my way to our new but unfinished office.

My gang was sitting around our conference table. I could see Agnes had started a map which she pinned to a whiteboard. She used four different colored markers to identify the murders.

"Guys let me turn the television on. The mayor is going to have a press conference in a few minutes," I said, walking in.

Father Dom asked, "About what?"

"They picked up some dumb bastard after an altercation at a store. It turns out this guy has pornographic pictures stored on his laptop, plus other related stuff," I replied, as I sat down at the table.

Dominic asked another question, "And they think this is our killer?"

I shook my head affirmatively. "They're going to use him as a suspect and announce for the first time that these killings are related."

It was Mr. Pat's turn to chime in. "And what do you think, lad?"

"It's bullshit. They'll couch the bad news with something positive,"

I was close to livid. I needed to focus on sharing the newest piece of information to the group. "Let me go over the profile I put together with Marcy and her partner, GQ Tony."

For the next few minutes, I went over my notes about the killer's description based on the nitty-gritty details Special Agent Tony described about narcissists.

Father Dom spoke up first after the discussion ended. "The data you just shared gives me a clear sign our unsub will not be pleased when the mayor makes his announcement. This guy, most likely, is going to produce another victim."

"Brother, that's exactly what I told the NYPD. I even mentioned that it might trigger an immediate response from this sicko."

Agnes said, "Let's hope not."

I turned to Mr. Pat. "You guys visit with Sally Anders, the room-mate of our second victim?"

"Yes, we did. Let Father Dom, tell you about it," Mr. Pat, replied.

Dom began, "We located her at a friend's place. I don't think she is moving back to that apartment ever again. Anyway, she has no recollection of being approached by anyone. The day before the murder, she and Mary Ellen Vickers, the victim, had drinks at Ernie's bar in Midtown. They met no one there while they sat at the bar."

"Did Sally remember telling Mary Ellen Vickers that she was going to be out of town the next day?"

Nodding back to me, Patrick pointed to Dom, who said, "I asked her that. She, in fact, told Vickers about a business trip that she'd be taking the following day, and that she would be out two nights."

"So, our unsub could have heard that Vickers would be alone for two nights. Don't you think?" I asked.

Patrick's info confirmed my suspicion. "This young lady, Sally, told us the bar was packed. So, yes, our unsub could have easily been sitting next to them and overheard the conversation."

"What does Sally Anders look like? Does she fit the profile of the victims?" I asked.

This time Dom pointed to Patrick. "If we assume this guy is going after attractive brunettes in their late twenties or early thirties no. Sally is a cute lady, but she's blonde and more like late thirties, or, early forties. However, she is an attorney. So, therefore, there is that connection."

"No, I think you have it right, Mr. Pat. So far, all the victims look alike. No blondes."

Agnes added, "I hate to say it, but all the victims look like Marcy." Wow, that was something I didn't want to hear. I widened my eyes, as I could sadly corroborate with Agnes's assessment. "You are right. I'm glad Marcy is staying home these days. That is an astute observation Agnes."

"We have nothing else on Sally Anders. Agnes, why don't you go over the map and the points you've marked?"

Responding to Dom's request, Agnes stood up and walked over to the whiteboard. "Believe it, or not, everything is happening near the precinct, Midtown South Precinct—your precinct, in fact, Joey. Around West 35th Street and 9th Avenue. If you look here," Agnes used her pen to point to an apartment building, "The first murder took place in this building on West 34th Street. The second murder just a few blocks from there on West 35th and 9th. The third victim was West 36th and 9th." Moving her pen to the last location on the map. Agnes continued, "And finally, our fourth, lived on the West 39th and 9th."

"You're right, everything is around the precinct," I added. "What did you say the name of the bar was that Sally and our victim, Vickers, went to? Ernie's?"

"Correct. Ernie's is on West 38th and 9th, close to your competition, Scallywag's Irish Pub," Agnes replied.

I sat back, crossed my legs, and posed my question. "Agnes, were you able to locate restaurants, or bars serving sushi and that drink, sōchū?"

"Right around this area, you have your choice of Latin, Indian, Pakistani, Italian, and a few others. The sushi places are on the east side, but still within walking distance to our victim's places. I found one place serving the Inari roll which is what one entree our victims ate. It's called Noriko. Other places don't list Inari rolls on the menu, but they'll make it if requested since it's so simple to prepare. One place that has both sushi and sōchū is at Shimizu on West 51st Street."

Patrick smiled. "Looks like we have to do our research, boss. I'm getting hungry as it is."

"Sounds like a plan, Mr. Pat. Father, are you in?" I inquired.

"You three go ahead. I need to get back to Saint Helens. I'll be in tomorrow after Mass. Enjoy."

"Very well. Let's have a drink at Ernie's, then, try this Shimizu place. Agnes, did you do any research on our victims?"

"Yes, I did. I also have pictures from their Facebook profiles. You want them now?"

"Let's review over dinner. Oh, there's the mayor now at his press conference. Let's listen to what he has to say," I said, turning up the volume on the television using the remote control.

In a crowded pressroom and over the sound of the gathered group, a news reporter captured the interest of TV viewers. Speaking slowly but distinctly, she relayed the latest news.

"This is Marlene Myers with WBYW, Channel Five, in New York City. In a few moments, we are going to hear statements by the mayor about four recent murders that, until today, had not been linked to a possible serial killer.

In the last three weeks, they murdered four young ladies in what seems to be the work of one man. Here is the mayor now. Let's listen in."

The mayor was introduced and began speaking, "Ladies and gentle- men. Today, we have apprehended a man whom we believe to be a prime suspect in four horrific murders that have occurred in the last few weeks in our city. Our police department has worked diligently on this case since the beginning." He paused, looking around the crowd.

"Until now, we had been following specific leads to these murders. So as not to alarm the public unnecessarily and prematurely, they kept information on the killings confidential for the case detectives to work on unencumbered. In a moment, we will hand out a press release with the names of the four victims," he said, nodding to an assistant holding the releases.

He went on. "I want to assure the citizens of our beautiful city that we will follow through on this case and bring to justice the brutal murderer of these young ladies. I will take some questions now."

"What a bunch of crap," I said, as I hit the mute button. "I hope our unsub doesn't take this bullshit personally. Otherwise, we are about to have a fifth victim real soon."

"Don't you want to listen to the Q and A, Joey?"

"Mr. Pat, I don't want to hear more fictionalized news. Let's concentrate on our findings. We've narrowed down the perimeter where this guy seems to operate in, and a few locations from where he might stalk his victims. I'm going to call Detective Lucy Roberts and see if she wants to join us for dinner."

"Joey, since these murders are all around the precinct, do you think the unsub is trying to send you a message?"

I looked at Mr. Pat. I had never given that a thought. It was plausible, but seriously, me? I uttered a weak reply, "Ah,... I sure hope not."

CHAPTER 9

We started at Ernie's which seemed to cater to the age group our victims fell into. Late twenties to mid-thirties and most professionals. Identifying ourselves as consultants with the NYPD, we showed pictures of the victims to the staff and got no hits. This wasn't unexpected. Ernie's was a high turnover bar in which most patrons came in for a drink or two but then moved on. A quaint little place—lots of mirrors and chrome. Unless a patron made some scene, no one would remember having seen anyone here. That, however, made a perfect place for our unsub to hang out, and begin his stalking process.

Detective Lucy joined us at Shimizu for dinner. Everything looked squared. The floors were squared with blue and green tiles, as well as the tables and doilies. The designer must have flunked geometry. That's all I had to say. While there, I brought up Lucy on the profile we had developed for our killer. Like me, she agreed that this suspect in custody was purely a move by the city administration to soften the news about a serial killer roaming the streets of New York.

"Agnes, you're the sushi expert. Why don't you order for us?" I said.

"How about we order what our victims ate?" She suggested.

Mr. Pat made a face, "I wished you hadn't put it like that, Ms. Agnes."

I laughed along with the others, "As long as it's cooked, I'll eat it."

After Agnes ordered, we began going over the research on our four victims.

Agnes opened her files and read from them, "These ladies have a very similar profile. They all have college degrees and were employed in some fashion in law-related jobs. There's a third category—something we have not mentioned. They're all white."

I asked, "What about their Facebook profiles? Are there similarities?"

Agnes flipped a few pages before replying. "Yes. They posted pics that would lead people to believe they were very promiscuous."

"Mr. Pat noticed that first. How so?" Lucy asked, glancing at Patrick.

Agnes smiled, "The pictures they shared of themselves were mostly in social settings. Such as bars like Ernie's, embracing guys and other ladies. Then, many of their other postings dealt with sex, love, one- night stands, stuff like that. Some other pics are not necessarily porno- graphic, but very sexually suggestive."

"And, of course, they all show their place of employment, age, and everything else about them, right?"

"Yes, they do, Joey," Agnes replied.

Patrick asked, "If our—" he paused, looking around, "if our person of interest is using Facebook as a resource for selecting his targets, how does he narrow then down?"

Agnes explained, "Good question. To answer your question, many people on Facebook join groups. For instance, Mr. Pat, you could join a group for 'New York Private Detectives,' or, in your immediate past life, 'New York Bartenders.' So, it turns out that these ladies were all members of various groups. What's interesting though, after doing my research on their profiles, I found that all of them were members of the same three groups at the same time. Namely, *'New York Social'*, *'New York Dating'*, and *'New York Attorneys.'"*

Patrick posed an important question. "Not all ladies were attorneys. Why would they join an attorney's group?"

Agnes smiled, "Ah, Mr. Pat, you're not looking to get married. But think for a minute. You're a single girl in New York City, employed in some fashion with the legal profession. You probably want to date, hook up, and ultimately find your Mr. Right. Why not join a group of local attorneys?"

"I would, honey," said Lucy.

We all shared a good chuckle over that comment. "How many members in all three groups?" I asked.

Agnes replied, " about three thousand, give or take a few."

"Can you see pictures of all the members?" I inquired.

"Only if you join the group and they accept you, yes," Agnes replied. "Then, it opens up the pages to all postings, etcetera."

Lucy took a sip from her warm saké before asking, "Do you think our perp is a member of these groups? And if so, is his picture on the group pages?"

Agnes looked up from the files. You could tell she did her homework. She knew exactly how to answer Lucy's questions.

"He would have to be a member to see the full profile of others. However, as to his picture, or his profile, well, he can put just about anything he wants. There is no verification of any kind. Profile pictures are optional."

Patrick made a face after tasting his saké. "Agnes, even if we studied all three thousand profiles, there's no telling if we are going to find the actual identity of the perp. Is that correct?"

"That's correct, Mr. Pat. However, I assure you he is in one group, or all three. But you're right. It's going to be a monumental task to find him that way."

Lucy added, sarcastically, "Well, that's a warm and fuzzy thought."

"I have an idea," I offered. "First, we should start looking at the members of the groups. But for the moment, only look at male members. As we do that, we should examine their profiles to see if there're any proclivities to an extreme and, or anal sex, whether explicit or implied.

Also, look at their 'likes,' such as restaurants, bars, and food types. Further, based on the profile we developed of this person as a narcissist. See if any of their postings show any of the characteristics we discussed."

Patrick raised his index finger. "You want us to join these groups so that we can get full access?"

"Yes, Mr. Pat. But develop faked identities. Each of us, including Father Dom, will become members of the three groups. That way we'll have fifteen different profiles. All fifteen profiles are going to be females, matching the description of our victims. Brunettes, in the legal profession, et cetera. And, let's be sure we are a little extra sexually permissive in our postings, including a propensity for extreme sex."

Mr. Pat smiled, "I don't know if I can be that creative."

I smiled at Pat, saying, "Come on, Mr. Pat, you can share those sexual fantasies you've had."

Agnes interrupted the light bantering. Now, it was her turn to be on a roll. "I'll take care of the profiles for all of us. You don't have to worry about them. Especially you, Mr. Pat."

"What about the additional fake pictures of us?" Lucy asked.

"I'll do that, too. I have my ways," Agnes produced the perfect Cheshire Cat smile before she closed her files and put them in her briefcase.

Our server arrived with our sushi. We agreed to share the various rolls that Agnes had ordered, family style. Somehow, eating the food that had been found in our victim's stomach contents, suddenly, became a little repugnant. I glanced around the table. Unexpectedly, everyone looked nauseated. "I think I'm going to have to get a burger on the way back."

"I'm with you, Joey, and a beer or two. This saké is not for me, " Mr. Pat added.

Lucy said, "You guys are so uncivilized. Eat your sushi. It's good."

"Back to our case," I said, "Agnes, get started with the profiles.

The sooner we join these groups, the faster we'll locate our unsub. At least, this is my hope. If our unsub is using this method as a menu to select his next—" I glanced around, "for his next date, we might be able to get ahead of him."

Patrick countered, "But how? You plan on contacting all these ladies?"

I thought for a second.

Agnes is sure that she has it all figured out. "I could post a warning on the sites, or, depending on how many, I could send a direct message."

Lucy chimed in, "And that could get your gig as consultants canceled immediately if the city admin sees it. Plus, our unsub is likely to see it."

"Lucy is right," I said. "We need to find another way. For now, let's gather the members fitting the profile, and join the groups. Then, we'll see how we go about it. We might need to add more faked profiles if we don't get a hit right away."

My right thigh vibrated, giving me an unexpected jolt. I pulled my cell phone out, and without looking at the caller ID, I answered, "This is Mancuso."

"Joey, Special Agent Tony here."

I glanced around the table, opening my eyes wide, "Hey, Special Agent Tony. How you doing?" I asked in my New York Italian slang.

"Did you see the press conference?" Tony asked, in a serious tone. Almost pissed, I would say. "I did. I did. Why?"

"Did you not share what we put together with the NYPD?" He asked, a bit agitated now.

"I was there when they interrogated this so-called suspect. I told them they had it wrong."

"What did they say? Hang on a second, Joey," Tony said, covering the mouthpiece, although I heard, "Thank you, Marcy." His tone became calmer, suddenly.

"Where are you, Tony?" I asked.

"Over at Marcy's. We went to the range today, and she asked me to stay for dinner. She made this incredible vaca frita. You know what that is? Shredded beef, pan-fried, a little garlic and onions—"

The hell with that. I interrupted, "I got it. I got it. How long are you going to be there? I was going to call Marcy," I lied. Now, I was pissed.

"I'm taking off in a few minutes. Anyway, they have this all wrong, man. That suspect does not fit the profile."

"I told them that."

"Well, they're going to piss the true perp guy off, and he's going to strike again. Soon."

"I told them that, also, Tony. I'm sure that by tomorrow they'll have to clear this guy."

"Yeah, well, tomorrow might be too late for the next victim. Do you have any updates on your own? Anything you want to share?" Tony asked.

"Nothing new. I've updated my group on the wonderful profile you put together. We're still working on this," I replied, stroking his ego and not wanting to share any additional information we had.

"Okay, Mancuso. We'll talk tomorrow, and I'll tell Marcy you're going to call her. She's making me a *cortadito* now. Take care," he said, and then hung up.

What an asshole. I said under my breath. Glancing at my group, I realized they were all staring at me, waiting for an update.

"So? You heard that was GQ Tony. He's upset no one paid attention to his profile."

Patrick added, "Rightfully so, I'd say."

"Hang on a second, honey," Lucy said. "What's that stiff necked, pompous ass doing at Marcy's again?"

"He's been helping her at the range. Marcy needs to take the FBI's firearm test soon," I replied.

Lucy quipped, "Helping her at the range? Yeah? You better put a target on that creepy ass guy, Mancuso. There's more than target practice going on there."

"Marcy assures me there's nothing going on there. At least, on her end," I said, in a hushed manner, looking at Lucy.

"Oh, darling. I believe that on Marcy's end, as you said. But this creepy crawler, Mr. Perfect, is a salesman, honey. He is selling, selling, all the time. Look out for that type."

"Point taken, let's get out of here. We'll reconvene tomorrow," I said.

Mr. Pat leaned over and whispered, "Burger and a beer?" I was more than ready. "You're on."

CHAPTER 10

I arrived at the Midtown South Precinct on West 35th Street at nine in the morning. The observation that Mr. Pat made yesterday about all the murders taking place within blocks of the precinct was intriguing. What I couldn't fathom was his other observation that the crimes were directed at me. Still shaking my head over this bizarre connection, I filed that last thought.

Detective Charles approached me, "Joey, we're meeting in the conference room. Join us."

Already in the office, Detective Farnsworth and Captain Johnson looked despondent. The captain pointed to a seat for me to take. "You were right, Joey," he began, "they released the suspect this morning. He had a legitimate alibi. He was nowhere near any of the murders when they occurred."

Pounding on the table, Farnsworth added, "Yeah, but he's still a pervert. Just not our pervert."

Ignoring Farns' comment, I asked the captain, "So, where are you now?"

The captain, in his brusque fashion, shoved the murder book aside, and replied, "We've wasted an entire day, and the mayor is pissed. Pissed. He says we made him look like a fool. The pressure is on."

I said, "So now, he's blaming you guys for them not being forthcoming with the news about a serial killer?"

"That's politics, right?" Johnson asked. "I hate to say it, but

"Pushing back from the table, Farns interrupted me, "Yeah, yeah,

Mr. Consultant, you said as much yesterday. What have you done?"

"We've been busy profiling our victims," I replied. I was about to explain everything we had uncovered, but then, I thought about Mr. Pat's, observation. "What if the unsub is in law enforcement himself? And, what about the fact that all the murders are happening within walking distance of this precinct?" I held back the information and plan of attack related to social media, now. So, simply, I said, "I'll have more later. My research lady is looking into the backgrounds of the victims for other clues."

Farns got up from his chair, "Fuck this. Charles and I have a few visits to make. We might as well start with other known sexual offenders we have in our files. We probably should have done that before."

That would have been smart of them to do. But again… both detectives left the room, leaving me alone with the captain. I asked, "Where's Lucy?"

"She should be here momentarily. She was delayed," he replied, sitting back. "Somehow, I think you have more than what you shared with us."

I glanced at the door to make sure we were alone, "I do. But for the moment this has to stay between us."

The captain leaned forward asking, "Why? What do you have?"

"All the victims lived within walking distance form this precinct. It involved all in the law profession or related field. And—" The captain's eyes opened wide. Interrupting me, he asked in astonishment, "Wait. You think someone in this precinct is the suspect?"

"No. I didn't say that ... well, at least, I hope he's not from this precinct. However, I don't believe in coincidences. I have a strong feeling our unsub is in the law enforcement field."

Placing his elbows on the table and covering his face with both hands, Captain Johnson said, "Shit, that's going to make the mayor blow a fuse." Raising his head and looking straight into my eyes, he asked, "Are you sure?"

"I'm not sure yet."

"So, why not share with the detectives?" You think one of them could be our killer?"

"All I know is that it is not you, nor I. Everyone else is a suspect until they're not. Also, we have a little sting operation going on, and, if we are lucky, we may trap the suspect. We're chumming the waters to see if our guy comes up."

The captain asked with a little apprehension, "Do I want to know what you're doing? Are you up to one of your charades?"

I sat back and laughed, "All of my charades, as you call them, have proved effective. Besides, we're not doing anything illegal. Look, we've uncovered, based on their social media profiles, that all these ladies were a bit sexually permissive. I don't want to imply they were asking for it. But anyone looking at their Facebook, Twitter, and Instagram profiles would think they were looking to get hooked up."

The captain leaned forward and whispered, "So, what's your plan?" I told the captain about our fishing expedition. Even though it was a long shot, and while it may take some time to develop, it was the only thing we had going. Hopefully, no more bodies will surface.

Although, my gut feeling was that the killer had something to prove.

Lucy walked into the conference room with a broad smile that flashed those pearly whites of hers. "Good morning, Captain, Joey. Sorry I'm late."

I said, looking at the captain, "This lady can walk into a funeral home and light up the room with that smile of hers. Makes everyone wonder what the hell she knows that they don't."

The captain smiled, "I know. I've enjoyed that smile for years. Got anything for us, Lucy?"

"Let me sit down and review this report from ViCAP, which I just got. Glancing it over, I do not see an exact match. No record of the same modus operandi. Either this killer is new, or, he knows to change his signature so they can't track him."

I wheeled my chair in closer to the table, and added, "He wants recognition, and his narcissistic behavior would show he wants credit for his acts. But perhaps he is smart enough to change signatures. Anything close to what we have here in New York?"

Lucy, keeping her eyes on the file, replied, "Unfortunately, quite a few unsolved cases are dealing with extreme sex. Only a few with anal sex, but none with a cross being cut into the breasts."

I had my arms on the table. Opening my palms, I inquired, "How about extreme sex, strangulation, together with anal sex, and cuts of any kind?"

"This is a long list," Lucy replied, looking up from the file, "I suppose I could rerun the program inputting those parameters."

"I think you should," the captain said, "start with two of those parameters, then add a third, and a fourth. Let's see what we get."

Lucy replied, "Yes, I'll do that." Then glancing at me, she asked, "Did you share anything on our fishing trip?"

Pointing at Captain Alex, I replied, "Only with him. No one else."

"Good," Lucy said.

"Let me ask," said the captain, "what happens if you get a bite on your social media profiles? What is your plan then?"

"We plan on being there to observe."

Johnson asked, "Wouldn't it be better to have an undercover cop play the role of your lady?"

I replied, "Absolutely. But she would have to meet the physical profile of our victims if it's going to work."

The captain smiled, "There's a young lady at the 25th Precinct in vice who just moved up from Miami. She wants to switch to homicide. I think she'd be perfect. She's blonde, but that can easily be rectified. What do you think?"

Lucy looked at me and nodded. I replied, "Let's meet her." Johnson pulled out his cell phone, "Want to meet her here?"

Shaking my head, I replied, "No, not here. Have her met us at the pub later this evening."

Lucy asked, "What's her name?"

Captain Johnson thought for a second, "Angela Asis. Originally from Barcelona, Spain. You'll tell her how she needs to look. She's young, attractive, and outgoing."

I searched for a picture of Marcy on my phone, handed it to the captain, and asked, "Do you think she can look like Marcy?"

"Why Marcy?"

I didn't want to reply. I hesitated, not wanting to tie the two together.

Lucy said, "Because all the victims have similarities to Marcy. Hair, eyes, a little younger, but not much. It's freaky."

Johnson couldn't take his eyes from Marcy's picture. "Angela is a perfect match. Amazing, I did not know—the similarities to our vics."

CHAPTER 11

I walked into the pub a little after five-thirty in the afternoon. It was lively with our first shift of Wall Streeters enjoying their premium drinks and cigars. A thin layer of white-grayish cigar smoke hovered above the back area of the pub. A second later, poof—the puff sucked up by our pricy exhaust system which had been an excellent investment on our part. No one ever complained about the smoke or smell of the cigars. Instead, what lingered was the natural aroma of the pub, that infusion of spirits of all kinds, and the occasional brewed espresso. The pub enjoyed a life of its own.

Sammy Davis's songs warmed up the crowd while waiting for the main act, Sinatra's 'New York, New York' which played every evening at seven, and to which the patrons sang along. They loved it.

Every time "a good-looking babe," as Sinatra would say, walked unaccompanied into the pub, the crowd went silent. I was standing at the very end of the bar when I noticed a lull in the room. It was as if the pub held its collective breath. I half expected to see Police Commissioner O'Malley, who occasionally stops in for a visit. But when I looked up and turned to my right, I immediately thought, 'Marcy?' Then, I realized this young primo looking fully loaded lady was a blond.

A Marcy look-alike. "Oh, boy," I said under my breath to no one.

Riley, our new pub manager, was at the entrance of the pub serving some drinks. He turned to face her, scratched his red beard, and with his Irish brogue asked, "May I help you, lassie?"

The young lady smiled at Riley and replied in a smoky voice with a slight Spanish accent, "Yes, thank you. I'm looking for Joseph Mancuso."

Riley turned and pointed his index finger at me, which, frankly, was what I was hoping for. Then, he turned back to the primo lady and said, "You mean Joey. See that rough-looking guy with the slick black hair behind the bar at the end? That's Joey."

I raised my right hand to wave at her, as she began walking towards me. Slowly, the crowd resumed their conversations, and once again, the pub resumed its natural sound.

"Hi, Joey. I'm Angela Asis," she said, unbuttoning her coat, and sat on a stool in front of me. "You're staring."

"Hi, Angela. Sorry about that, but you look very much like someone I know. She's not blonde."

"You mean Marcy? Yes, I know."

"You know about Marcy?"

"They have briefed me. And, I have read all the press reports from earlier this year when Marcy was shot on the plane at Newark. Preventing those radical Islamists from creating a mass shooting was quite a heroic act on her part. How is she doing?"

"Unfortunately, a US Federal Marshal was killed in the incident. But yes, it could have been devastating if the two shooters had started their killing spree in the plane. Marcy is doing much better, thank you. She is getting ready to take the FBI fitness and firearms test and be reinstated."

"Sounds good. Now, tell me about this case."

"Are you still on the clock?"

"No, I'm off-duty now?"

"How about an adult beverage?"

"A beer, thanks."

"One Brooklyn Lager coming up. Glass or bottle?"

"Bottle is fine, thank you."

I reached to my right and pulled out two locally brewed Brooklyn Lagers from one of the many ice packed buckets that we kept with various brands of beers around the pub. I wrapped a paper napkin around her bottle, popped the top, and handed it to her. I did the same to mine. "How much do you know about the case?" I asked, looking around to make sure we had some privacy.

Angela took a sip from her beer, put it down, peeled the napkin back a bit to look at the label, and replied, "I'm aware of all the incidents. I've reviewed the murder book and have been read in as to the trap you want to set."

Not all Spanish accents are the same. I've heard my share here in New York. Spaniards have a distinct accent when speaking English. Angela's was no exception. It sounded like a female romantic and a melodic version of Julio Iglesias, the Spanish singer. I could listen to her for hours. But no. Back to business. "Okay, so you know we have read only a few people into this, right?"

"I do."

"As you know, we are posting many profiles on social media, and some group pages. All with the characteristics of the victims, from physical to like. As well as preferences," I said, glancing around.

Angela flashed a smile, "Some of which are going to be quite explicit about sexual permissiveness."

"Is that a problem?"

"Joey, I've been in the Vice Squad in Miami PD for a few years.

This is like playing dolls again. Although, I have two questions."

I leaned forward on the bar to ask, "Which are?"

"First, you are going to post multiple profiles. What about pictures? You can't post my face in all of them."

I motioned with my hand for her to stop there. "We're going to do it in such a way that we don't show your frontal profile. Well, not your face anyway. You're going to have to pose for a photo layout. What's the next question?"

"How are we going to filter for the many perverts that are going to respond to these postings? All these social sites are full of them."

"I know," I replied, and noticed she had finished her beer. "How about another beer?"

"Sure."

Handing her another lager, I replied, "We know the guy is local. We are pretty sure he is in law enforcement like our victims. And he, most likely, is a member of one of these social groups. So, now, we'll ignore the other perverts, as you say."

"Great, I'm ready to start. Tell me something about that photo hanging on the wall behind you," she said, pointing past me at the wall. I didn't have to look. I knew the photo she was referring to. I smiled, "That's one of the twenty-two black and white photos we have around the pub. That one is the oldest one of the bunch. In 1948, Captain O'Brian opened the pub. That photo is of him with Truman Capote when Capote released his first novel, *'Other Voices, Other Rooms'*."

"I love it," Angela said, and asked, "Have you visited Cuba?"

"Only Little Havana in Miami. Otherwise, no. Why do you ask?"

"The Hotel Nacional de Cuba in Havana has four bars within the property. One of them called *'Vista al Golfo Bar'* has pictures of celebrities who visited the hotel going back to the 1930s. Your pub reminds me of that bar."

"So, you've been to Cuba?"

"I've kept my Spanish passport, so it was easy. Yes."

"Pleasure or business?" I inquired, only because I was curious. It was none of my business.

She smiled, glanced around and replied, "If I tell you—" she paused. "Okay, I got it, you'll have to kill me."

"Exactly. When do I meet the rest of your team?"

"Be here at nine tomorrow morning. I'll have the team assembled, and we'll do the photo shoot in our brand-new office, which got new flooring today. Finally."

"What should I wear?"

"Bring a change of clothes. We need various pictures. Be sure to bring your Miami Beach wear."

Smiling, she said, "That fits in my little purse. Is your brother, the priest, going to be here?"

"*El Padre* Dominic, yes. But I'll make sure he leaves before the photo shoot if that makes you feel better."

"It would, *Sí*. You know, Joey? I could bring some of my photos of me in bathing suits."

Yeah, but that would not be as much fun. "You could, but then we have to crop and experiment with Adobe Photoshop. We'll just do new photos." Now, who's the pervert?

Mischievously, she asked, "Are you taking them?"

"No, Agnes will. I'll direct," I said, trying to sound toneless.

"Great. Tell me a little about your background. How did you end up owning an Irish pub?"

"My background, you ask, huh? So far there are three chapters, and we're on chapter three," I said, taking a sip of my beer. I went on, "Chapter one, I guess I'll call it, was growing up with an Irish mother, and an Italian father. A loving family. That's my recollection. Chapter one ended with my father getting shot in a bar in Little Italy when I was sixteen."

"Oh! I'm so sorry to hear that. You don't have to go on," she said, shaking her head.

"It's okay. I'll give you the short version. My dad, second generation Italian, born in Little Italy, like myself, followed his dad's chosen profession back then. I was headed in the same direction, until that day," I replied, in a low voice glancing around."

"So, what happened?" She asked, leaning forward on her stool. "Father Dominic happened. That's what happened. Dom is me Mom's first born from her first marriage to Brandon O'Brian. Father Dom became my surrogate father from that point on. It was his persistence that started me on the right path, and the start of chapter two."

"That's when you joined the NYPD?"

"Exactly. And for sixteen years, I did that, until—" I paused, not wanting to get into too many details, "Dom and I took over for his Dad running and managing the pub. And here we are in chapter three."

Angela began putting her coat back on, "Chapter three could be interesting. I mean, you guys are running a pub and a cigar bar, and as private investigators consulting for the NYPD."

"Could get very interesting, yes. We're, also, going to be taking cases from a criminal law firm here in New York. Therefore, it could be a fun chapter," I said, dropping our bottles in a recycling bin below the bar.

"Okay, *hasta mañana,* baby," Angela said, in her smoky voice while buttoning her coat.

"Thank you for volunteering for this, Angela. We have to stop this guy quickly."

"I know. Listen, I've been seeing your manager make espressos.

Would you mind asking him if he can make me a *cortado*?"

"You mean steamed milk and expresso?"

"Yes, why? What do you call it?"

"I call it a *macchiato*, and Marcy calls it a *cortadito*. All the same, I guess. I'll make it. One *cortado* coming up."

As she began her walk to the front door, the pub went systematically quiet again. It was seven in the evening, as the front door closed erasing all traces of Angela, the crowd erupted with *'New York, New York.'*

CHAPTER 12

I love taking my Shelby Mustang out on weekend drives—the only time I get to enjoy it. Since parking during the week is at a premium in New York City, particularly in the Financial Center where the pub is located, it makes sense for me to use a car service. Today, I was in a Toyota Corolla. My Uber driver, Lucio, was dealing with a thin layer of snow on the ground, which was a carryover from the early morning precipitation.

I was looking forward to reaching the pub and setting up for the photo shoot with Angela. My instinct kept telling me that planting the fake profiles on the social media pages would generate a lead for us. It was a risky proposition. Specifically, if it stirred public apprehension over the idea that a serial killer was running rampant terrorizing the city. Unexpectedly, my cell phone rang, startling both Lucio and me. The ID caller read Capt. Alex. "Good morning, Captain."

"Not quite. We have another victim."

"Shit," I said, looking at the phone. "Where?"

"West 8th and 32nd."

"That's just east of the precinct?" I asked, looking out the window, but not focusing on anything. "Can you go there, now?"

"On my way. Text me the exact address," I replied. I asked Lucio to change course and take me to the scene of the newest murder. Next, I called the pub and alerted everyone where I was headed and why. I asked them to stay put for a bit.

They taped the entrance to the small apartment building off with the all too well-known yellow crime tape. I inspected the exterior. Sure enough, there were no cameras of any kind visible on the exterior of the building. Walking up two flights of stairs, I found Officer Sanchez, and his partner, Officer Edwards, standing outside the entrance to the victim's apartment. The same two officers that had been first on the scene at the last murder.

I don't believe in coincidences, but they do occur. So, I asked as I walked in, "How come you guys are here?"

Sanchez, the tall and gangly one, replied, "We got the call, sir."

"Are you guys out of Midtown South Precinct?"

"Yes, we are, sir."

Edwards, the hefty one with another tight tapered shirt, noticed that I had become pensive. He frankly said, "This is not just a coincidence, Mr. Mancuso. This is our shift and our area of patrol. Plain and simple."

I turned to look at him, "Got it. Tell me what we have here." Sanchez swallowed hard, and replied, "The precinct got an anonymous call about a dead body at eight this morning, and we responded to the call. The building super opened the door, and that's what we found." He pointed to the inside.

I stuck my head in and saw a small studio apartment. Again, as in the others, the room temperature was frigid. A window was opened allowing the outside temperature, which was in the thirties, to invade the interior of the studio apartment. The bed was towards the back and in the middle of the room. Two doors were on the right of the bed. One of which I assumed to be the closet. The other was the bathroom. A small kitchenette area was towards the front left. On the right was a sitting area comprising a settee, coffee table, and lounge chair in front of desk positioned by the wall with a small television on it.

The body of our victim lay on the bed, naked, facing down with her legs dangling down at the end of the bed. *'Same MO,'* I said to myself. "Did you guys go in?"

"I did, sir," replied Edwards. "I wanted to see if our victim was dead."

"I assume she is."

"She is," said Edwards.

"Where did you step?" I asked, looking at Edwards.

"Yes, sir. I went in and purposely walked close to the walls on the right side."

"Excellent, Edwards. Were you wearing gloves and booties?"

"Yes, I was."

"Any sign of forced entrance?"

"No, sir. The door was locked."

"Let me see," I said, closing the front door halfway while bending down to examine the lock. It was a Schlage antique brass lock that had accumulated a thin layer of rust and turned darker with passaging time. I noticed small scratched lines around the entry area of the keyhole that revealed the original antique brass coloring. I looked closer to examine the lock.

"Do you need a magnifying glass, sir?" Sanchez asked.

"Sanchez, I have an app for that," I said, smiling and pulling out my phone.

Both patrolmen glanced at each other and chuckled.

I activated my 'Mag' App and, not only enlarged the view of the lock to see new markings but also snapped some pictures. "One could only imagine to what extent Sherlock Holmes would have gone to get an app like this."

"That's cool," Edwards said.

I finished taking a few pictures of the lock when the posse, comprising Captain Alex, Farnsworth, and Charles arrived.

Farnsworth was the first up the steps. "Mancuso, how did you get here so quick?"

I wasn't stuffing my face with jelly doughnuts at the precinct.

Was what I would have loved to have said but didn't. "I was a few blocks away," I replied, instead.

The captain asked, "What you got, Joey?"

Before I could respond, Detective Farnsworth said, "Let me in there."

"Just wait for a second," I said, blocking the entrance, like a left guard protecting the quarterback.

"Mancuso don't forget who's lead here," Farns said sternly, trying to push through my block to look inside. "My God, this lady has a big ass."

Ignoring that incredibly disrespectful comment, I spouted, "Just wait a minute." I stood tall in front of the door. Farnsworth was so close to my face that I could smell the onion bagel on his breath again. "Captain," I added, "I noticed some fresh footprints on the carpet. Moist prints. This door was picked opened."

The captain grabbed Farns left arm and pulled him back from me. "You're saying our unsub was just here?"

Quickly, I shifted to a parade rest stance before replying. "Someone was just here, and they picked their way in. So, more than likely, yes. Our unsub may have been just here."

"But the killer would have risked running into the uniforms when they arrived," Detective Charles said.

I replied, "Not quite. Our unsub made the call himself after he left." Then, I asked," Did they trace the call?"

"No, it was quick," Johnson replied.

I questioned, "He called the precinct. Not 9-1-1, right?"

Charles replied, "Yes, our precinct. What's the difference?"

Detective Charles, you dumb ass, was at the tip of my tongue. Instead, I came back with, "Had he called 9-1-1, there would be a record of where the call came from." I knew the moment the words left my mouth that Charles would catch flack for raising the question. I, suddenly, felt bad for making Charles look like a fool. "I'll bet you dollars to doughnuts that if we could locate the source of the call, it would be from one of the few remaining public phones on a nearby street."

Farnsworth was breathing heavy like a racehorse just moments before the gates open. His nostrils expanded and contracted. I think foam was forming around his mouth. He couldn't wait to get in the studio apartment.

Captain Johnson noticed the same thing. "Detectives take a walk outside and locate public phones within a two-block radius. Tape them and have a forensics team check for prints."

Farnsworth erupted, "Captain, we can have uniforms do that. This is where we need to be."

Raising his voice, Captain Johnson said, "Get to those phones before we lose any good prints. Take Sanchez and Edwards with you. I'll take over this scene."

Huffing and puffing, Farnsworth walked down the stairs followed by the others.

"The CSU team should be here momentarily," said Johnson. "How did you notice the moist footprints?"

Now that it was only the two of us, I was more relaxed, "When I bent down to examine the lock, I noticed a certain glimmer on the carpet. Upon further review, I could see wet footprints going from the front door to the bed. Then back out."

"Do you think this murder just took place?"

I replied, "I think the coroner is going to tell us it happened late last night or early morning."

"So, why'd he come back?"

"My guess is he left something behind and came to retrieve it. Fearful it might expose him."

"Very possible. Did he finally make a mistake?" The captain asked.

I wanted to reply that, yes, he had finally made a mistake. But I wasn't sure if that was indeed the case. "Captain, I'm photographing the footprints before they dry up. Otherwise, we'll lose them."

"Do it."

I walked in wearing my booties and latex gloves, and turning back to Johnson, I said, "Have CSU check for prints on the lock and knob. He might have left without cleaning that. Although, I doubt it."

Kneeling and bending over, I tried to get as many photos

of the moist prints as I could. Hopefully, they could lead to a clue later.

"I'll wait here."

The freshest footprints were the first ones our unsub made as he walked in. If he forgot something, and then went outside before coming back in, he would have stepped on the thin layer of snow the city had received overnight. The glimmer I noticed on the carpet was, in fact, shoe prints.

The small studio apartment mimicked the same scenario from the previous murders. Clean and undisturbed, everything was in order, no clothes laying anywhere. Even though I wanted to inspect the lady's breasts to see if she had been cut, I waited, instead, for the crime scene unit to arrive. I decided in the meantime to check her mail that sat on the small kitchen counter.

"Captain, come in. Look for her purse while I check her mail," I said, perusing her stack of mail. Examining the opened mail on the counter, I said, "Her name was Darlene Rogers."

Johnson wearing his booties and gloves opened the closet and found her purse hanging from a hook. Other empty bags and boxes of shoes were lined up above the clothes. "Joey, she's twenty-nine, and she's DEA."

I lifted my head from the stack of mail. "She's an agent?

Johnson walked over to me to show me her shield. "Yes, she is."

"Dammit, we've got to get this fucking guy."

The captain glanced around at the whole studio as he stood next to me. "You were right. I think we pushed him to strike again this quick."

"Belford called it."

"Belford?" Johnson questioned.

"Yeah, Special Agent Belford, he's the one helping us with the profiling. He's been right on, so far."

The coroner and the CSU crew arrived. We stepped aside and said, "Guys, I need to see if her breasts are cut, and I need a TOD," I mentioned to them. "Also, make sure you check for prints on the lock, and measure the wet shoe prints on the carpet, immediately. There," I said, pointing. "I marked them where my pen is."

They looked at me with absolute disdain. It was apparent I didn't need to tell them what to do. These guys and gals are professionals. I was just trying to be extra careful with the little evidence we had. I overheard one of them tell the other, "This guy is going to tell us to hold our dick when we piss, next."

"Excuse me. Did you get the measurement of the shoe prints?" "Thirteen inches, sir," a CSU member replied.

After completing the preliminaries, taking photos, and videoing the scene, two of the members of the crew turned the body on the bed facing up, as others began checking for prints.

Sure enough. Our victim had two crosses cut into each breast. Curiously, not much blood on her or the bed.

Alice Winfield, the coroner, said, "Same MO, guys. Superficial cuts on the breasts."

"How come there's so little blood?" I questioned.

The coroner replied without raising her head, "The blood coagulates within minutes of death. Based on her position, the blood flowed to her lower body. I have a feeling they had sex. Then he strangled her during sex, as he did the others. But he cut her a few minutes after she was already dead."

"What about a time of death?" Johnson asked.

"This asshole knows what he's doing," the coroner began, "I can only guess it happened late last night, or the early morning hours, based on her body temperature, which is cold right now. She's still not in full rig."

I said, "Correct me if I'm wrong. Rigor Mortis starts about two hours after death from the neck down. And you said she is not in full rigor. So, is it possible that she was killed four or five hours ago?"

Alice, the coroner replied, "I'd say between midnight and four in the morning. But again, with the temperature in the room being so cold, it affects all my calculations."

"What about COD?" Johnson asked.

Alice motioned with her right hand to the neck area. "I'll know better when we do a full autopsy. Preliminarily, same as the others, strangulation. Same size contusion around her neck, and you can see the little red satin fibers."

"Alice, we need to know stomach contents as soon as possible," I said.

"Mancuso, we'll do an autopsy as soon as we can. Unfortunately, this is not the only body we have to deal with today," Alice replied, as she leaned down and inspected the right breast. "Look here," she pointed with her right index finger, "there seems to be some indentation on the left side of the right breast."

Both Johnson and I moved in closer to observe. "That's weird, an oval shape?" I examined.

"Let me see how big it is," Alice replied, as she measured the oval indentation. "It's one and a half inches by an inch. It has a little marking in the center."

"Allow me to take a picture with my magnifying App," I said, as I pulled my phone out and photographed the indentation. I took various photos, some standard size, others magnified.

Johnson moved back, "What could that be?"

Alice called for one of her guys to take pictures. She observed, "She's still wearing her earrings. Maybe it's a ring, or a brooch?"

"No, no," I said, "whatever it is, it belongs to the killer. That's why he came back. He left after killing her, then realized it was missing, whatever it is, and he came back to retrieve it. Otherwise, he was leaving us a clue."

"Shit," the captain said, "we need this guy to make a mistake."
"Yeah, well, he's five to zero, so far."

CHAPTER 13

I made it back to the pub after they had completed the photo shoot. Father Dom, as agreed, had not stayed for that.

Angela was not comfortable sporting her mini bikini around Dominic. I had no such issues. Unfortunately, a new murder had occurred, and duty called. Mr. Pat, Agnes, and our undercover model, Angela Asis, were waiting for me. The tension was in the room. I could cut it with a knife. It was that thick.

Angela, now dressed in her usual wear, asked in a somber tone, "I heard the killer struck again."

I needed to relax. Once I sat down, I put my legs up on the conference table and crossed my ankles. "I'm afraid, he did. And, I'm sure the mayor's press conference pushed him to do it. This animal wants credit for his horrific actions."

Mr. Pat inquired, "Same MO, Joey?"

"Same. Except for this time, he made a mistake. But could correct it before we found the body. He left footprints from which the CSU team could estimate the size of the killer's shoe to be an eleven."

"Anything else?" Patrick asked.

I pulled out my phone, searched for my photos, and handed Mr.

Pat the phone. "You're looking at a photo of an imprint on our vic's right breast. Slide the photo to your right, and you'll see an enlarged imprint."

Angela and Agnes both walked behind Mr. Pat to look. Pat moved the phone to the right so that they could take a better look.

Angela commented, "It's an oval-shaped something or other. What do you think it is?"

"We have no clue," I replied, frustrated. I got up to light a cigar.

Agnes sat down at the conference table. "Send me the pics so that I can file them on my laptop, would you, Mr. Pat?"

"Here, Patrick, I'll do that," I said, taking the phone back and slightly biting down on my cigar with my front teeth before lighting it. "I'll send you photos of the scene and the footprints, as well."

Angela, joining Agnes at the conference table, asked, "So, what do you think happened? That imprint results from something that was under her breast. For the imprint to form, it had to have been there for a while before the killer removed the item."

I turned on the exhaust system over the office area, the same type we had at the bar and the new cigar club. With a torch-type lighter in the shape of a pistol, I fired up my cigar and returned to the conference table. "My observation and deduction are that the item was under our vic's breast after he strangled her and sliced her breasts. First, he strangles them, and then he turns them over, slices their breasts as a cross, and then turns them over, face down, again. During that process, whatever the item is, it got caught by the victim. After all that, he goes around the apartment, cleans and removes any evidence, and then leaves."

Patrick was making a frown when he pulled a chair out to sit. "What am I missing?"

"Sorry, Mr. Pat, my fault. I was not specific," I replied. "In this last instance, it seems the unsub realized that he left something behind after he left the apartment. That's when he came back, picked the lock, went in with wet shoes, looked for the item, and then removed it. A little after eight in the morning, the precinct received an anonymous call about the dead body with an address."

I looked around the table and continued, "That call, I'm sure, he made himself from a public phone in the area."

"So, we know the item is his. Otherwise, he wouldn't have bothered to come back for it."

"Exactly, Angela," I said, letting out some cigar smoke. "At the crime scene, someone suggested a brooch, or possibly an earring. They both make sense, but the likelihood of them belonging to the killer is low. What we need to figure out now is what kind of item would a man be carrying that has that shape and can fall off so easily?"

Agnes opened her laptop. "I'll start a list."

As if on cue, Angela, Agnes, and I flinched and then turned our heads toward a snapping sound in the room. It was the seal on a bottle of water that Patrick broke.

"Jaysus Mary Joseph, you guys, are jumpy! "The comment would have customarily produced a chorus of chuckles. Not today. A surreal surround sound of nervous sighs filled the room while Patrick took a sizable gulp before he resumed the conversation. "So, how big is the imprint?"

"We measured the imprint to be one and a half inch by an inch," I replied.

Another lull. This time everyone became pensive, trying to wrap their heads around this mysterious object our unsub used. Angela was the first to break the silence.

"Could it be a pin that's attached to the killer's lapel, or, maybe a medal?"

Patrick opined, "A pin, perhaps. But a medal? Who carries medals?"

"Guys," I warned, "don't limit yourselves. Think outside the box. It may be nothing obvious."

Agnes had now flashed the picture of the imprint on our seventy-inch television screen. Angela got up from her chair, scrutinizing the photo, she made an acute observation.

"It's obvious to me that the unsub didn't want to leave it behind. I'm sure it's a personal item of his."

Patrick put the bottle down, got up, and moved closer to the screen, "Agnes, can you improve the quality of the photo?"

Agnes, right on it, was madly ticking in dimensions to adjust. "Working on editing as I speak."

"What are you seeing, Mr. Pat?" My curiosity suddenly peaked. "Come here a second," Patrick said. "Look in the middle of the oval. There seems to be a couple of lines, maybe a logo, or a letter."

I got up, put my cigar in the ashtray, and moved in for a closer look.

Agnes said, "Hang on a second. I'll put up a lighter enhanced version of the pic."

We waited a couple of seconds as the new photo flashed on the screen.

"Agnes, enlarge the image. Just show us the section Mr. Pat is referring to."

While the new image had lost some of its resolutions, it embossed some logo or lettering on it. It wasn't obvious, but it was a new clue. I said, "This is good. It may narrow it down."

Angela smiled and patted Mr. Pat on the back. She added, "Good pick up, Pat."

Mr. Pat gave her thumbs up.

"How did the photo shoot go?" I asked, pointing to Angela.

She smiled, "Great. You missed my Miami Beach look."

I didn't reply but noticed Mr. Pat and Agnes gave each other curious glances.

Agnes added, "I'll be putting up the profiles, across all social media, in a few minutes. Also, I'll request joining all the groups, using various other profiles. I have those ready to go."

"Perfect. I hope this works. We need to find this guy. Now." For the first time, I was feeling like we were getting somewhere with the case. I picked up my cigar and moved it to the side of my mouth.

Angela leaned forward on the table, "I have a question. If you are under the assumption that our unsub may be a member of yours, and hopefully, soon my precinct, isn't he likely to recognize either you or Detectives Farnsworth and Charles while you're spotting me? Assuming he makes contact."

I had accumulated a long ash on my cigar which is a sign of a good cigar. Flicking it off on the ashtray, I replied, "That's why I'm bringing in Larry and Harry, whom you haven't met yet."

Are they part of the team here?" Angela asked.

"They were private detectives working for Bevans and Associates, a criminal law firm. Now, they work for us. So, the moment you get a bite on one of the social media sites, they'll be tailing you with us in the background."

Patrick asked, "What are the detectives from the precinct doing?"

"Yes. Cagney and Lacey. They very upset those two this morning.

The captain had them check for prints and locally known sex crime suspects. Instead of what they wanted to be doing, which was investigating the latest crime scene. He, also, sent them to find public phones within a two-block area. They may be pissed, but look at it this way. If the unsub made a call from one of those, we might get lucky. Patrick joked, "That should keep them busy for a while."

"I hope so, Mr. Pat," I replied, laughing.

Agnes said, pointing to me, and then Patrick, "Back to the imprint. I need to look at what you guys carry in your pockets to get an idea as to what may have been the imprint. Okay? So, empty your pockets."

I smiled, "Good idea, Agnes, except you will not find much on us, but I'll comply, anyway."

Both Patrick and I began taking things out of our pockets.

I put a four-inch pocketknife on the table that I keep in my right front pocket. My wallet from my left back pocket, a handkerchief from my right back pocket, and some cash and keys from my left front pocket. "Not much there, Agnes."

Angela looking at the items, asking, "How many men carry a handkerchief these days?"

I smiled, took the cigar out of my mouth, and replied, "Right? Very few, I think."

Patrick emptied his pockets. Other than an iPhone, he had the same items in his pockets, including a handkerchief.

"Look at that. Two out of two," said Angela, laughing. "You're no help, guys," said Agnes.

"Here's what you need to do, Agnes. Wait until we get our first shift of regulars, the Wall Streeters, at around four-thirty, or five. They're wearing suits. So, more pockets. Have a couple of them empty their pockets to see what they have."

Patrick in his Irish brogue said, "These lads may hesitate to do that. You never know what they may have in their pockets."

We all laughed.

I added, "I'll corral a couple and get 'em to do it here in our office."

CHAPTER 14

The rest of the day went by uneventfully. Larry and Harry had stopped by to meet Angela. I gave them the background on the case. Plus, their roles to play if we got a bite on the social media chumming we were doing.

Being so busy with the recent crime scene and later at the pub, I hadn't realized Detective Lucy was nowhere to be found. I picked up my iPhone from the conference table and called the precinct to speak to Captain Johnson. "Captain," I said, when he answered the phone, "where's Lucy, I haven't heard her or seen her."

"My fault, Joey," he began, "I've had her working with the FBI's office. They were helping her with the ViCAP research and the profiling of the unsub. I should have mentioned that to you."

"No problem. Does she have anything new?"

"On the profile, it's almost identical to what Special Agent Belford laid out for you. He's pretty good."

I made a face but didn't comment on that. "What about ViCAP?"

"They found some fascinating stuff. Nothing exact, but something to work with. Why don't you come over and we can review it together? She's on her way back?"

"I guess I can do that. What about Detectives Farns and Charles?

Did they get anything on the public phones?"

"No, that was a dead end. They're out visiting the usual suspects. By the way, they're not thrilled with their assignment."

"Well, someone has to do it. Tell you what, we have the social media profiles up on all the sites, and we are monitoring them for any hits. Why don't you and Lucy come over? I'll order lunch. We can review the ViCAP information here."

"Works for me. I'll divert Lucy to the pub. See you in a few." Wanting to check up on Marcy, I called her while I waited for

Lucy and the captain.

"Hi, Mancuso, how're you?" She sounded chipper. "All's good. How are your firearms exercises coming along?

"Great! Tony and I are going out to the range now to practice one more time. I plan on taking the FBI's test in a few days."

"Aren't you rushing that?"

"I feel good where I'm at with it. I need to get back to work."

"Is Tony there now?"

"He's on the phone. You need to talk to him?"

"Not really. Don't want to bother him while he's in his "Spock with the Enterprise" mode. You know, the Wi-Fi, black tooth thingy that lives in his ear?"

"It's Bluetooth, Joey. And, he's not using it."

"Really? Well, that's unusual. Just tell him his profile seems to be right on."

"You got it."

"Be well. Love you!" I said, hoping for a like response. What I got wasn't what I expected.

"Talk to you later."

***

Our pub was opening at two in the afternoon. For the time being, it was quiet, with only the staff getting ready. I was in the mood for beer. Reaching into the cooler, I pulled out a freezing Brooklyn Lager.

Lucy and Captain Johnson arrived together. As usual, the sound of the city rushed into the pub as the front door opened along with an artic flow of air. The temp was down in the twenties.

"Welcome," I said, "let's go to the office. I have sandwiches ready for us. Tell Riley your drink preference."

They greeted Agnes, who was working in her area with four monitors tracking the activities in the various social media sites.

"Where's Angela?" The captain asked.

"She went to meet with her husband," I replied. "She said something about renting an apartment."

As we walked into the office and left the pub behind, Lucy asked, "Joey, when are you opening the cigar club?"

"O'Brian's Cigar Club and Spirits is almost ready. I am hoping to open in a couple of weeks."

"Membership going well?" Johnson asked.

"Very well, I think. With no advertising, just from our patrons by word of mouth, we have over one hundred members signed up. Have billed no one yet, but we don't expect anyone is dropping out."

"What's it going to cost me to join?" The captain asked.

"The regular membership is one hundred twenty-five dollars per quarter. But for you, gratis. Just keep it to yourselves, okay?"

"Well, sign me up," the captain said, jumping at the chance.

The food I had ordered had just arrived—a variety of sandwiches cut in half, tuna, ham with cheese, turkey with cheese, and chips. "Sit around the table. I want to hear about this ViCAP research. In the meantime, help yourselves. Mangiare, mangiare," Joey encouraged them to eat in Italian.

We ate for a few minutes, as Lucy got ready to brief us on the research. Wiping her hands on a napkin and taking a sip of her Diet Coke, she began.

"There are no exact matches for our unsub's MO. However, once we opened the search parameters, we uncovered similarities. Let me get to the bottom line. By the way, these are all unsolved murders. Murders or deaths involving an extreme sex such as choking. There's a bunch around the country. Many of these, though, are thought to be accidents. Just people just going too far with the choking. Now, if we add actual strangulation, the numbers drop. Then, if we add anal sex, the numbers drop even more. We took those and searched for a sliced breast, or breasts, as a cross."

"What happened?" I asked, putting down my ham and cheese.

"No hits, other than our murders. So, we went back and inputted any cuts with a knife of any kind," Lucy paused.

"And?" Johnson inquired.

"We found a couple of gruesome murders, where the victim's throats were sliced, and they bled to death."

"Although, the conversation is not conducive to eating, I hope you're enjoying your food," I briefly interrupted. "Lucy, what's the bottom line?"

"Okay, Mancuso, here it is. We have unsolved serial killers that fit some of our killer's MO's in Philadelphia, Prince William County in Virginia, Washington, DC, Chicago, and now, New York."

I was just finishing my second beer when I posed another question. "Which is the closest in form to our unsub's MO?"

Lucy looked down at her notes, "Chicago. There, the victims all had like checkerboard cuts on their backs. They were strangled with what seemed like a satin band. Not red, but blue and anal sex only. The apartments were cleaned like ours. Nothing left behind. No prints. *Nada*."

"How about Philly?" I asked.

"Two victims. Very similar, but no cuts," she replied, perusing her notes once again. "Let me go on. Prince William County—"

I interrupted, "That's Quantico, Virginia, right?" Captain Johnson replied, "Yes, that's correct."

Flipping a page, Lucy read from her notes. "In Quantico, they found three victims with a straight line cut on their backs. Whereas, in Philly, they had no cuts and were strangled by hand—both hands—using Latex gloves."

I thought for a minute. "What about in DC?"

Lucy flipped another page. "Two ladies in DC. Same M.O., including cuts on their backs as a tic-tac-toe."

I drew a tic-tac-toe emblem on a piece of paper, looked at it, and then asked, "The tic-tac-toe—could those be crosses next to each other?"

Lucy considered it. "Maybe, yes. I suppose they could be."

I asked, "So, all had a cuts, except for the murders in Philly. Is that correct?"

"Yes, that's correct," Lucy replied.

"And" making sure I understood her correctly, "the Philly murders were strangulations with gloves. Right?

"Correct," Lucy replied, and asked, "Are you thinking of ruling out the Philly kills?"

I nodded affirmatively. "They don't fit. I think I'd omit them. What do you guys think?" Glancing around the table.

Everyone agreed.

"Okay." I pulled myself closer to the table and rested my elbows on it. "I assume all the victims were females. Right?"

"Yes," Lucy replied, nodding her head. "White females and single?" I queried.

"No, not all white. The two young ladies in DC were African Americans."

"Were they all employed in some form of law enforcement?" I was exploring every angle I could think of.

"No, they were from a variety of fields. We found no correlation there." Lucy was reading from her notes again.

I covered my face with both hands, thinking for several seconds before I concluded. "If our killer is tied into one, two, or more of these murders, most likely, he's changing his signature so that he can be untraceable."

Johnson added, "You think this guy, our killer, is in law enforcement. Right, Mancuso? If that's the case, he may do that on purpose. Knowing full well that we can research this kind of thing."

"Lucy, did you give us the cities in chronological order?"

"Yes, I did, honey. Why?"

I replied, "As soon as we have a suspect, if we can place him in any of these cities at the time of the serial murders, boom, we have him."

The captain got up and walked around the table. "Assuming he's involved in these other killings, why is he only killing ladies in law enforcement related fields now?"

I pushed my sandwich plate aside, "Something triggered the need to go after law enforcement. Some frustration. Maybe, a new infatuation."

Mr. Pat walked in with a tray of *cortaditos*. "Hey gang, it's three in the afternoon. Official Cuban time to drink espressos or cortadito*s*. How're you all doing?"

"Hey, big guy, thank you, and how do you know that?" Lucy asked.

I was deep in thought, but I replied, without looking up, "He's been hanging around Marcy too long." Then I thought of something else. "Lucy, all our victims are brunettes, late twenties, or early thirties, good looking—both faces and bodies. What about the other victims? Any correlation?"

Lucy put down her cortadito. "No, they don't match our victims. There was not one outstanding feature in the group. Just, good looking females in the same age group, and all white females, except for the two in DC."

All I had pictured in my head was an unfinished puzzle. The frame was mostly intact, but the pieces were scattered. Not to mention it was the wrong color scheme.

"Joey, I'm going to have to get back to the precinct," Johnson said. "I think we made progress."

"I agree, Captain. I was hoping to show you the new club before you leave? Do you have a few minutes? How about a cigar for the road?"

"I'd love to see it. I'm going to pass on the cigar for now since Mrs. Johnson doesn't like it when I walk into the house smelling like a stogie."

Mr. Pat, in service mode, chimed in. "No cigar for Captain Johnson. Joey, I'll get you one. How about you, Mrs. Roberts, do you smoke cigars?"

"No, baby, thank you," Lucy replied.

We walked through a set of double doors towards the front of the office. I was very proud of our new enterprise that was about to open.

"Wow, this looks nice, Joey. How big is it?" Johnson asked.

"We have just under two thousand square feet. Look to your right. Those French doors with the opaque glass, they lead to the pub."

"So, anyone at the pub can walk in here?" Lucy asked.

"Only, if they're members and have their key card," I replied.

The captain looked around, "You kept the same dark plank flooring as in the pub, but with a lighter stain. Man, this is like a vast living room. So cozy. I love it."

"All the seating is in leather. The sofas. The club chairs. We set it up, so there are five different sitting areas. We can move things around to accommodate a big group." I added, "You'll notice, no over- head lights, just table lamps."

"I love the ambiance. You know who's going to like this place?" Lucy asked, smiling.

"Sergeant Major Harold. Your hubby," I said, pointing at Lucy. "By the way, Lucy. Captain thinks I made up the story of you folks naming your three sons Frank, Dean, and Sam after the Rat Pack." I have a feeling he needs to hear it straight from you.

Lucy laughed, "Yes, we did. Harold loved Sinatra, Martin, and Davis Junior."

"That's so funny," Johnson said.

"However," I interjected as I faced Lucy, "being the top-notch investigator that I am, my deduction has always been that. .." I paused for effect, "they inspired you at conception. So, to keep the fantasy alive, you named them accordingly. Am I good, or what?"

The room broke out in laughter.

"Lucy bantered, "You're so full of shit, Mancuso. Well, I got work to do. I gotta get moving. Thanks for lunch and the tour."

We were walking back to the office when Agnes almost ran into us. "We have a hit on one of the social media groups. Some guy wants to meet up with Angela. Tonight."

CHAPTER 15

Our sting was on. Everyone was excited and hoping our first bite could land the big one. I asked Agnes, "Is Angela ready with her cover story?"

As we all moved back to our office, Agnes replied, "She is Carmela Navarre, law student, working for the District Attorney's office in Manhattan as an intern. We are using her own background story, born in Barcelona, et cetera."

Mr. Pat asked, in his Irish brogue, "Couldn't you have picked a name that I didn't have to roll the r? Come on, now. Give the lad a break, why don't you?"

Everyone cracked a smile. I know Mr. Pat was trying to lighten the mood, but not now. We needed to keep focused.

Captain Johnson added, "Joey, I have the cooperation of the DA's office. We set up a bogus employment profile for her, just in case our unsub has access to it."

"Where does she live?" I asked.

"I have that covered, also," said Johnson. "We have her staying at a suite hotel near our precinct. One we use for witnesses. We have cameras, microphones—the works. Plus, we will position Detectives Farnsworth and Charles next door. She'll be safe if we get that far."

I nodded, "Let's hope we get that far, and we can nab this guy."

Lucy added, "We need a little luck on our side. So far, our unsub is like 'The Invisible Man.'"

Looking at Agnes, I asked, "Who is this person that contacted Angela? What does his profile say?"

Lowering her head to the laptop screen, and reading from the Face- book page, Agnes replied, "According to this, his name is Peter Gruntel, a law professor at NYU. No pictures of his face, but photos of the campus library, and some classrooms. Age forty-two. He posts quotes from Socrates, Aristotle. Nothing very personal."

Mr. Pat asked, "Does such a person exist?'

"Yes, Mr. Pat, there is a professor with that name at NYU. I checked. But keep in mind, just like we added some bogus profiles, I doubt, if this is truly our unsub, that he would use his actual identity. It's effortless to copy someone else's profile and start a new page."

"But" Lucy asked, "is there another profile for a Peter Gruntel?"

"No, just the one," Agnes responded.

I looked at the captain, but before I said anything, he said, "I'm on it, Joey. I'm dispatching two other detectives to check up and follow Mr. Gruntel. I'll tell them to only observe. For now, no contact."

I nodded.

Lucy inquired, "What happens if this is not our guy, and he's just there for a date that might, or might not, lead to sex? Just asking."

We all looked.

Looking at each other in bewilderment, I offered a response. "I guess we'll leave that up to Angela, right?" I made eye contact with everyone in the room when I said that. All I got back were blank stares. There seemed to be more questions than answers.

The questions continued, this time from Mr. Pat. "If this Gruntel proposes sex, Angela can just say no, right?"

"Problem is," I began replying, "how do we know that he's our guy if she says no?"

"Okay, I got it," said Mr. Pat.

Lucy asked, "Sure sweetie, but what about the cameras?"

Agnes said, "Perhaps, Angela can have a word, or phrase to alert us to turn off the cameras."

I said, "Look, from what we think, our killer proposes the sex before he gets to the vics' apartments. That's how they go directly to the act without any foreplay. So, Angela will have plenty of warning before she gets in the room. I'm not worried about that," I said, and asked, "Where are they meeting?"

Agnes replied, "Interesting enough, this guy picked Ernie's at seven in the evening. I messaged back and forth with him, pretending to be Carmela. He said, *'if we hit it off, maybe we can have dinner.'*"

Johnson asked, "Joey, do you think Larry and Harry are a good fit

for this assignment, or should I get two others?"

"Captain," I began, "Larry and Harry are as inconspicuous as their names. No one will know they are there. Trust me. By the way, is Angela going to be wired?"

"Not wired. What we've done is configured our listening devices with a wireless Bluetooth phone headset. She'll be wearing that. It allows for two-way communication. Even if she takes it off, we can still hear her."

"What about us? Are we going to be outfitted with listening devices?" I asked.

"Yes. We're all going to have the same Bluetooth devices. I'll get 'em to you before we start the sting," Johnson replied.

"Okay, that sounds perfect. Here's what I think we should do if you agree, Captain. You and Lucy pair up and hang outside in your car. Mr. Pat and I will do the same. In case they get in a car, we can follow them. Larry and Harry will be inside Ernie's at six-thirty, and Farns and Charles, at the hotel suite. Works for you?" I asked, looking at the captain.

"Works for me. Has anyone called Angela?" Johnson asked.

"Yes, I did. She's ready," Agnes replied. "I also called Larry and Harry. They'll be here at five-thirty to get briefed."

There was something I wanted Agnes to check on, but for the life of me, I was drawing a blank.

She noticed the confused look on my face. "Joey? What's on your mind?"

I slapped my hands, "Got it! I want you to check up on the two uniforms that arrived first at two murder scenes. Officers Sanchez and Edwards. The captain can get the full names."

She looked surprised. "You want me to do a full 'cybernoscopy'?"

I loved that word! That was Lucy's term for doing a complete search, whether legal or not, about a subject. "Yes, please. Just start with where they've been before New York. Pay attention to the locations of the other serial murders. Do that for now. Then we'll see."

"On it, boss."

Lucy came over to me, and asked, "I haven't seen your sweet brother, Father Dom, where's he? He would love to be involved in this."

"I know. *El Padre* is at a parish retreat designed for couples. He's stuck in a Holiday Inn somewhere."

The captain abruptly cut in, "Okay everyone, we're all set. Keep your fingers crossed."

Lucy and the captain left the office. I had about an hour before our duo of inconspicuous PIs arrived for their briefing. That brought me time to touch base with Marcy. I promised her that I'd call and inquire about her firearms dry-run test at the range.

Marcy answered, "Hi, Joey. How's your day?"

I sat back and put my legs up on the conference table. "My day just got exciting. But I called to hear about your day, not mine. Tell me, how did it go at the range?"

She sighed, "Wow, Tony worked my as off."

I interrupted, "Excuse me?"

"You're such a pervert, Mancuso, he—"

I interrupted again, "Perhaps, but that's an interesting choice of words, considering the case I'm involved in. Go on, sorry I interrupted."

"I was going to say, he put me through the entire test, all phases, short arms, long arms, the works. I think I'm ready."

"I don't want to rain on your parade, but I was hoping to hear 'I know I'm ready', as opposed to, I think. You know what they say… you think, you don't know. Which is the hardest part? I'm guessing the shotgun, right?"

"It has been because of the pumping action required. But I could still do it in the time allotted. My right arm is killing me, though."

"It's easy for me to say this, but I think you should wait a couple more weeks before taking the test."

"You've said that. I'm just anxious to get back to work. I can't stand sitting on my ass. It's been almost a month."

"Fine, you're a better judge than I am. I'm sure you'll do fine. Is Special Tony there now?"

"No, he dropped me off about two hours ago. He said he had a date tonight."

"A date? Can I ask you a personal question?"

"Can I stop you?"

"No, but I'm serious. Is he still coming on to you? I know you've said he'd asked you out a few times."

There was silence. No reply. "Marcy?"

"No, he doesn't stop asking. And, frankly, it's bothering me a lot. If it weren't because he's been helping me on the range. ...," her voice trailed off.

"Has he been rude about it?"

"I don't know about rude, but he assumes that there is a relationship that doesn't exist. He's like possessive about me. He even asks about my relationship with you."

"I told you from the get-go that this guy is an asshole. I don't like him one bit, and it has nothing to do with you. He's too perfect."

"Listen, the sooner I get back to work, the better. I'll be done with him at that point. And, for your peace of mind, I'm not partnering up with him. I can assure you of that."

"Marcy, I've got to get ready for a little sting at Ernie's Bar we have planned for tonight. I'll share more tomorrow with you. I wanted to alert you that one similarity all of our victims have—and don't be alarmed—is that they all physically look like you."

"Are you serious?"

"I'm afraid is true."

"What are you saying?"

"All I'm saying is, I want you to be aware of your surroundings. The other similarity is that our vics are all in some form of law enforcement related work."

"That's freaky. At least, I'm not socializing out there."

"I'm glad to hear that. For more than just that reason."

"By the way, I'll be visiting my parents in Jersey for a few days. Mom's birthday is coming up. I think my brother wants to take the family for a couple of days upstate."

"Sounds wonderful. I'll call you. Say hi to the family. When is this trip happening?"

"Tomorrow."

"Great, have a wonderful time. I love you, Marcy," I said, again hoping for a like response.

There's was a momentary silence. Finally, I heard a faint, "Me, too." And the line went dead.

I closed my eyes, sat back, and smiled at her response. Even though she had said it in a low and very timid voice, I heard it loud and clear. As if she had shouted it from the top of the Empire State Building down to the sidewalk. I had decided for the third time in our relationship to bring up the marriage. This short period we had been apart convinced me. I was hoping it, also, assured her we belonged together. I mean, all I did during the day was long to be with her. And it was not just our sex life, which was great and exciting. No, it was my need to be with her. We just enjoyed each other's company. Even if we were just sitting together at a movie and occasionally rubbed arms. I needed to be in her space. End of story.

I was relaxing in the office with my legs on top of the conference table when Larry and Harry walked into the office. While I was dealing with the maddening tingling sensation that comes with your legs falling asleep, I was trying to figure out who was who. It's like walking into an accountant's office with twenty identical-looking accountants lined up in twenty identical cubicles. That's equally maddening.

Grunting, I said, "Hi guys, I need to brief you on our operation, have a seat, please. First off, Larry—"

"Yes?"

It was very fortunate that the guy on the left answered. While I explained Larry's role and then repeated the process for Harry. There was one thought that lingered in the back of my mind. Whether we could successfully pull this off and finally nab our perp.

CHAPTER 16

The surveillance mission was on. I was genuinely hoping this guy who contacted Angela's Facebook page was our perp. It was a long shot, though. How lucky could we get?

We sat and waited. I wasn't comfortable wearing this crap in my ear. It felt like it weighed a pound. I had this picture in my mind that my ear was drooping down from its weight. I thought of those photos in National Geographic of people from African tribes who wore big ass earrings in the lobes of their ears, the size of a fifty-cent coin. I turned to my left and looked at Mr. Pat. He was sitting in the driver's seat wearing the same Bluetooth earpiece. His, however, seemed miniscule. Natural, even against his enormous face covered with his bushy red beard and mustache. Of course, it helped to be six-foot-plus, also.

Our surveillance was on two sides of Ernie's Bar. We were parked on a one-way street heading south on 9th Avenue. We were about one- half block away at the corner on West 38th and 9th Avenues by Il Punto Italian Restaurant. The captain was on 38th Avenue, which is one-way going east. We would be ready to follow Angela if she and her date got in a car.

We had a perfect view of the bar even though it was dark outside.

Patrick's eyes were fixed on the front entrance of Ernie's. Without looking at me, he asked, "What's bothering you?"

"This shit in my ear," I replied, ripping it off.

"After a while, it's like wearing an earring. You don't feel it. Put it on, laddie. You need to be connected."

"I don't wear fucking earrings, do you?"

Patrick turned his face to look at me, and in a severe tone, replied in his Irish brogue, "Only when I wear high heels, but don't tell anyone."

He remained serious for a moment. Then we busted out laughing.

A few minutes later, as we kept our surveillance on, we noticed

Angela, aka Carmela, walks into the restaurant. She spoke softly, "I'm entering Ernie's."

"We see you," replied Larry, who was already inside Ernie's.

Mr. Pat turned to face me, "Joey, you're not listening, Angela just reported. She's in."

"As long as you're listening, we're good. I keep looking at this gadget, and I see something."

Keeping his gaze on the entrance to Ernie's, Mr. Pat quickly looked to where I was pointing, "What? I see nothing."

"An Arepa vendor," I replied as if I had uncovered a cure for the common cold.

"We're on a stakeout, and you want an Arepa?"

"Stay put, keep listening." With that, I got out of the car trying to be inconspicuous, walked over, and bought an Arepa.

"Did you get me one?" Mr. Pat inquired, as I sat down and closed the door.

"You can have this one after I'm done."

"I don't think so. Smells good. What's an Arepa, anyway?"
"Columbians and Venezuelans make it. It's a flat cake made from corn. You add cheese and butter, then grilled, and *Voila!* An Arepa."

"Looks like a pancake. Why the sudden urge for one?" he asked,

still looking at Ernie's front door.

"It was either using your ass or finding something else."

Patrick gasped, "My ass, or, an Arepa? What the hell are you talking about?"

"Anything going on inside Ernie's?"

"All quiet now. Angela is having a glass of White Beringer with ice," replied Harry.

"With ice?" I asked.

Patrick ignored my question about the wine with ice. "About my ass and the Arepa. What's up with that?"

"I've been looking at this gadget, this Bluetooth thing. As I looked, I realized I was looking at the imprint of our last vic's right breast."

"Hah, but how does my ass get into this conversation?" Patrick asked, covering the earpiece.

"I needed something to make an impression on. I could have had you sit on it, and then take a picture of the impression, or find a substitute to make an impression on."

"I'm glad you chose the Arepa."

I had pressed the outside of the Bluetooth earpiece into the Arepa. My hands were a little greasy, but since I always carry a handkerchief, I took care of that. Removing the earpiece from the Arepa, I cried out, "There!"

Patrick flinched in his seat, "What now?"

"Look, there it is." We both stared at it. It was the same imprint on both the Arepa and our last victim's breast. "Hold it a second. Let me take a picture."

"Guys," the captain's voice came over the earpiece, "we're all connected. But no one understands what's going on in your car."

Lucy, who was with the captain, chimed in, "All we heard is something about Patrick's ass, an Arepa, and an implant."

"There's a story there, for sure. Sounds like the making of a new Aesop Fable, doesn't it? It has a nice ring to it, too—Patrick's ass, an Arepa, and an implant. What do you think? Okay, you don't have to answer that," I said in one breath. I paused briefly before I continued. "What I'm holding in my hand is indeed an imprint. Anyway, we'll explain later," I replied. I cleaned up the gadget and placed it back in my ear.

"Perhaps, you can keep that between the two of you," added Angela, from inside the bar. "Nothing going on. No sign of our professor."

I asked, "Anyone approach you yet, Carmela?"

You could hear Angela chuckle, "You don't need a membership in eHarmony if you sit here long enough. I've had a few offers already. Some quite interesting, I might add. But our professor is AWOL."

The captain's voice came over the earpiece again, "Let's give it thirty more minutes."

Angela replied, "Roger that. Wait, a moment. I just got a Facebook message on my phone."

"Who from?" asked Johnson.

"Our professor," Angela replied.

"Saying what?" I asked.

Angela replied, "It reads, *'Sorry Carmela. Can't make it. We'll reconnect.'* That's all he wrote. Except he added a smiley face."

"You think he's at the bar?" I asked. "Never mind, there's no way to know. Larry and Harry, hang back, just in case he's looking. Wait a few minutes, then leave. Angela, you can go now."

"This is Captain Johnson, I'm setting up a surveillance of Professor Gruntel's home. We'll do a full background check on him. Detectives Farnsworth and Charles, you're done at the hotel for now. Joey, are you still on this thing?"

"Yes, I am."

"What's up with the Arepa?" Johnson asked.

I replied, "I'll go back to the pub and compare pictures. I might have found what our killer left behind and later retrieved. Captain, make sure you check if the professor has been where the other murders took place."

Johnson ignored my request, and said, "That'd be a huge break if you found out what the killer left behind. Call me when you know more. We're done, folks." The captain was about to drive off when he saw a familiar face. He cut the ignition and sent a message to the crew. "Wait, wait. Everyone stay put."

I asked excitedly, "What's up, Captain?"

"Patrolman Sanchez is walking out of Ernie's Bar?"

Lucy inquired, "Sanchez? That's one patrolman that kept showing up at the crime scenes, right?"

Johnson replied, "Correct. Joey, you had a suspicion, didn't you?"

"Yes. But their explanation made sense. I mean, it is their shift and patrol area. Of course, that could be part of the plan."

"Lucy and I will follow Sanchez and see where he leads us. In the meantime, we'll end the surveillance of Ernie's as of now."

Detective Farnsworth spoke over the com system, "Captain, you want us to hang around the hotel?"

Johnson, already on the move along with Lucy, replied, "No need to since our unsub broke contact with Angela. You guys go home. Thanks."

I removed the earpiece and put it in my pocket. "Mr. Pat, let's head back to the pub."

Patrick said, "That would be a miracle if we could tie the killer to the earpiece? The problem is that it's going to be like finding a needle in a haystack. Do you realize how many people have these? They're popular gadgets, lad."

"You're just full of encouragement, aren't you? One thing at a time, my dear friend. I have an idea." I took my phone out and dialed Doctor Frankie, the medical examiner."

After a few rings, the ME picked up. "This is—"

I cut in on his greeting. "Doctor Death, Mancuso here."

"Don't tell me we have another body," he said, somewhat alarmed.

"No, no, thank goodness. I need you to look at some photos of our last vic. Her name was Darlene ..." I paused, "Forgot her last name. Sorry about that, Doc."

"Rogers," he said. "Okay, I have the file. What do you need?"

"Look at the photo of her right breast."

"Okay, and I'm looking for what?"

"I know there wasn't much blood from the cuts. I do remember seeing a trickle that flowed down her breast in the area where we found the imprint."

"There are a couple of trickles. What about them?"

"Isn't there one that stops at the top of the imprint?"

"I'm looking at it. The phone went silent, except for Doc breathing a few times before he spoke again. "Yes. The trails don't go any farther than the imprint."

"Great! So, is it possible the item that made the imprint may have had some of our vic's blood on it?"

"It would have to. Yes. Did you find the item?"

"No, but we may know what it is," I said, taking the damn gadget out of my pocket and examining it.

"Your killer probably threw away the item, or, at the very least, cleaned it to remove traces of the blood."

"If he threw it away, we're fucked. But if he kept it, I think we can place him at the scene of the crime."

"What is it?"

"The pictures I took of the vic's breast and imprint I believe match an imprint for one of these Motorola black tooth gadgets. I'll know better when I can blow up the photos."

"Bluetooth, Mancuso," Doctor Frankie said, with a chuckle.

"Blue. Black. Whatever the fuck color they are. This thing has little holes and crevices around the housing. If it had blood on it, I'm sure there are blood traces inside the gadget."

"And here I said before that forensics would not solve this crime. Significant work, Joey."

"It's a long shot. Bunch of other pieces has to fall into place before this is confirmed."

"You well know that's how it all starts. One piece at a time. Keep me posted, brother."

I clicked him off, looked at my watch, and made another call. "Agnes, are you still at the pub?"

"I was just leaving our office. Yes. Why?"

"Stay put. I'm on to something. Order a pizza or something for us. We have work to do."

CHAPTER 17

A few minutes after the surveillance ended, something was bothering me about the message from our supposed Professor Gruntel. "Pull over, Mr. Pat."

"What's up?"

"This guy is not following his MO," I said, closing my eyes, putting my head back on the headrest, and thinking. I reached for my cell phone and dialed. "Angela, are you still at the bar?"

"No, I just left. You need me to go back?" She asked.

"No. Head over to the suite hotel where you're supposed to be staying."

Angela paused before responding. "Okay, I can do that. But why?"

"From what we know, our unsub stakes out his victims before he makes physical contact. It is likely that he was at the bar and now is probably going to follow you to see where you live. Let's make sure we play his game."

"The detectives already left the hotel. You just want me there. .. by myself?"

"Go in the front door. Then, make sure no one sees you, and leave through the back door. Mr. Pat and I will be there to pick you up. If you see anyone suspicious enter the lobby, do not, I repeat, do not go to your room. Call me, if that's the case. *¿Entiende, Carmela?"*

"*Sí.*"

Without hanging up, I turned to Mr. Pat, and said to Angela, "He's going to want to make sure there are no cameras, et cetera. That's what we think he's done in the past. The message canceling the date was just a ruse. He needs to survey the location."

"I'm on my way," Angela replied.

Mr. Pat put the car in gear, pulled out unto traffic, and said, "Okay, headed to the back of the hotel. Man, your mind is always working, isn't it?"

"I'm fully engaged when I'm on a case. Fully engaged."

I dialed the captain, but his cell phone was going directly to voice- mail. "Fuck, Johnson is not answering his phone."

"What do you want to know?"

"The whereabouts of Sanchez," I replied.

"You think he's headed to Angela's place?' Patrick asked.

"Let me call Lucy." As she picked up, I asked, "What's happening with Sanchez?"

"I'm driving behind. Johnson is trailing Sanchez on foot."
"What's he doing?"

"Sanchez is strolling, window shopping at the moment."

"Lucy, in what direction is he walking?" I asked, looking at Patrick. "As if he was going back to the precinct," she replied.

"Well, that's the same direction as the hotel suite," I muttered. "Yes, but Angela is driving back to it. This guy is not following her," Lucy commented.

"I know, but what if he heard something at the precinct about our surveillance plans, and knows what we're doing?" I asked as Patrick drove to the back of the hotel.

"Well, if he did. Is he stupid by showing up at Ernie's, knowing our plans?"

I responded, "Keep in mind we are dealing with a narcissist. In his mind, he's smarter than all of us. He could taunt us, at this point."

"I'll let you know as soon as Sanchez arrives at his destination."

We had arrived at the hotel suite and waited for Angela. It was taking a little too long for Angela to walk out, and I was getting anxious. The hotel had been a small apartment building that had been converted into a quaint suite hotel, and it was perfect. No cameras anywhere. A few minutes later, I was about to step out of the SUV when Angela walked out the back door.

"Anyone suspicious?" I asked her.

"No one there," she replied, getting in the back seat of Patrick's SUV.

"Okay, good. Let's head to the pub and brainstorm."

Once Angela got in the SUV and buckled up, she asked, "You think he followed me?"

I turned back to face her, smiled, and replied, "If it's not Sanchez, I bet you cannolis to dollars he did. This guy needs to see where his potential victims live. If he feels safe, he'll make contact again."

Angela inquired who Sanchez was, and I brought her up to date.

Patrick parked in the alley behind the pub, in a space designated for deliveries, and we walked in the back. Dean Martin's old hit *'You are Nobody 'til Somebody Loves You,'* was playing in the background. Marcy's smiley face flashed in my mind for a second. The place was buzzing with activity. I gave Riley, our manager, a thumb's up, and after saying a few hellos, shaking a few hands, I made my way to our office.

Agnes had two pizzas waiting for us. Pepperoni and sausage, tomato and onions. An iced bucket of beers sat next to the pizzas. I grabbed a Heineken, nodded to Angela, and Mr. Pat, to do the same.

Johnson was calling me on my cell, "Yes, Captain."

"Joey, this guy walked right in front of the hotel without stopping. Then, he went back to the precinct, retrieved his car and drove away."

"Are you following him?" I asked.

"I have Farnsworth and Charles on his trail now. They'll follow and see if he goes to his home."

"Okay, let us know if anything changes on your end. In the meantime, we're trying to find out what the imprint could be."

"Roger that."

Handing Agnes my iPhone, I said, "Agnes, take the last few pictures I took, and blow them up on the screen. The ones with the impression of the phone gadget on the Arepa."

"On the what? Did you say Arepa?" Agnes questioned. Mr. Pat laughed, "It's a long story."

Agnes uploaded my pictures to her laptop and then flashed them on the big screen. We all stared at the photos.

I sat back in my chair, took a paper plate, a napkin, and a slice of pepperoni pizza. "Agnes, can you show the impression on the Arepa next to the one of our vic's close-up of the breast?"

"Give me a second," she replied.

And there they were. On the left, the impression on our vic's breast, and on the right, the one on the Arepa. "What do you think, guys?" I asked.

Patrick replied, "Almost identical."

Agnes added, "Really."

Angela chimed in, "Wow!"

Putting down my beer bottle, I smiled and said, "Ladies and gents, I think we know what the unsub left behind."

My cell phone rang while still connected to the laptop. Looking at the picture that flashed on the phone's screen, Agnes said, "It's Marcy, Joey."

"Answer, I'll talk to her a second," I said, looking at Mr. Pat. "I'll be a minute. Marcy is leaving for a few days upstate with her parents."

"Take your time," Patrick said. "We'll eat."

"Hey, Marcy, how you are doing?" I asked, walking to a corner of the office.

"Good, good. Listen, we're not leaving tomorrow. We delayed the trip one day. My brother is tied up. So instead, I'm going to the range one more time, and go through one more dry run of the FBI firearm's test."

"Want me to go with you."

She hesitated, "You can join us, but so that you know, Tony wants to conduct the test. He's been working with me all this time."

"I understand. You guys go," I said, wanting to say something nasty. Instead, I asked, "Does he keep all the guns with him?"

"He keeps them at his place but brings a duffle bag when we go to the range."

"I see."

"I spoke to him earlier. He was asking where you were."

"Really? Why would he do that?" I asked, baffled by Tony's question.

"I don't know. He's never done that before."

"Strange. What did you tell him?"

"I told him you were on a stakeout at Ernie's Bar in Midtown." Alarmed, I asked, "How did you know it was Ernies where I was?"

"You told me earlier when we spoke. Why? You didn't want him to know?"

"Ah, no, that's okay. I didn't realize I told you where we were going to be."

"You did. Otherwise, how would I have known?"

"You're right. I just don't see why he would care."

"He asked about your case. He wanted to know if I had an update."

"If the Special Agent wants an update, tell him to call me next time."

"He means well, Joey. Anyway, he's going out of town the day after tomorrow. So, he thought we'd do the test one more time. I'm ready. I can't wait to get back to work."

I closed my eyes and said, "I want things to get back to normal. You back at work, and us back together again. We miss you both of us."

"Hah, you tell your little friend to hang in there. Who knows?" she replied with a chuckle.

"He's been hanging, and that's about it."

"I miss your perverted sense of humor. Talk to you soon."

"All the best, Marcelita. *Te quiero*." I said as she clicked off.

CHAPTER 18

Walking back to the conference table, I grabbed another slice of pizza and sat down. I noticed Agnes had printed two enlarged copies of the photos. One with the Arepa and the other with the vic's breast. She had connected lines on what seemed like a letter imprint on the indentation of the item.

Agnes smiled, "Look here," she said, as she slid the photo of the Arepa towards me.

"You're good," I said, taking out the Bluetooth gadget from my pocket. "It's the Motorola logo. The letter M."

Patrick put down a slice of pizza, swallowed, and said, "So, we have confirmation of what made the indentation. Now, we have to hope we can find it on our perp."

I added, "This guy has made no mistakes. If he kept this gadget, that's the first mistake he's made."

"The gadget impression on the vic's breast is so far-fetched. I bet this guy figures his plan is foolproof even to the most astute detective. So, I bet he cleaned it and still has it."

"I hope you're right, Angela," I said. "By the way, you haven't been to the precinct, right?"

"No, no. The captain told me to stay away. I still need to be undercover assuming our unsub works there."

"Good!" I was relieved to hear that Angela was staying clear of the precinct. "Okay, folks. Thanks to Mr. Pat for cleaning up. Now that we've filled our bellies, let's review what we have."

As Patrick disposed of the garbage, he said, "If you'll give me a minute, I'll make some espressos. Cigar, Joey?"

"That'd be great. Make it Gurkha Heritage Robusto, Pat."
Pointing to Angela, I asked, "Do you smoke cigars?"

"Occasionally, but I'll pass today. Thanks."

"While Patrick works on the espressos, let me ask you," I began. "You found a place to rent?"

"It's a corporate owned apartment. My husband's company is going to let us use it for a while. This way we can take our time finding out where we want to be."

Agnes inquired, "What does your husband do?"

"Mark is going to be managing the commercial real estate office in New York. He's with SBRE. They're a worldwide company involved strictly in commercial real estate."

I asked, "He was in Miami with the company?"

Angela replied, crossing her legs and sitting back, "He was managing the Miami office. New York City is their biggest office. It's a great opportunity for him. For us, I should say."

Agnes turned to her laptop, hearing a ding, and without looking away from it, she asked, "And, are you going to be working in homicide for Captain Johnson?"

"I hope so. I'm tired of vice. Especially, now that I'm married," Angela replied.

"We just got an email from Lucy," Agnes said, as Patrick walked in with four espressos and two cigars.

"What's it say?" I asked.

"Let me open the attachment," Agnes said, as she made a few clicks on her laptop. "Did you ask her to check on past work locations of people in the precinct?"

"I did. Just four of them for now."

"This email is from her just now. Joey, you asked, she says. And she had not done it until now. She apologizes. Okay, so, the two uniforms that keep showing up first at the scenes, Sanchez and Edwards. Edwards has been nowhere near the locations of the other unsolved murders. Edwards is a local guy from Queens. Sanchez was born in Greenville, Illinois. A city of less than seven thou- sand in population. Joined the local police department there that comprised thirteen. He trained with the Chicago Police Department. Later, washed out of the FBI Academy training in Quantico. Then, joined the NYPD two years ago."

"Does it say why he failed the Bureau's Academy? I asked.

Eyes on her monitor, Agnes replied, "No, nothing on that. She adds that the dates coincide with the killings in both Chicago and Quantico."

Patrick added, "Well, that can't be a coincidence."

"What about detectives Farnsworth and Charles?" I asked.

Agnes replied, "Also, from New York. Detective Farnsworth is from Brooklyn, but we knew that from his accent, right? Detective Charles is from Buffalo. Neither has worked in any of the cities in question."

Angela, raising her eyebrows, turned to me. "Joey, you had a feeling about these four. Right?"

"Edwards looked too young to have been anywhere else, but the thing is that he and Sanchez kept showing up at the scene of the crimes. There is something about Sanchez that made me think twice. First. I just wanted to make sure. Concerning the detectives, I wanted to confirm we didn't have a wolf in the henhouse. Understand?"

"What now?" Patrick asked.

"Now ... now, we need to monitor Sanchez twenty-four seven. He may be our man."

Patrick had another question. "So, you're leaning in his direction as our unsub?"

"I don't know, Mr. Pat. Let's review what we do know. Agnes, on the whiteboard, please, start two columns."

Agnes got up, and with an erasable blue marker drew a line down the middle of the board. "Shoot," she said.

"Okay. On the left, label that as 'Known Facts'. On the right, label that as 'What We Think'."

Agnes did as I asked and waited for more instructions.

I started, "Beginning with the left side, add 'Female Victims Employed in Law Enforcement Related Jobs.' 'all brunettes,' and 'all late twenties, or, early thirties.'" I leaned back, "What else folks? This portion is interactive." I thought of Marcy, again. Except this time, I got a bad feeling when her face flashed in my mind.

Patrick added, "Same-sex act,' and 'extreme."

Angela said, "'All active in social media,' and 'Members of the same groups within Facebook,' and 'All single.'"

Agnes jumped in, "And 'permissive,' based on their postings."

I added, "So, that makes 'em easy targets, or, at least, targets."

"And..." Patrick said, "'all, but one lived alone.'" I asked, "Anything else on the vics?"

Everyone looked at each other, but there was no response until Angela chimed in.

"White."

"Okay, I think we saturated that side. What do we know about our unsub?"

Angela replied, "According to both profiles we have, your friend, the FBI agent, and the profile Lucy had the FBI office do, our unsub is a narcissist."

"We know he's male, right?" Patrick asked.

"According to the medical examiner, yes," I replied.

Agnes wrote "Bluetooth" on the board. "We now know he has used this gadget. Possibly owns one."

"Let me ask," said Agnes, "do we know, or just think that our unsub suffers from OCD?"

I replied, "Based on the profiles, we think he is obsessive-compulsive. Based on the crime scenes, we also think he's the one cleaning up after the crimes. It's inconceivable that all our vic's kept their apartments so organized and cleaned."

"I'll put OCD, on the right side for now," Agnes said.

Angela said, "We should add 'Other unsolved serial killings in the cities Lucy reported.'"

I responded to Angela's comment. "I have a strong feeling that most of these murders are related. The only issue is that we just don't know for sure."

Agnes said, "I'll add that we think he's in law enforcement himself." Patrick looked deep in thought. "I've been thinking about the characteristics of the unsub. One profile said that the unsub might think that the type of sex he has with the vics, not the extreme part where he strangles the woman but the other. The other as abusive and wants to inflict anguish."

"So, what's the question?" I asked, intrigued by Mr. Pat's observation.

"The question..." Patrick replied, pausing slightly for effect, "the question is this. Is it possible they molested our unsub as a child?"

The team went quiet. Everyone went into deep thought for a minute.

I stood up, "Patrick, that's an amazing question. I'm sure our profilers missed that." Walking around our table and taking a hit from my Gurkha, I said, "Agnes, add that to the right side, please."

Angela pulled herself close to the table. "That's a scenario, but how does that help us find the unsub?"

"It all helps, Angela," I replied, "this is a puzzle, and this is just another piece that could link our unsub to these murders."

"I know," Angela said, "but first, we have to have a suspect. Only then, can we tie these together. I'm afraid that just thinking, or, even knowing they sexually abused our unsub as a child does not lead us to anyone in particular."

"You're right," I said, "but again, we're building our case. The more we know about this killer, the better. Please add that the killer wears the same cologne to every murder."

Patrick asked, "We know that?"

I replied, "Dr. Frankie confirmed he detected the same scent of cologne on every vic's back."

Angela asked, "So, he gets close enough to them? Like his chest on the vic's back, and transfers his cologne?"

"Exactly," I responded.

Agnes added, "One more piece of the puzzle. Or, at least, a clue."

I looked at my watch. It was eleven in the evening. "Folks, let's go home and reconvene here tomorrow morning at nine. We'll pick up where we left off."

Agnes asked, "What do you want me to do if I get another hit-on Carmela's Facebook profile?"

I turned to Agnes, "Call me, immediately. No matter what the time. Now, everyone go home but don't stop thinking. Thank you."

CHAPTER 19

It exhausted me from the long day and all the brainstorming. Patrick gave me a ride back to my place which I appreciated. During the ride, we made small talk and discussed the progress of the cigar club. Patrick was a co-owner, now. So, he was very much into that part of our relationship.

This puzzle was still far from coming together. Maybe, just maybe, we had the corners placed down, but there were still a lot of pieces laying on the table without a home. My apartment that Marcy had called a big locker room with a bath, and a kitchen looked better after I had put a few things away. Now that I had been forced to sleep here every night.

My mind was racing with all the observations we had made. I had this awful sensation in my stomach again. The icy vacuum that I couldn't figure out why I was feeling. Once in the apartment, I jumped into bed knowing full well I would not get much sleep. The blanket felt like a lead blanket. Kinda like the ones they put over you for x-rays.

I heard this twinkle sound next to me. Trying to focus and think, I realized it was my iPhone's wake-up alarm. My body felt as if I just gone to sleep. I had it set to go off at six in the morning every week- day. I mumbled a few cussed words in Italian, rolled out of bed, and made my way to the bathroom. I was eager to talk to my brother, Father Dom. He'd been away on a retreat, and I had not brainstormed with him about the case. I dialed his cell phone. "Brother Dom, how you are doing?"

"Good morning, Joey. How have you been?"

"Working hard on this case. I can't wait to talk to you about it. Getting ready for Mass?"

"Sounds like you're in a submarine," Dom said, then added, "indeed, six-thirty, and seven. How's Marcy?"

I ignored the statement about the submarine. I was sitting on the toilet in my bathroom. Folks always say, 'You sound like you're in a submarine.' How many people have talked to someone on the phone who is in a submarine? What does that sound like? I replied to Dom, "I spoke to her yesterday. She is doing the firearm's test routine for the last time today. Tomorrow, she's headed up state with family for a few days. Listen, can you come over to the office after Mass?"

"Yes, I'll come over. How's the cigar club coming along?"

"You'll love it. We're almost ready to open. But I want your brain power in this case. See you about eight?"

"I'll be there," Father Dom said.

I arrived at the pub a few minutes before eight. I made espresso and waited for brother Dom to add the steamed milk for our *cortaditos*. The temperature outside today was in the mid-thirties with clear blue skies for a change. I was eager to share with Dom our findings, and the many thoughts that had kept me up most of last night.

Sitting on a stool at the bar, I read the New York Post's front page, as a chilly breeze swept the pub. In came Father Dominic with a refreshing smile on his face.

"How goes it, brother? *Va bene*?" I asked, turning to face the front door.

"All good. What's up with you?"

"We have a lot to discuss. We've missed you. How was the

retreat?"

"I enjoy spending a couple of days with couples. It gives me a chance to connect with reality, and the challenges they face in today's world."

"I'm sure you shared your wisdom, and the twenty-first century approach to the Catholic Church."

"That I did. Although, I learn more from them than they do from me, I think. It was very rewarding."

"I'm happy for you. Let's sit at a table. I'll bring you up to date on these murders. Ready?"

"Let's do it."

We sat in the pub area just as we had done many times before. Our pub had been in the family for almost sixty years. It was a refuge for us during the early morning. The memories in photographs surrounding the walls with celebrities like Truman Capote dating back to Captain O'Brian, Dom's grandfather, and later his father, were plentiful. Our décor was homey, comfortable, and relaxing.

For the next hour, I reviewed the profiles of the perp, the victims, and the clues we had developed. Dom was quiet, absorbing everything I covered. He displayed a variety of facial expressions as I described the crime scenes.

"So," Dom said, "you're looking for a man who wears a Motorola Bluetooth device. A man who has narcissistic characteristics and is more than likely in law enforcement. Plus, you assume he's a repeat serial killer."

"That pretty much sums it up. Out of over eight million people in New York City that should narrow it down," I said, smiling.

"None of what you have is going to lead us to a suspect. What you have is only going to help after we find a suspect."

"I'm afraid you're right. I feel like a dog at a dog's convention sniffing everyone's ass to find the one that farted."

Dom reacted with a frown, "I get the picture, but I would have used a different simile. Have the detectives at the precinct come up with anything?"

"They're all working hard, looking at the usual suspects. They brought in detectives from the SVD to help out with the case."

Dom enquired, "SVD?"

"Sorry. Special Victims Division. They deal with sex crimes." He squinted and asked, "They were not on this from the start?"

I replied, "No, the powers that be brought in the homicide division first. Remember, they didn't want the publicity about a serial killer."

"Got it."

I told Dom about the night before and the sting we had set up at Ernie's Bar. How we had everyone was in place and how it all fizzled out until we spotted Officer Sanchez.

"So, you think he might be your man?"

"You know what they say about coincidences, right? What are the chances we're expecting our sting to pull in the unsub, and this guy shows up?

"The bar is a few blocks from the precinct. Therefore, it is conceivable.

"We're going to monitor him. Let's assume he is not. What are your other thoughts?

Making a few observations on that, he said, "I think you were correct in thinking that the killer surveys his victims beforehand. He must have followed Angela to her suite hotel to check the layout. And, of course, to see if there're any cameras. So, he's going to call again, if he was satisfied."

"I hope you're right. Because right now, we have a bunch of ideas and clues, but nothing that leads us to anyone. This guy can continue killing, and unless he makes a mistake, we have nothing that can give us his identity. This is becoming personal. Patrick thinks he might taunt me."

"Why you?"

"I don't know, but I keep having this icy feeling in the pit of my stomach. I can't explain the reason why."

We both went quiet thinking about what I had just said.

Dom asked, "Getting back to Marcy. You think she's ready to take the firearms test?"

"She's very resolute, and she's been working hard at it."

"What if she doesn't, Joey? You think she'll drop back into a depression again?"

"Man, I don't even want to think that. I'd rather think of the other ending. The one in which she passes and goes back to work. And we get back together."

I wanted to share that Marcy screamed, 'I love you,' on the phone the other day. But she hadn't. I knew better. And I too had to manage my expectations, or it could be me that goes into a depression. I replied, "There was a slight hint she might be ready the other day on the phone. So, I'm optimistic about our getting back together."

"Alright, she goes back to work, you guys get back together, and all is back to normal. Works for me, Joey."

"I tell you what, brother. The second we find our killer, and assuming the positive results with Marcy, I'm not wasting any more time. Get Saint Helens ready for a wedding, a big wedding," I smiled that. "I can't imagine being without her. And, every time I think about the future, I see us together in a loving and gratifying relationship."

Dom smiled to himself. "God willing, that will be your fate."

We sat there for a while, saying nothing. I know I've said this before, but we both enjoy sitting in the pub early in the morning. There's such a big contrast to the evenings when the patrons are in full force. The sounds of glasses clinking, the music in the background, the laughter of the patrons, and just the buzz generated by the energy in the room. All that compared to the mornings when all we hear is the sound of a drip of water from one faucet behind the bar.

Dom broke the silence, "What's on your scheduled today?"

"I'm going to spend some time at the precinct and bring everyone up to speed on what we have uncovered. Why don't you join me?"

"I'll do that. Yes, let's go," Dom replied. "So, I take it you're feeling good about the future?"

"Yes, and no. I can't shake this feeling inside that something bad is about to happen."

"That's just anxiety, Joey. You're feeling anxious about the case, and about Marcy's test. That's all."

"I hope you're right, brother. I hope you're right."

CHAPTER 20

Yesterday was a nothing day. Dom enjoyed being in the precinct and spending time in the squad room. We discussed both profiles. All the clues we had uncovered were looked at and added to the ones the detectives had developed on their own.

Officer Sanchez was now a suspect and under surveillance twenty-four seven.

We were back at the pub this morning, and we were in a wait and see mode. Hoping for no more murders, and trying to make more sense of what we had.

Dom prepared some espressos while we waited for the rest of the team to arrive. "Should we add more profiles to the social media pages?" Dom asked.

My cell phone rang. The ID caller read 'Alberto Rodriguez'. "Hold that thought, brother. It's Marcy's stepdad," I said, pushing the green icon on my phone. "Mr. Rodriguez, good morning. How are you?"

With no pleasantries, Alberto got to the point, "Joey, do you know where Marcy is?" He asked, agitated.

"No, I thought she was leaving with you guys today. Why do you ask?"

"We haven't heard from her since the day before yesterday. Her mother called her last night, but she hasn't called back."

"She was practicing at the range yesterday for her firearm's test. Then, she was driving to you guys in Jersey this morning. Have you called her cell?"

"Of course, Joey. She was supposed to be here around seven in the morning. We're all here waiting, but she doesn't answer her phone."

I shook my head, and said, "It's not like her. I can go to her place right now."

"No need. Her mother and brother already left to go to her apartment," Alberto said.

"I'll call Tony Belford. He was with her at the range yesterday. I'll call you back as soon as I speak to him."

"I don't like that guy. Okay. Call me or I'll call you as soon as I hear something,"

"I'm sure she's fine, Alberto. She'll probably show up at your place any minute," I said, trying to believe that myself.

"What's going on?" Dom asked.

I looked at my watch "Marcy was supposed to be at her parent's two hours ago. She's not answering her phone since yesterday." I looked through my contacts quickly for Belford's number.

"This is Special Agent, Tony Belford." I interrupted, "Tony, this is Joey."

"I'm not available to answer your call right now ..." Belford's message went on.

"Shit, he's not picking up," I said, staring at the phone. I hung up. Immediately, my phone rang. Without looking at the caller ID, I answered.

"Joey, this is Farnsworth."

"What's up, Detective? I'm in the middle of something," I replied, impatiently.

"Excuse me, Mr. Consultant. I thought I do you the courtesy of letting you know that our professor, Peter Gruntel, is not our man. We questioned him this morning, and after checking his past location, he's never been in any of the cities our unsub may have committed prior murders. Plus. .."

I interrupted, "Farnsworth, sorry, man. Just that everyone is looking for Marcy. We haven't heard from her since yesterday, and she's two hours late in arriving at her parents in Jersey."

"You want me to check for any accidents this morning?"

"Yeah, yeah, great idea. But check since yesterday, just in case."

"I'm on it. Call you back," Farnsworth said. "Wait, Joey, Still there?"

"Yeah, what's up?"

"Listen, this guy, Gruntel, if you look in the dictionary under nerd, his picture is there. Skinny tall dude, black wide rim glasses, and a black bow tie. Plus, he abhors any social media. He's a recluse and wants the Facebook page down rapido."

"No can do. We need page up. Otherwise, the unsub will suspect something's up. Tell him not to worry about it. We need his cooperation for a little longer."

"I don't know, man. He's likely to contact Facebook to have them take it down."

"Scare him or something. Don't let him contact Facebook. I gotta go."

That icy vacuum in my stomach I felt yesterday was back. An idea popped into my head. I looked through my contacts again and dialed.

"This is Victoria Stewart. How can I help you?"

Victoria is the Special Agent in charge of the New York's FBI White Collar Crime Division. Marcy's and Belford's boss.

"Victoria, this is Joey Mancuso," I said, without giving her a chance to ask anything. I went on, "We hadn't heard from Marcy since yesterday when she was with Tony at the range. Have you heard from Tony today?"

"Tony was on his way to Chicago, his old posting, to clear something up. Have you called him? He may be on a plane."

I didn't reply. "Joey?" She asked.

"Chicago, you said," I replied, as my mind went into gear. "Victoria, do me a favor. Can you check to see where Tony has been? assigned before Chicago? Would you mind doing that and call me back?"

"I don't have to check, I know where. After the academy, they assigned him to Atlanta. After that, he went back for more training with the Behavioral Analysis Unit at Quantico. Then, they assigned him to the BAU in DC for a year. Then, he went to Chicago. Why do you want to know?"

I was stunned. Was this our guy? I asked myself. I looked at Father Dom sitting next to me and mouthed the word, fuck.

Father Dom just frowned.

"Victoria, do me another favor. Have Tony call you when he lands.

Leave him a message to do so. Make something up, I'll explain later."

"Sure, Joey. But what about Marcy?" She asked.

"I'll call you back in a few minutes and thank you."

Detective Lucy walked into the pub flashing her wide infectious smile. She greeted Dom and hugged me. "Good morning, boys."

"Let's walk over to the office. We may have something developing here," I said, in a somber tone.

I saw Lucy exchange glances with Dom. Her smile vanished. Just then, the rest of the team walked in. Mr. Pat, Angela, and Agnes. I waved them over to come into the office.

We all sat down at our conference table. I think my face showed the concern I was feeling. No one made any small talk, or funny remarks, as we usually did.

Patrick asked, "What's going on?"

Just then my phone rang. I raised my index finger at Pat motioning to give me a minute.

"Mr. Rodriguez," I said, as I answered the call. "Any news?"

"She's not at her place, and she's still not answering her phone. And Joey, her bags for our trip are still there. Packed. Just sitting there."

"Okay, Alberto. I have the police checking for any accidents yesterday or today. I'll call you with any news. You do the same. I'm sure she's fine."

"Joey, her car is there, also…" he said, as his voice trailed off.

I didn't know what to say. I sat there looking around the table. All eyes were on me. "Alberto, I'll keep you posted. Hang in there."

There was dead silence in the room when I clicked off the phone and stared at the floor.

Lucy broke the silence asking, "Joey, what's going on?"

Looking up, but beyond anyone present, I replied, "Marcy is missing."

CHAPTER 21

I pushed back from the table, leaning back in the chair. I covered my face with both hands. When I looked up, my gaze was straight up at the ceiling.

Angela broke the silence, "Joey, what are you thinking?"

"I'm not liking what I'm thinking," I replied, pulling myself back to the table. Turning to Lucy, I said, "Lucy, please, call Victoria Stewart. Find out what flight Agent Belford is on. Then, call the airline, and have them check the manifest. I have a bad feeling he didn't check in for the flight."

Patrick rubbed his red beard, "Why, lad? You think it involved this Belford character in this?"

I opened my palms facing Mr. Pat, I answered, "I hope not. But last night, all these thoughts kept creeping in. One after the other. It was as if someone was whispering to me."

Agnes added, "That's your subconscious working. You are talking to yourself."

I heard Agnes, but I wasn't listening, "What?" I probed, turning to Agnes.

"You've been thinking about those ideas, but you haven't verbalized your thoughts. That's why they're in your subconscious. Tell us."

"You may be right," I alleged. "I think I didn't want to believe my thoughts."

Lucy broke in, "Belford was scheduled to take American Airlines Flight 289 at seven-thirty this morning from La Guardia to O'Hare," she said. Frowning, and shaking her head, she added, "He was a no- show."

Everyone's gaze went from Lucy to me. I looked around the table, starting to my immediate left, Dom, followed by Lucy, Angela, Mr. Pat, and sitting to my right, Agnes. "Okay, here's what I've been thinking."

As if choreographed, everyone leaned forward.

"Marcy has been complaining about Belford being very possessive of her. He's been pressuring her to go out socially. Advances that she has rejected every time. When we were together, and Belford was profiling our unsub, I noted a couple of things he said. Things which, until now, meant little. For instance, when we talked about letting the press and the public know about a serial killer, he personalized it by saying, *'might as well be on our terms.'* He insisted that the killer wanted credit," I said, as I softly pounded the table.

Dom asked, "What else?"

I pointed at Lucy, "It was something you said." I looked to my left. "Lucy warned me about this guy, Belford, as it related to Marcy. She said something like, *'be careful with this guy, he's a salesperson, and is always selling, selling.'* Remember, Lucy?"

"I said that," Lucy replied, "but how does that tie in?"

I responded, "Back when we were profiling, Bedford made a crude joke. He said, *'the difference between love and rape is salesmanship,'* or some shit to that affect."

Angela noted, "That is crude. Although, we know our killer is successful in enticing our vics into sex on their first date, right?"

I nodded, "Hopefully not all his dates agreed. But there's more. When we spoke about ViCAP, the FBI's database for crime search, he said, *'we'll be able to search for similar crimes, assuming the killer used the same signature.'* So, he's very much aware of that."

Lucy said, "And we know that none of the unsolved murders looked at having the same signature. They have a signature. Just not the same one. Clever."

"Agnes," I said, "you were the first one to observe that all our victims looked like Marcy."

"I know," Agnes said, almost apologetically.

Father Dom added, "So, you're saying that this guy is obsessed with Marcy. And, since she has rejected his advances, it triggered his killing spree?"

"Perhaps, brother," I replied, "but we need a psychiatrist to answer that one."

Mr. Pat asked, "Assuming we are right, and this Belford character is our unsub, what caused this abduction of Marcy? I mean, why now?"

Everyone looked back at me. I thought for a second, and replied, "By accident, I told Marcy of our stakeout at Ernie's. Innocently, she told Belford about it after he asked her where I was. He asked how the case was unfolding."

"When did she tell him?" Lucy inquired.

I replied, "The same day we were going to do the stakeout."

Angela broke in, "So, he knew we would be at Ernie's before we went on the stakeout?"

"Precisely," I replied. "Maybe, he saw us outside Ernie's. If he knew we were there, then he had his reverse stakeout."

"I need to ask," Angela said, "does Belford use a Bluetooth device?"

I nodded, "He doesn't just use it, he wears the freaking thing all the time."

"Let me ask another question," Angela retorted, "does he know we know about the device being left behind? If so, he got rid of that piece of evidence."

I shook my head, "I did not share that with Marcy. So, it's not likely he knows we know that."

"Good," Angela said.

Patrick asked, "We need to locate Marcy. Have you tried finding her phone?"

Agnes replied, "I did, Mr. Pat. Joey has her iPhone password. Her phone seems to be off."

"Can we locate Belford?" Angela asked.

I reached for my phone and called Victoria Stewart. "Victoria," I said when she answered, "I need to bring you up-to-date on some- thing, and I need your help."

She replied, "Joey, I figured something is not right. I'm right outside your door. Let me in."

I motioned to Pat, "She's outside. Let her in."

"The pub's door?" Patrick asked, surprised.

I nodded and pointed to the pub.

Victoria walked into our office, and I made some quick introductions of the team members gathered. "Victoria," I said, "we need to locate Tony Belford."

"Tell me what's going on?" She asked, sitting down at the conference table taking the chair Patrick had been seated at.

I started by telling her we had concluded Marcy was with Agent Belford, and not of her own free will. I then gave her the down and dirty of the case we were working on.

Not wasting any time with more questions, she called her office and put a tracer on Belford's phone and car. I knew that it would be a waste of time, but it was a place to start. If Belford had abducted Marcy, his phone would be off, and he would not be driving his car.

"Could they be back at the range?" Victoria asked. "I know Marcy was dead set on taking the test in a few days."

"No," I replied, "if they went yesterday, she wouldn't be back today. Too much stress on her arm and shoulder. Besides, she was leaving on a trip with her parents today."

"What range was she going to, Joey? I'll send a patrol car to check, just in case," asked Lucy.

"I know they go to a couple of them. Try Westside Gun Range on West 20th, that's the nearest," I replied.

"There has to be an explanation," Victoria began. "I just can't believe Belford is your man."

I pounded both my palms on the table. Pushing back, I got up and walked away. Speaking a bit too loud, "Shit, this is all my fault, shit!"

My sudden reaction took aback everyone.

Dom said, "Joey, you can't blame yourself—"

I cut him off, "Don't you see? I, inadvertently, told Marcy about our stakeout. Belford found out from her, and it set this whole thing in motion. Of course, it's my fault."

Lucy said, "This is not the time to play the blame game. We need to find Marcy."

"Patrick asked, "How about a BOLO?"

Lucy replied, "We don't have enough for a *'be on the lookout'* call. Plus, we don't know what car they're in yet."

Victoria added, "Once we know if Belford is in his car, we could rethink that."

I sat down again, "You can bet they're not driving around. He could have abducted her yesterday, before or after the range. She might be. .." my voice faded. I couldn't finish the sentence.

Victoria answered her cell phone. Everyone kept their eyes on her. "Well, there's no trace of his phone. And, his car is at his place," she said, glancing around the table.

"Great!" I said, "We can't trace either their phones or their cars. He could have her anywhere, for all we know."

Lucy broke in, "Joey, the officers that are at Westside Range report Belford and Marcy were there yesterday until three in the afternoon. They left together."

"Are the officers still there," I asked.

"Yes, they are," Lucy replied.

"Have them asked if anyone saw them drive away. Ask if anyone remembers the car they were in," I said, looking at Lucy.

"Mrs. Stewart," Father Dom said, "could you check into Belford's background before he joined the bureau? Go back as far as you can. From birth, if possible."

I turned to Dom, "What're you thinking?"

Dom replied, "one theory we're working on is that the munsub may have had a traumatic upbringing. Possibly suffered from molestation or abuse. Let's find out about Belford's."

"Good one, Father," Mr. Patrick observed.

"Agnes," I said, turning to her, "get a map of the tri-state area. Let's begin with the idea that Belford drove out of the city at about three in the afternoon. If Marcy was an unwilling participant, then he must have drugged her somehow. He must have had a place to go to in mind. Right?" I asked, looking for affirmations.

Father Dom started to ask I didn't want to hear, "Joey, what—?"

Thrusting myself away from the table, I interrupted Dom. "What if nothing? No! He didn't kill her. I think he's obsessed with her. That's why he's acting out and killing these other look-alike. In his bizarre way, he loves her. The sick bastard."

Lucy looked at her phone as it chirped. She clicked it on, listened for a minute, and said, "Nobody got a license number. However, they saw Marcy get in a white SUV with Belford. He was carrying a duffle bag."

I was too agitated to say anything. I knew what was in the duffle bag.

Victoria said, "So, Belford must have borrowed or rented an SUV. You think he's driving to Chicago? His old home?"

Having calmed down a bit, I replied, "No, if he drugged Marcy to take her somewhere, he only drove for a few hours. They're in the Tri-state area, for sure."

Agnes said, "I can start calling car rental agencies. But that's going to take a while. Plus, they will not give me much information."

Lucy snapped, "They will if it's Detective Lucy Roberts from the NYPD calling. Get a list going, Agnes. Let's you, Angela, and I call. Maybe, we'll get lucky."

My phone rang. Detective Farnsworth was calling. "Yes, Farnsworth, anything?

"No, I have nothing. You have anything on your end?" He asked, sounding genuinely concerned.

I explained what was developing.

He asked, "How can we help?"

"Are you still surveilling Officer Sanchez?"

Farnsworth replied, "Joey, we just got through questioning his partner, Officer Edwards."

"And?" I asked.

"It seems Edwards and Sanchez were together, drinking and eating, on two of the nights our killer struck. So, it's unlikely Sanchez is our unsub."

"So, you're dropping the surveillance?"

"The captain was going to cut it back to after his shift for one or two more nights."

"I got it. Makes sense, I guess. I'll keep you guys in the loop. Thanks, Farns."

"No problem, Joey. This FBI agent, Belford, you think he's our man?"

"It's looking that way," I paused, closed my eyes, and finally said, "call you later."

CHAPTER 22

Marcy turned her head from side to side realizing as she did that, she had a massive headache. Trying to open her eyes and focus, she woke up from what felt to her like a drug- induced sleep. She heard words but couldn't make any sense of it.

"Welcome back, sleepyhead," said Special Agent Tony Belford a second time.

Marcy didn't respond. Her first reaction was to wipe her face with her hands. As she attempted to do that, she noticed that they strapped her to a bed face up. They fastened both her hands with handcuffs to the back of the headrest. Raising her head, she noticed her legs tied with satin red ribbons to the bottom frame of the bed.

"Here, let me make you more comfortable," said Belford, as he slid a second pillow below her head.

At first, she thought she was dreaming, but as things came into focus. She started shivering from the cold temperature in the room. Slowly, she raised her head again and gasped when she realized she was completely naked.

"What have you done?" She shouted, as she dropped her head back on the pillow. She was pulling and shaking both arms, trying to free herself from her constraints.

"Nothing, my darling. You slept well. I didn't think you would sleep this long," Belford replied, sitting a few feet from her on a leather Lay- Z-Boy smiling.

"Tony, you don't have to do this," she said, avoiding being confrontational.

He shouted, "They pushed my hand. It's not my fault."

She took in her surroundings. Glancing around a rustic wood cabin, she found herself in. Leafless trees surrounded the windows, as the wind howled through the small gaps. Ignoring his comment, she asked, "Where are we, Tony?"

"I'm in paradise, looking at you."

"I'm cold, could you cover me, please?"

Reluctantly, he got up from his chair. From the closet, he pulled a beige wool blanket, "You look beautiful just like I imagined," and put it on her.

"How did you drug me?"

"Rohypnol in your fruit juice when we left the range. Perhaps, I gave you too much. Sorry about that."

"You said, *'they pushed you.'* Who exactly pushed you?"

"Your ex-boyfriend, that Man-cue-so guy. His team and the NYPD," he said, sitting down again across from her.

The realization hit Marcy, "Oh, my God! You're the serial killer they're looking for!"

"It's okay. We're finally together. So, I have them to thank for that."

"Tony, you don't have to do this. We can talk about it."

"Talk, talk, talk. There's nothing to talk about. We're finally together to make love to each other. Not to talk about it."

"Tony, please. Stop this now."

"How many times have you rejected me? Five times. That's how many. You've never even noticed me. We're soul mates, Marcy. You'll see. My love for you knows no boundaries. And, I know you'll love me back. Just as much as I love you."

Marcy's mouth was dried. She needed to think of her next move. "Can I have some water?"

"Of course," he replied, as he stood reaching for a metal container. Raising her head with his left hand, he brought the container with his right to her mouth and poured in some water.

As she dank, water slid from Marcy's sides of her mouth. Looking at him, she said, "Tony, you need to end this. You know they'll be looking for me. I was supposed to go on a trip today with my parents."

He smiled, "We can send them a postcard to tell 'em we're enjoying our honeymoon."

"Can you turn the heater up? I'm still freezing. Please?"

Marcy watched as Tony got up and shut a window. He walked over to the right side of the cabin where the gas fireplace was located and clicked on the starter button. Immediately, a blue and yellow flame sprung from the fireplace. "Thank you," Marcy said. "You said I rejected you five times. I don't remember that."

"Five times I asked you to go out with me socially. All I wanted was to enjoy a romantic dinner so you could get to know me better. And, five times you brushed me aside like if I was an insect not worthy of your attention."

"Tony," she began, still not wanting to be confrontational, "I never meant to hurt you or brush you aside. We are co-workers and friends. I have a rule not to socialize with co-workers."

"That's swell because we're no longer co-workers," he said, sitting back in his chair across from her.

"My five rejections. .." she paused, not sure she wanted to ask the question. She went on, "The five victims. Are they in any way tied to my rejections?" She asked, closing her eyes, hoping for a negative response.

"I had to gratify my ego after you crushed it each time. See, they didn't reject me. They wanted to be with me."

"Oh, my God. But why kill them?"

"Ah, that's a long story. Maybe, I'll tell you someday. Are you hungry, my darling?"

Marcy ignored his question. "Where are we?"

"At a friend's cabin. Nice and private for us to be together."

"Those are pictures of your family? She asked, looking at mantel above the fireplace.

"My family? Yeah, right. I told you. It's a friend's cabin."

"How long was I out?"

"What you really want to know is how far are we from the city? Right! Well, far enough, and secluded enough that no one will bother us."

Marcy needed to make a move. "I need to use the restroom."

She saw him, looked at her with skepticism. "We don't want you to have an accident on our honeymoon bed, do we? But if you try anything, I mean anything, I'll put you out again. Understood?"

"I just need to use the bathroom."

He walked over to her left side of the bed, and uncuff her left arm, leaving the cuffs around her hand. Holding her arm behind her back, he reached over with one hand and undid the handcuff from her right arm. Again, leaving the cuffs on around her right wrist. Pulling her right arm behind her back, he connected both handcuffs.

Marcy sat up with his help. The top of the blanket fell on her legs, exposing her breasts. Her legs were still spread and tied to the bed. She noticed the red satin ribbons he used for her legs. Glancing around the wood cabin, she saw the place was immaculately clean. Everything seemed to be in perfect order. The mantel above the fire- place had a few family pictures. She doubted it was anyone related to Tony. Other knickknacks adorned the shelf. The small dining table for two had white plastic doylies on it. Something her mother would have on her table. It was a summer cabin. Probably belonged to someone in the city. She noticed all the furniture and adornments were aged. Every- thing was old, as if they had not updated the cabin since the 90s. A photo of smiling President Clinton hung from a wall.

Tony came around the front and began untying her left leg while momentarily glancing at her breasts. He sighed. Marcy felt very uncomfortable, but she ignored his glance, planning her move.

"I'm going to need to use my hands in the bathroom," she said.

He looked at her and smiled. "One hand will have to do. You're a lefty, so I'll undo your right hand. Slide over and get on your back."

Marcy stayed seated, thinking for a moment.

Tony got up raising her left leg with one hand and pushing her back by the shoulders. He then turned her over on her back, exposing her derriere.

"What are you doing!" She exclaimed.

"Nothing yet," he replied. He took the red satin ribbon and bound it to her left handcuff. Immobilizing her left arm. He then untied her right leg, leaving the ribbon loose. Sliding her down on the bed, he pulled her up by her shoulders to a standing position. Standing behind her, he embraced her by her breasts and pulled her close to him. She was shivering, not only from the cold, but from the thought of having this animal touching her as he was.

"I need to go, please, Tony."

He whispered, kissing her in her right ear, "I never noticed your little parrot tattoo on your neck."

"Let go of me!" She exclaimed.

He kissed her ear again, and said gently, " darling, this is how it will be. The two of us as one."

Marcy moved forward to get away from Belford. Quickly, she attempted to kick him using her freed right leg. Belford was too quick for her. Still cupping both her breasts, he moved his lower body back. Her kick just barely brushed his right leg.

"Marcy, Marcy, relax. I'm a patient person. You won't want to reject me again, darling. I promise you."

"Don't touch me. You're crazy," she said, realizing right away that she made a mistake.

Tony quickly turned her around to face him. Marcy could see that his face was now flushed and red with fury. His eyes were burning with anger. "I'm not crazy. Don't you ever say that to me again," he said, so close to her face she could smell his breath.

She toned it down, "You're right, and I'm sorry. Now, can I use the bathroom?"

Tony turned her around and held her shoulders. He walked her to the restroom just off to the left side of the cabin.

"I need some privacy," Marcy said, noticing the duffle bag behind the Lay-Z-Boy chair Tony had been sitting in.

"You can close the door, but noticed I removed the doorknob. So, try nothing stupid or I'll drug you again."

Marcy sat on the toilet without opening the lid. She needed to calm down and plan her next move. Looking around the small bath- room. She noticed a small window with laced curtains above the tub, a small pedestal sink on the side, a little basket containing pot-pourri, a bar of soap, and a couple of hand towels. No medicine cabinet. Nothing she could use as a weapon. Her thoughts wandered off to her parents and to Joey. What could they be thinking, and how could they find her? She looked at the glass mirror and wondered if she could break the glass and use it as a weapon. Instead, she turned on the water and wet her hand. With the soap, she wrote on the glass MM and today's date. At least, she would leave a clue behind.

"Are you done?" Tony's voice brought her back to the realization of her captivity.

"One more minute," she replied. Then a plan came together. "Coming out."

She opened the bathroom door and saw Tony get up from his chair and begin walking towards her. She rushed Tony, like a line-backer rushing the quarterback. Her freed right arm folded in front of her, with her elbow pointing outwards. She hit Tony in the middle of his chest with all her might. Pushing him back all the way to the opposite side of the cabin.

Tony's legs got stuck in the area rug in front of the gas fireplace and fell backward into the fireplace. Marcy could remain standing and ran to the duffle bag containing the firearms. She knelt behind the chair and reached for the duffle bag. She saw Tony get up from the floor with the back of his flannel shirt on fire rushing towards her.

CHAPTER 23

I sat at the conference table with my head down. I was drained. My mind was racing, but it was like a closed-circuit race going around and round with no end to it. Where could Belford have taken Marcy? The *'why?'* made me feel a little better. If he was obsessed with her, he was not likely to kill her. But what was he planning to do to her?

Riley MacClenny, our pub manager, stuck his head in our office. I did not know time. The pub was already opened, which meant it was two in the afternoon or later.

"Joey, there's a city inspector here." I raised my head, "What?"

"There's a city inspector here," Riley repeated.

"What the hell does he want?" I asked, somewhat irrelevantly. "He says he needs to check licenses," Riley replied.

I looked up at the ceiling as if asking the heavens, a question, - What the fuck?

"I got this," Lucy said. "Don't worry, honey. I'll send him on his way," she said, motioning me to stay put.

I turned my chair in the direction of Agnes' desk area. "Any luck calling the rental agencies?"

Both Agnes and Angela shook their heads. "Nothing yet, Joey," Agnes replied.

"This bastard is too smart to rent a car under his name. We're wasting our time with that."

Angela said, "Nothing else to do now. We'll keep at it, for now."

'Nothing else to do now,' I repeated to myself. I looked around the table. Patrick was reading from a file. Victoria was on the phone. Father Dom was looking at the map of the tristate area Agnes had put on a wall. Angela was by Agnes's desk area making calls. Everyone was involved in some activity. None of which, I thought, would lead to uncovering where Marcy was being held captive. I kept thinking of the hundreds, maybe thousands, of unsolved abductions of women and children. Some of which would never be solved, and the ones that were led either to murders of the victims, or horrible stories of years spent in captivity. I reached for a wastepaper basket, brought up it to my face, and threw up.

Father Dominic came over, "Are you alright?" He called for a server to collect the trash can and take it away.

I looked at him, had it been anyone else, I would have answered with a wry remark. I held my tongue and ignored the question. "Brother, I'm at a loss. This son of a bitch has us on checkmate. Anything on the map?"

Dom replied, "Not really. I keep looking for a sign, but I don't see anything. I'm assuming he drove for no more than five or six hours. So, if that's the case, he's no more than four hundred miles away at the max."

"That's assuming he drove and stopped somewhere after a few hours. If he resumed the trip this morning, there's no telling where they might be by now. This is all my fault, Dom," I said, lowering my head.

"That's nonsense, Joey. You had nothing to do with this."

"We should have been married by now. In love and living together. None of this would have ever happened."

"What kind of illogical conclusion is that? Things happened to postpone or delay a potential marriage. Even that would not have stopped this crazy person from acting out as he has. This Belford is deranged. We're not dealing with a normal person. So, stop blaming yourself, and start thinking like you do, and let's solve this case."

I got up, and hugged Dom, as tears emerged from both my eyes. "I love her, brother. I can't live without her."

"Yeah? I'll stop lecturing if you start thinking. We'll find this bastard and bring Marcy back safe and sound."

Victoria had watched Dom and me from her peripheral vision while she talked on the phone. She clicked her phone off. "I got some background information on Belford's childhood," she said.

Everyone gathered around the conference table.

"I think we are on to something," Victoria Stewart began, "Belford was raised by his mother and a stepfather. A Reverend. His father passed away when Belford was only a year old," Victoria said, looking up from her iPad around the table. She proceeded to read a report that had been emailed to her from her office. "Belford ran away from his home at age sixteen. He went to live with his paternal grandparents, after which, his stepfather was charged with sexually molesting him. The case never went to trial because allegedly, his stepfather killed his mother, before committing suicide."

"How did they die?" I asked.

Victoria read on, "Six months after being charged, the stepfather shot Belford's mother in the face, then shot himself in the head."

Lucy added, "We may have the trigger that led to Belford's deviant behavior."

I thought for a second, "Was that how the deaths were, in fact, ruled, a murder, and a suicide?"

Father Dom knowing my inquisitive mind asked, "Why Joey, are you thinking that Belford had something to do with their deaths?"

"Just asking, brother. Who knows how long Belford suffered through that? I wouldn't put it past anyone not wanting to kill their offender. Especially for sexually molesting him."

Angela inquired, "What about his mother? Would he kill her, also?"

Lucy replied, "If Belford thought his mother knew what his stepfather was doing to him. It's very possible, right?"

I didn't wait for anyone to answer that question. "Folks let's not get sidetracked by that incident. I think this information is key to what we thought before. Belford is our guy. The question remains. How are we going to find out where he has taken Marcy?"

Agnes had her laptop at the table, looking up from it, she said, "There's no record of Belford or Marcy using their credit cards anywhere, for anything."

Victoria broke in, "How are you getting that information?" she asked, staring at Agnes.

I said, "Victoria," she looked at me. Shaking my head, I said, "Some questions need to go unanswered."

Victoria said, smiling, "Disregard my question."

Mr. Pat said, "Belford must have rented a car. Very few places, if any, are going to let you do that with cash. They want a credit card. Plus, if he's driving, he needs to buy gas, food, and a place to stay. I suppose he can do that with cash. But somewhere along the line, he'll need to use a credit card. He may be using a credit card not issued under his name. Don't you think?"

Lucy asked, "He's using an alias?"

Special Agent Victoria said, "I'm not going to ask a question, but allow me to think out loud for a second," glancing at Agnes and opening her eyes wide. "Could there be a record of Belford buying supplies for like a camping trip somewhere that someone could find?" Agnes smiled, looked at me, as I pointed to her laptop, and nodded.

Angela added, "Even if we find out he bought supplies, that's not going to tell us where he might be headed. Although," she paused, "he might have rented a place to stay ahead of time."

I looked at my watch. I had set the stopwatch counter to correspond with the last time Marcy was seen which was yesterday at three in the afternoon. It read twenty-six hours. I didn't want to think of the anguish Marcy must be going through. I swiveled my chair to face away from the table and all assembled there. My stomach was churning, and I thought I was going to throw up again.

Lucy pointed at Victoria, and asked, "Mr. Stewart, what was Belford's stepfather name?"

Victoria opened her iPad, scrolling through a few pages, she replied, "Reverend Thomas Stiles. What are you thinking?"

Replying, Lucy said, "Perhaps Belford is using that name. Or, at least, the last name."

"As a matter of fact," Victoria said, "Belford was adopted by Stiles and given his last name. For a while, he was Anthony Stiles. He changed it back to his dad's last name of Belford when he went to live with his grandparents."

Agnes said, "I'll start a search of Stiles to see what comes up."

I was listening to the discussion, swiveling back to face the group, I said, "No, wait. Don't do that—"

Lucy interrupted me, "Joey that could be a possibility." I said, "Peter Gruntel."

CHAPTER 24

Marcy, with one hand tied, and fully naked, struggled to run behind the chair where Belford had the duffle bag with the weapons they used for her firearms training. She knew if she could open it she would have the advantage. She glanced to see Belford running towards her, with his red flannel shirt on fire.

Tony stopped, realizing his shirt was burning him. He took it off and stomped on it with his right foot. Ashes flailed everywhere. Raising his glance at Marcy, he smiled.

Marcy's free hand trembled as she attempted to open the zipper and reach for one revolver in the bag. His sudden stop and smile confused her. Then, she realized the duffle bag had a Master Lock attached to it.

"Good try, Marcy. I should never underestimate you. But that's what I like about you. You're a fighter," Belford said, stepping on all the little ashes on the area rug.

Marcy was kneeling by the chair, dispassionately looking at the duffle bag. She looked up at Tony, who was now standing in front of her. His shaven chest was striking. He was white as fresh snow. Shivering from the cold and trembling with fear, she remained quiet.

"I told you not to try anything. I don't want to drug you again, but you're not giving me many choices, now are you?"

"Tony, you don't have to do this. You won't get away with it," she said, as she made a fruitless effort to cover herself.

"Oh, but we're going to be together forever, darling. We're going to have little Belford's running around our house. You'll see."

"Let me go now, and I'll tell everyone we're out in the woods practicing for my FBI test."

"Marcy, you're insulting my intelligence. There's only one plan left. We go forward with our lives together. I wish it could have been different. We could have been together, working and enjoying our lives as a couple. I tried."

"Can I have my clothes? I'm still cold."

"Here," he said, reaching for a backpack on another chair, but monitoring her, "I brought your favorite clothes to lounge around. Sweatpants and a top."

As Tony reached for the backpack, Marcy saw his exposed back, and she was horrified. "My God! What are all those scars?"

Tony turned to face her, dropping the clothes he retrieved for her on the chair, he reached in and pulled out a tee shirt for himself. "Those, yeah well, that's a family album," he said, as he put on the tee shirt.

Marcy couldn't believe the many scars on his back. His entire back was like a checkerboard, little squares from just below his neck, to his waist, the width of his back.

"Get up, and try nothing. I'm going to untie your arm so that you can put these on," he said, reaching for her sweatpants and top.

She didn't want to be drugged again, so she went along for the moment, and not try anything. She put on the pants, followed by the top. "Can I just sit here?"

Tony thought for a moment, "Yeah, you can sit there, but the cuffs go back on," he said, as he cuffed her hands in front of her, and connected the handcuffs to the cuffs around her ankles.

"What happened to your back?"

Belford picked up the backpack that was in the other chair, threw it on the floor, and sat down across from Marcy. Sitting back, he squirmed from the fresh burns on his back. "You mean besides the blisters from you pushing me into the fireplace?"

Marcy just nodded.

"Three hundred twenty-seven crosses," he said, glancing at the floor with a look of shame.

"I don't understand," Marcy said, "what does that mean?"

"Is your stepfather good to you? Alberto. Seems like a delightful man, is he?"

"The best. So much so, I call him Dad. He loves both my mother and me."

"Love. Now there's a word that requires definition. Doesn't?"
"What are you saying?"

Tony's facial expression changed as he closed his eyes. He was deep in thought. Anger was visible in his eyes when he opened them once again. "Well, my stepfather loved me, too. Three hundred and twenty- seven times."

"Oh, my God," Marcy said, "Did he ..." her voice trailed off.

Tony looked up at Marcy, "Since he married my mother, I was fourteen until I left the house at sixteen."

Marcy asked, "Each cross, did he do that each time?"

Belford, still looking towards Marcy, but through her, replied, "Every Tuesday and Thursday when my mother was out supposedly playing cards with her girlfriends."

Marcy wanted to probe some more but was concerned about his reaction. She remained quiet.

Belford, his eyes focusing on Marcy, asked, "You wanted to know about the scars?"

She nodded.

Belford looked down at the floor, "Every time he molested me, the Reverend would cut me as a cross. Deep enough to scar me."

"Did you count them? The crosses, I mean."

"I didn't have to. I kept count of the times he abused me."

"What happened to them?"

"I ran away to my grandparents, and when they saw my scars, my grandfather pressed charges against my stepfather," he replied, in a somber tone.

"Did he get what he deserved?"

"Oh, they both got what they deserved. However, just not from the authorities," Belford said, taking a deep breath.

"What do you mean?" Marcy asked with concern.

Belford didn't reply right away. He sat there unresponsive for a few moments. "I snuck back into their home one day and waited for them. I was almost seventeen..." he said in a whisper.

"Did you..." Marcy began asking but stop short.

He looked at her again, "He kept a revolver on his side of the bed in the night table. At first, they thought I was there to visit since I had not seen them for almost a year. Then, they saw the gun. I remember my mom's face. She knew why I was there," he paused, "I had them sit in the living room. Standing behind him, I put the gun on his head. I can still hear my mother asking for mercy for this animal. I wanted to look into his eyes before I pulled the trigger. So, I moved to face him, still holding the gun touching his forehead," he paused again, looking up at the ceiling and taking a deep breath. "In one quick motion, I moved the gun below his chin, pointed it upwards and pulled the trigger. The bullet went through his brain, and out the top of his head. I never had, and have never seen again, so much blood spurt out of the top of a head. It was like a broken sprinkler just gushing blood upwards."

"Oh, my God. What about your mother?"

"My mother, you ask?" Tony said, glancing back at Marcy. "My dear mother, it turns out was not playing cards on Tuesdays and Thursdays. No, she was fucking around with various men while this animal had his way with me. She knew what he was doing to me, but to say anything, would have interrupted her devious acts. Right? I followed her for weeks after I ran away from home and saw more than I needed to see. The bitch," he said loudly, and closing his eyes.

"What did you do?" Marcy asked.

"I stopped her screwing around. That's what I did. After I shot the bastard, she sat there motionless, almost catatonic. I wrapped the revolver around the animal's hand, pointed it at my mother's head, and pulled the trigger," he said and sighed.

Marcy couldn't believe what she was hearing. She trembled from the fear of being in this room with such a cold-blooded killer. She had seen little or no emotion from Belford, as he recounted this experience.

"So, Special Agent Martinez, you're probably wondering if I got away with it, right?" He asked, now smiling sarcastically.

"I assume you did," she replied.

"The perfect murder suicide scenario. See, I had pictures of my mother entering various motels with men. I displayed them on the coffee table in front of where I had him and her sitting. So, I left home, called the police from a public phone a few blocks away, and reported hearing gunshots. It was an easy conclusion for the authorities. Husband shoots wife for infidelity, then kills himself in remorse. Case closed."

"Were you ever questioned?"

"My grandparents told the authorities I had been in my room, and in bed all the time. They never knew I snuck out of their home through my bedroom window."

Marcy felt hopeless. Her captor had been emboldened at the age of sixteen and had gotten away with two horrific murders. Besides the recent crimes in Manhattan, she knew there had to be others before. She glanced around the small one-room cabin, searching for a way out. A way to stop this madness that befell her. She closed her eyes.

"By the way, darling," Belford said, as his voice shocked her back into reality, "we need to get ready to leave. I want to be out of here in an hour. I have tuna sandwiches. I made fresh for us. Are you hungry?"

"Yes, I'm," she replied. But she wasn't. Her stomach was in knots. Buy time was her only thought. "Where are we going?"

Belford looked at Marcy, and thought for a second, "I don't know if I should tell you—"

She interrupted, "What difference does it make now? I want to know," she said softly and not in a demanding way.

Belford smiled, "We have about three days of travel ahead of us. Our destination is the beautiful Northwest. Whistler, British Columbia."

Her immediate thought assured her that this animal was not thinking of killing her. At least, not immediately. "Why there?"

"Mr. and Mrs. Nichols own a quaint one-bedroom cabin there.

Very much like this one. Only bigger, and on two acres."

"The Nichols?' she asked.

"That's us, darling. John, and Mary Nichols," he said, grinning. "Now then, let me fetch your sandwich. We need to eat and run," Tony said, walking over to a small refrigerator near the bathroom wall.

"I would like to take a shower, please."

"A shower, now? No, I don't think so. Here," he said, taking a bottle of cologne from the backpack. "Splash some of this on. You'll feel better."

She looked at the bottle without glancing at him. She said sternly, "I would feel better if I took a shower."

"I like you just the way you are. Did you know Marcy, one of the biggest love stories in history, was that of Napoleon Bonaparte and Josephine in the late 1700s?"

"So, what about it?"

"As Napoleon returned from his many battles, they say it, that he would send a messenger ahead to Josephine, with a simple message, *'don't wash.'* He loved her 'au naturel' smell."

Marcy didn't know what to make of her situation. Was Belford crazy? What was going through his mind? How many victims are out there? Will she ever escape, or was her fate sealed?

CHAPTER 25

Lucy asked, "What about Peter Gruntel? That's the professor, Detectives Farnsworth, and Charles questioned. He's been cleared?"

I had an idea, and I felt right about it, "Yeah, he's been cleared. But that's the profile Belford has been using on Facebook and other social media." Turning to Lucy, I asked, "Please, call Farnsworth, get Gruntel's address. Agnes," I said, pointing at her, "start researching Gruntel. I want to know everything about him, pronto, Agnes, please."

Father Dom said, "I think you're on to something. Let's hope this

Gruntel fellow has some answers."

I stood up and walked away from the table. An adrenaline rush overtook me. I shivered. I felt like a lion who just got a sniff of his prey.

Lucy was standing a few feet away said, "Joey, I have Gruntel's address. Farnsworth wants to know if he should meet us there?"

"Ah," I thought for a second, "no, no need. You and I can handle this." I went over to Patrick, "Mr. Pat, you and Angela follow us in your SUV. We'll go to this guy's home. Oh, and Pat, bring the backpack."

"You want me to go along?" Dominic asked.

"Brother, how about you help Agnes with the research? Call me the moment you have something. Okay?"

Lucy took the Lincoln Tunnel, pulled onto Interstate 85 North on our way to Paramus, New Jersey. Mr. Pat followed behind with Angela. My mind was on Marcy. I looked at my watch and the stopwatch counter I had started when Marcy was abducted. It read thirty-two hours. A few minutes later, we arrived in Paramus and located the home of Professor Peter Gruntel.

Lucy knocked on the front door. Professor Gruntel answered. Farnsworth had described him as a tall skinny nerd, with broad black rim glasses, and sure enough, a Woody Allen look-alike said, "Yes, how can I help you?"

Lucy flashed her creds, introduced me and inquired, "Can we ask you a few questions?"

"Sure, please come in. What's this about?" He asked, as we followed him to the living room. "Have a seat," he said, pointing a sofa.

"Mr. Gruntel," I began, "you spoke to Detective Farnsworth, about

a profile on Facebook."

"Yes, I did. But I had no idea the NYPD would follow up on these things."

"Yes, sir. There seems to be more than just a Facebook profile. Have you ever heard the name Anthony or Tony Belford?" I asked.

He hesitated, thought for a second, and replied, "No, I can't recall ever hearing that name. Why? What's the issue?"

His hesitation made me think twice. "Mr. Gruntel, is there anyone else in the house with you now?"

"Why, what's going on?" He asked, nervously. Lucy took my cue and sternly asked again.

He replied, "Just my wife in the kitchen."

I asked, "Do you mind if we look around your home, sir?"

"No, go ahead. But please, tell me what's going on."

I had already called Mr. Pat, who was parked outside with Angela Asis. Lucy had requested that Mrs. Gruntel join us in the living room.

"Detective Asis and Mr. Sullivan are at your front door. Would you mind if I let them in?" I asked.

Mrs. Gruntel looked distressed, drying her hands on a kitchen towel, she asked, "What's going on, Peter?"

Lucy said, "There's a possibility that someone has stolen your identity, Mr. Gruntel, and they may be committing some crimes."

Mrs. Gruntel asked, "Oh, my God, in our home?"

"No, madam," replied Lucy, "but it's the procedure that we secure your home. Can Detective Asis and Sullivan check your home?"

"Please, go ahead," said Peter.

I nodded to Angela and Mr. Pat, as they began a walk-through of the home.

Patrick asked, "Do you have a basement?"

"Yes, through here," replied Mrs. Gruntel, pointing to the stairs leading down to the basement.

Lucy and I sat with the Gruntel's, as Angela and Pat made their way to the basement.

I asked Mrs. Gruntel, "Do you know an Anthony Belford?"

She turned to her husband, then, shaking her head, she said, "No, I don't."

Gruntel asked, "Is that the person who stole my identity?"

Both Angela and Patrick walked back into the living room. Mr. Pat looked at me and shook his head. He pointed to the stairs going to the second floor; I nodded.

"Very possible. Yes, sir," Lucy replied.

I asked, "Have you noticed any activities on your credit cards that are not yours? Or anything else out of the ordinary?"

The Gruntel's looked at each other. Then back at me. Peter replied, "No, we haven't."

Lucy asked, "Do you own a white SUV?"

Mrs. Gruntel replied, "No, just our two cars outside."

"How about other property? Do you own any other homes?" Mrs.

Gruntel replied, "No, this is our only home."

Putting his hand on her knee, he said, "Well, yes. We inherited a cabin from my mother last year."

I jumped at the answer, "Where, sir?"

"About an hour from here in Wawayanda State Park. Well, not in the park itself, but bordering the park by Wawayanda Mountain and the Appalachian Trail."

Both Lucy and I looked at each other, and our eyes opened wide at the same time.

"That's it!" I said.

Mr. Gruntel moved up in his chair, "they only opened The park from Memorial Day through the end of October. Everything is closed there, now. We only go in the summer months."

"Can you give me an address, sir?" I asked.

"Not really, I can draw you a map. The cabin is secluded in the woods," Peter replied.

I frowned as my phone rang. The ID caller showed Agnes photo. "Excuse me a second," I said, getting up and walking a few feet away. "Yes, Agnes, what do you have?"

Agnes was very agitated, "Joey, I found a white SUV rented by a Peter Gruntel the day before they abducted Marcy at Enterprise Rent- A-Car in Paramus, New Jersey. How are you doing there?"

I ignored her question. Walking into the kitchen and away from the Gruntel's, I said, "See if the car is equipped with GPS. If so, find out where it is now." I thought for a second, "Wait, they're not going to give you that information. Maybe Lucy should call."

"Sweetie, I'm already using Lucy's creds. Otherwise, I would not have gotten any information. I'll get you the location and text you in a moment. Hang in there."

I smiled. That's my Agnes. I walked back to the living room just as Angela and Mr. Pat were coming down from the upstairs bedroom. I looked at them.

"All clear," Angela said, as she and Mr. Pat, joined everyone else in the living room.

"Lucy, can I talk to you in the kitchen for a moment?"

Lucy looked at the couple and asked, "Would you excuse us for another second?"

The Gruntels nodded, looked at each other, and remained quiet.

As we entered the kitchen, I said, "Agnes found the SUV rented under the name of Gruntel."

"Do you think these two are involved?" Lucy asked.

"I don't know. It was rented right here in Paramus."

"Shit, what a coincidence," she said.

"That, or Belford, is pointing the finger at this guy to throw us off."

"What do you want to do?"

"You and Angela stay here with these folks. Question them separately. Who knows, they may be involved. I'll drive to the cabin with Mr. Pat. We'll check it out and call you back."

"Honey, I don't want you going up there without backup. Besides, this Belford must be armed. I can call the New Jersey State Police."

"No, no. I don't want a posse showing up. Marcy could be there. We'll be fine. Then again, they may not be there at all." As I said that, my phone chirp. I took a quick look, Agnes had texted me the location of the SUV. I noticed Lucy looking at me, but she said nothing.

Lucy said, "Okay, get the map from Mr. Gruntel, and let me give you my second weapon I have in the car."

I didn't share with Lucy that we had located the SUV. "The map, yes, I'll take that. But I don't need your weapon, thanks."

"Joey, you can't go up there unarmed."

"I just said, I didn't need your weapon. I didn't say we were unarmed."

"Baby, be careful, and bring Marcy back," she said, as she kissed me on the cheek.

We walked back to the living room. Mr. Gruntel had drawn a map of the location of his cabin.

"Tell me about your cabin, sir," I said, as Peter handed me the handmade map.

"One-room cabin. It's like a studio apartment. But it has every-thing we need."

"Happy to hear that. Where does it face, north, south, where?" I asked, hurriedly.

"Faces east. We have some beautiful sun rises through the forest. You should see the sun rays break through the trees—"

I needed to interrupt, I'm not buying the cabin. "Mr. Gruntel, I don't need a picture. Just specifics. Tell me more about this map."

The professor gave me the layout of the cabin and the surrounding area. He mentioned a mailbox that had a wooden eagle on top of it. That's where we turn into the dirt road to reach the cabin, he told us.

I walked close to Patrick, "You have the backpack?"

"In my SUV, lad."

I whispered in his ear, "Let's go get Marcy."

CHAPTER 26

Patrick and I got into his SUV. "What's in the backpack?" I asked. As he drove out of the Gruntel's driveway, Patrick turned to me, and replied,

"Same as always. Two Colt forty-five, and two Remington 870 shotguns."

"Enough ammo?"

Looking forward, and smiling, he replied, "Plenty to save the Alamo, this time."

"Good."

"We're we headed?" Patrick asked.

"Do you have a navigation system in this car?"

"Of course, lad. Open the glove compartment and take out the folded map. This is an old bucket. I do it the old fashion way."

"Got it. I have an app for that. It's called Waze. I'll set it up."

"Of course, you do."

My app was on, but we didn't have a specific address to plug in, so I said, "North and west to Wawayanda State Park. We'll follow these coordinates that Agnes sent," I said, showing him my phone. "That's where the SUV Belford rented is. Take State Road 17, south to the 288. Then, head northwest. We're about forty-five minutes away."

Patrick glanced at me, "Some of those roads may not be opened this time of year, as we get closer to the park."

"You have four-wheel drive, don't you?" I asked, glancing back at Mr. Pat.

"Sure do. What's the plan?"

"At the moment, my only plan is to get Marcy. I'll make up the rest as we get there."

Patrick smiled, "Works for me."

We had been on the road for one hour, and we still had about twenty miles to go. I was anxious. Agnes kept us posted from the pub. She was able to see the GPS on her computer. We were not. I looked at my watch. Thirty-five hours, it read. Marcy had been with this killer for thirty-five hours. *'My God, what could she be thinking,'* I thought.

It was very dark. The moon was out. The skies were clear. If I had time to look. The sky was coated with a million stars. At least we had the advantage of surprise. "Fuck, there. There's the eagle!" I said as Patrick drove past it.

"You want to go up the dirt road?" Mr. Pat asked, coming to a full stop.

"No, no. Let me see if Google maps work here. If so, we can get a layout of the area," I said, as I tried to connect to the internet. "I have no fucking service. See if you do."

"Nothing, Joey. No bars, nada. How far did Gruntel say the cabin was from the road?"

"About two miles. Keep veering right on any forks, he said."

"I think we can drive up a mile, or more. I won't turn on the lights."

"Okay, let's do that. Also, let me disconnect the interior light," I said, as I ripped the bulb from the socket inside the car."

"Easy, boss," Mr. Pat said, looking at the light.

Patrick drove slowly, as we both sat forward on our seats, making sure we stayed on the dirt road.

"Joey, we've gone a little over a mile."

"Okay, stop here. We'll walk the rest of the way."

"Let me drive this rig off the road, and hide it, somewhat."

"The hell with that. I want you to block the road. Find a spot where no one can drive around the car. Then, block the road. There! On the turn."

We got out of the SUV. We holstered our Colts, with shotguns in hand, began a double step towards where the cabin was supposed to be.

Walking up an incline after a few minutes, I saw a small shimmer of light. "You see it, Pat?"

"You think that's the cabin?" He whispered back.

"It has to be. This place is deserted. I'll take the north side. You take the south. The front door is facing east, according to Gruntel. Let's make sure the white SUV is there."

"Got it. Joey, take a minute and mute your phone. I just did mine."

"Good point. If the car is there, I want to get close to the cabin and see if we can hear or see something. We can't go blasting our way in."

"Roger that."

We walked another hundred yards through the brush and into the forest. There was about an inch of fresh snow on the ground. I have always enjoyed hearing the crunching of the snow as you walked on it. Except tonight I was unaware of it. The interior light was just barely visible through a small crack of what had to be window curtains.

"Stop!" Patrick whispered. "Is that Belford?"

I squinted my eyes to focus, "Shit, yes. What's he doing? Loading his SUV?"

"Sure, looks that way. Is he carrying?" Mr. Pat asked.

"I can't tell from here. But this would be a good moment to blow his ass away, right?"

"Yes, but we're too far away," Patrick said.

"Let's move in, see if we can isolate him. Before, he goes back inside."

As we moved in, Mr. Pat stepped on a dry branch, breaking it. The sound, in the forest's quiet, was like a plane had just crashed a few feet away. We both knelt, keeping our eyes on Tony Belford. Belford stopped moving, put his hand on what we could now see was his pistol, and slowly did a clockwise three-hundred-and-sixty-degree turn, pivoting on his right leg. Seeing nothing, we hoped, he threw a duffle bag in the car and went back inside the cabin.

"Shit, we missed him," I said, whispering.

"Sorry about that, Joey," Patrick said, apologetically.

"Let's go back to Plan A. You go to the south side of the entrance, I'll come in from the north side. If he's leaving, he should come out with Marcy any moment."

"Roger."

We moved from both sides, towards the front of the cabin. We waited. Sticking my head out partially, I could see the door of the cabin opening out. A few seconds later, a partial figure of a female emerged. It was Marcy. Someone turned off the light on the porch. Here was my chance. If Marcy walked out, followed by Belford, we had him.

Marcy appeared very erect. Her head was almost immobile, she was treading very carefully, as she stepped out onto the small front porch. It was dark, the porch's roof covered the area where Marcy was standing still. And then I saw it. Almost entirely covered by Marcy's long hair was the barrel of a rifle. A shotgun that extended back into the cabin. 'Fuck!' I said to myself. Belford was still in the cabin, holding the other end of the shotgun, for sure.

"Joey, Joey, come out, come out, wherever you are," said a voice from inside the cabin.

'How did, he know we were here?' I asked myself.

Marcy was looking straight ahead. She stood there like a mannequin. I now saw her hands cuffed in front of her and connected to a pair of leg cuffs.

The voice said, "Joey, I'm coming out now. Show yourself. Oh, and please note that Marcy's head and the end of the barrel are tied together. Any stupid moves well, we both lose Marcy."

'Always a step ahead this asshole is,' I thought. Marcy's head moved forward. Then, she took a step forward herself, being pushed from behind by the barrel on her head. Belford was now in full view. His right hand looked as if it was also tied to the shotgun. His index fingered bordered the trigger.

"Belford," I said, stepping out of the dark, "let Marcy go, and you can walk out of here. Simple trade Belford. Marcy stays, you go."

Belford glanced to his left and looking down from the porch. Our eyes met. He smiled. "I wish it was that simple, Mancuso. You and your little makeshift team of investigators brought this on yourselves."

Marcy shouted, "Whistler, Bri—" Her head jerked forward, as Belford pushed the barrel into her head with a sudden move.

I froze. What was she trying to tell us? I asked myself.

"You stupid little girl, shut up!" Belford said, loudly. "Who else is with you, Joey?" He asked, without looking at me.

"I'm alone, Belford. Now listen—"

"Sure, you are," he said, interrupting me. "Is your brother, the priest, with you? If so, he can perform the ceremony here. We have everyone we need. The bride and groom, the witness, and the priest. Then, Marcy and I can be on our way... to our honeymoon."

"You're a sick bastard, Belford," I said, holding my Colt pointed down, and moving towards the front steps of the porch. "You can't get away with this. Think about it. Walk away, now. Leave Marcy behind, and just go."

"Man-cue-so, don't take another step. Toss that gun away into the woods. Do what's best for Marcy. I have nothing to lose. You," he paused, and shouted, "throw your gun away. I'm warning you!"

"Okay, okay, calm down. Here," I said, holding the gun up by my fingertips, "I'm throwing the gun away." I tossed the gun into the woods.

"Now," Belford said, "whoever else is with you, better show themselves. Oh, and Mancuso, that other weapon strapped to your back, toss it away."

I did as he asked. He was holding all the cards, and he was right, he had nothing to lose. "Mr. Pat, come out and throw your gun out."

Belford swiveled his head one-hundred eighty degrees, looking for Patrick.

Fearful that Patrick's move could scare Belford into pulling the trigger, I said, "Mr. Pat is on your right, and he's coming out slowly, unarmed."

Belford glance to his right, and down below the porch, as Mr. Pat showed himself. "Ah, the bartender. Did you bring your shaker?" He asked, mockingly.

I could see Patrick holding his anger in check.

"Drop both your weapons, Mr. Bartender. Now!" Belford shouted. "Easy lad, I'm dropping both of them, now," said Patrick, raising both his hands.

Belford ordered, "Both of you, move to the front, where I can see you."

Patrick and I converged in front of the cabin about ten feet from the steps of the porch. The scent hit me. The smell of the cologne I had picked up at the murder scenes was very pungent.

Belford asked, "Anyone else with you, Mancuso?"

"No one else. Just the two of us," I replied.

"Good, good. Now, boys, I know it's cold. But I want you to strip to your underwear," he said, laughing, "I mean, I hope you're wearing underwear. Oh, and, take off your shoes, too."

We did as he asked.

"Then, Mr. Bartender, take all the clothes and throw them in my SUV's back seat. But before you do that, where's the key to your car?"

"In my pocket," Patrick replied. "Which pocket, Mr. Bartender?"

"The right pocket of my pants," Mr. Pat, responded.

"Very well. Joey, very slowly, reach into his right pocket with your left hand, and retrieved the keys for me. Once you do that, slowly walk over to my car, and place them on the roof of my car just above the driver's seat. Can you do that, Mancuso?"

Again, we did as he ordered. I placed the keys as he requested on the roof of his car, and Patrick collected our clothes and threw them in the back seat.

"Well done, boys, well done. Now, I want you to move back to my right, there," he said, pointing to a spot with his left hand, "by the fire pit. Lay face down with your hands behind your heads."

As we walked towards the fire pit, Patrick said, in a low voice, "Joey, if he picks up any speed coming out of here, he's going to crash with my SUV, as he makes the turn."

"Shit, you're right," I said.

"No talking boys. Just lay face down on the ground, and Marcy and I will be on our way."

"Wait, Belford," I said.

"What now, Mancuso?"

"Our car is about a mile up the dirt road," I paused, thinking if I should tell him.

"So, what?" Belford asked.

I told him. "It's right before the first sharp left turn. It's blocking the road, and you'll crash into it."

Belford smiled, "Well... that's very thoughtful of you, Joey," he said, as he pushed Marcy forward, and began coming down the steps from the cabin porch.

"Tony, there's still time to end this," I said, from my position. "Mancuso, we're beyond that. I have a question for you, though," he paused, "how did you find us?"

As little as it meant now, I wanted to find out if he had help in this abduction, or in his whole serial killing routine. "Your partner told us."

"My partner?" he asked, surprised. "I don't have a partner", he laughed, as he said that.

I raised my head and looked at him, "Professor Peter Gruntel, your partner."

"That little shithead is not my partner. You thought I had a partner? He was just a convenient asshole whose identity I used. Oh he's quite the porn enthusiast. You should look at the websites he frequents."

"I'm sure you both have a lot in common then," I said, trying to look at Marcy.

Marcy glanced at me. Her eyes were filled with fear.

Belford ignored my comment. "Here's what's going to happen. Marcy and I are going to get in my car and drive away into the sunrise."

He took a few steps forward, "I could kill you both, but I want you alive to ponder on the beautiful life Marcy and I are going to have together. The children we'll have."

With that, he made Marcy, with her neck still strapped to the shotgun, get into the car from the driver's seat, and climb over into the passenger's seat. Turning the ignition on, he drove out onto the dirt road.

The ground felt cold, like a tundra. Both Patrick and I got up.

"Mr. Pat," I said hurriedly, "go in the cabin, see if there's a landline."

Patrick ran to the cabin's steps. He asked, without looking back, "What are you going to do?"

Before he finished asking, I was already running up the road, bare- foot and in my underwear. I picked up Patrick's Colt he had dropped by the steps. I could see the red taillights of Belford's SUV, as they got smaller and smaller. *'He's going to have to move our car out of the road, I might catch up,'* I thought. I ran as I've never run before. My adrenaline was pumping. I could feel every rock, pebble, and branch as my bare feet tread on them. My legs were becoming heavy, but I continued to run with all my might. It was dark, I couldn't see but three feet in front of me, but I ran. I ran for Marcy. I ran to save her life.

CHAPTER 27

A dense fog was passing through. I lost the view of the taillights, as Belford veered left to make the turn. I was two hundred yards behind. Then bright red lights. He stopped! I said to myself. I tripped over a branch. Without wasting a second, I rolled and picked myself up. I was limping. "Fuck!" I shouted. My legs were giving out. They began feeling rubbery. I had no strength left in them. Then, I heard a crash. Then a second one. Then another.

Finally arriving at the location where we had left Patrick's SUV, I couldn't see anything. I was momentarily confused. Did Marcy drive one vehicle out of here with Belford in the other? But how? Why? What the hell is going on? A cloud cover that had turned the already night sky into a perennial black hole gave way to a sliver of moonlight, and there it was. Now, I knew what the sound of the crashes was. Belford had pushed Pat's SUV off the road into a narrow creek that ran the length of the path on the right side.

Looking up the road, I no longer saw any red taillights. I saw nothing. And with that, my hopes of saving Marcy became a nightmare again. Sitting on a boulder by Pat's overturned SUV, I could feel my left ankle was swollen.

It felt like an hour had gone by as I sat there disconsolate, and without a plan. But it had only been a few minutes when Patrick arrived, covered in a blanket.

Throwing another blanket over me, he asked, "What happened, Joey?"

"There," I pointed to his SUV, which he had not seen, "the bastard pushed it into the creek. He's gone, Pat, and he's got Marcy," I said, grabbing the blanket as I shivered uncontrollably.

"There was no land-line in the cabin," Mr. Pat said, almost apologetically.

"Is your car equipped with GPS?"

"No, I'm afraid not. It's old for that," Pat replied.

"Agnes knows where we are. She, also, has a fix on Belford's SUV."

Patrick pointed out the now obvious. "Yeah, but that animal is too smart. I'm sure he'll disconnect the GPS on his rental."

I looked around hoping to see something. Another cabin, anything. But there was nothing for miles. "Help me up, let's see if I can walk to the road where we came in."

Patrick helped me up and found a sturdy branch I could use as a walking stick. He asked, "Where do you think he's headed?"

Walking slowly and carefully, watching where I stepped, I replied, "I don't know if he slipped, or, he meant to confuse us. But Belford said, 'we'll ride off into the sunrise'."

Patrick had a hand on my shoulder to help me, and said, "It is almost sunrise. So, he could have taken the saying 'riding off into the sunset', and just changed it, no?"

"Yes, or, he could drive east, towards the sunrise. Maybe, northeast or southeast. Fuck, I don't know," I said, frustrated at my inability to deduce.

Patrick asked, "What was it that Marcy tried to say? Something like, whistler bree before Belford stopped her."

I looked at Pat, opening my eyes wide, "That's it, she was trying to give us a clue. But what did she mean?" I repeated, "Whistler bree." I kept repeating it, but nothing came to mind.

After a few minutes, we reached the main road. Looking around we saw nothing, just the mailbox with the eagle on top. I said, "Do me a favor, Pat. See if there's any mail in the mailbox, would you?"

Patrick looked at me a little funny but did as I asked. He walked over to the lone mailbox on the road and pulled out the content.

"There's a letter address to Peter Gruntel. It's an advertisement from a cable television company."

"What's the address on it?"

"Fourteen Laurel Road, New Jersey."

"Alright, at least, we know where we are. Look around, is there another home, or cabin nearby?"

We both looked around. Nestled in the woods, I could see the silhouette of a what seemed to be a home to the south of us about one hundred yards away. "There Patrick, is that a home?" I said, pointing toward what I had seen, as I held on to my walking stick.

"Seems to be, but all these homes are closed for the winter." "Better yet. No one is going to let us in dressed in blankets. Maybe they have a phone and some clothes for us. Let's go over there."

"Stay here. I'll go."

"No, I need to get out of the cold. Help me up," I said, as Mr. Pat and I made our way to the home.

We knocked on the door to cover the basics. We could tell the home was vacant. Within a few minutes, Mr. Pat was inside the house, having climbed through a window on the side of the home. Opening the front door for me, I could feel the temperature inside the home was cold, but not the frigid cold of the outside.

"Patrick, see if you can find some clothes for us. I'll look for a phone."

I tried a couple of light switches. There was no electricity in the home. Patrick went in search of clothing. I looked around for a land- line bumping into a few pieces of furniture as I searched. There was a musty odor in the home that coincided with the house probably being vacant since the closing of the park in October.

Minutes later, Mr. Pat showed up in the living room sporting a New York Jets tee shirt, and a pair of jeans that were a little tight on him. "Here, Joey. These will probably fit you better," he said, handing me another pair of jeans, and a tee shirt with the Princeton Tiger's big P in the front. "I take it the phone is dead," he said, glancing at the phone on the table next to where I was sitting.

"Deader than dead, my man. Did you find any shoes?"

"Not my size, but here, try this pair on," he replied, as he gave me a pair of old worn loafers."

"Cuddly plush pink slippers?'' I asked, glancing at his feet. "Cute, right? Nothing else fits these size thirteen feet of mine."

I was sitting in a very old recliner in the home's darkness. Just a slight shimmer of light from the moonlight outside that projected through the window.

"How's the ankle?" Mr. Pat asked.

"Swollen, I wish we had some ice. Listen, I've been thinking about what Marcy shouted out."

"Whistler bree," he said.

"Exactly. What if she meant to say two different words? Such as whistler, and bree?

"Whistler" he paused, "bree." Again, he repeated, "whistler, bree."

I listened to his words and kept repeating them to myself. Suddenly, it hit me, and I said out loud, "Whistler, British Columbia!"

Pat said excitedly, "That's it, Whistler, British Columbia. You think that's where Belford plans to go?"

"I bet you there's a place there under Gruntel's name. Likely a rental. Unless the professor has another place there."

"Agnes could find out quickly, except, we have no way of calling anyone. You think Belford changed his mind after what Marcy could get out?"

"He might. Except, he doesn't have too many options. He's on the run. It's not like he can call a travel agent and change plans."

"You think he's going to drive? What? three, or four days across country with Marcy, an unwilling passenger?"

"I don't," I stopped, "Look, what are those lights outside?" I said as I got up.

"Stay put. Let me look," Patrick replied, as he got up, and

swiftly walked to open the front door. "Police, Joey,' he said, excitedly, "a bunch of them."

"Help me up," I exclaimed.

"I'm running out after them. They're headed to the cabin probably."

Patrick helped me up and ran to the street in his slippers, under-sized tee shirt, and tight jeans. As I got to the front door, I could see a stream of New Jersey State Police cars with their lights on, but no sirens.

He flagged down one of the last cars that were going by. Within seconds, he was surrounded by officers. He put his hands up. I wondered what the police thought at the sight of this immense redheaded man with his red beard, an expose belly button, tight jeans, and his cuddly plush pink slippers. I smiled. A renewed sense of hope rushed through me.

Still using my walking stick, I began making my way outside towards the road. Never mind that it was in the thirties, and I was freezing. I had to meet them. Patrick had his hands down and was pointing at me, then in the direction of the cabin.

Before I made it to the police cars, other official cars had gathered where Patrick was, and where I was headed. The red and blue flashing lights from all the vehicles was an eerie sight on such a night.

"Are you Joey Mancuso?" One of the officers asked.

"Yes, Officer, I am," I replied, as I approached the police car.

Noticing my hobbling around, Officer Cardenas, as his name tag read, told me "Have a seat in the car. We have an EMS vehicle coming behind us. I'm sure they can assist you."

"Thank you, but I'm alright, Officer Cardenas," I said.

Patrick chimed in, "No, he's not. He may have a broken ankle."

"Cardenas, we need to put an APB out for a white Jeep SUV. He

left here about," I stopped to look at my stopwatch counter, it read thirty-seven hours, "about one hour ago. So, he's not more than sixty miles away."

Cardenas asked, "Did you happen to get a license number?"

I could see Patrick frown, and I replied, "New Jersey plates, CBL-

EL, I missed the last digit. But if you call Enterprise Rent-A-Car in Paramus, New Jersey. They'll be able to give you the whole plate number." I glanced at Patrick and saw a wide grin on his face.

I went on to explain other details. Captain Johnson and Detective Lucy had already given the state police all other specifics of the abduction.

Cardenas asked, "Is this Belford armed?"

Mr. Pat replied, "Very much so, yes."

The EMT vehicle arrived, and Patrick grabbed my arm and walked me towards it. "Check his left ankle. It may be broken," he told the paramedic that had stepped out of the truck.

I sat on the back of the truck, as my ankle was being inspected by the paramedics. Cardenas came over to me, "I have to ask this. Was Ms. Martinez cooperating in any way with the suspect?"

I held back from saying something stupid. Cardenas read my face, and said, "Sorry, Mr. Mancuso. I have to ask."

I calmed down, and replied, "Call me Joey. I understand. Belford had a shotgun strapped to Ms. Martinez's neck when they left here. So, yes, she was cooperating, but under duress."

"I see, thank you," Cardenas said.

"Cardenas, we need to get some helicopters in the air. This guy is too smart to keep the same car. If we don't catch him quick, we'll lose him."

"Joey, I'm aware of your relationship with Special Agent Martinez. Trust me, as soon as there's daylight, we'll have them up there. Any clue where they were headed?"

I looked up at Cardenas from my sitting position. The paramedics had strapped a tight bandage around my ankle, "We think, Whistler, British Columbia. But that may have changed."

"That's over three thousand miles. You think that's where they're headed?" Cardenas asked.

"I don't know, man. That's what we think. I need to make a call. Can I borrow a phone?" I said, as I got up from the back of the EMT truck and thanked the lady who worked on my ankle.

"Here," Cardenas said, "use my cell."

Thanking him, I called Agnes. After a quick update, I asked her to check and see if Peter Gruntel owned or had rented any property in Whistler.

"Joey, everyone is here. Your brother, Father Dominic, wants to talk to you. Do you have a minute?"

"Put the *Padre* on."

"Thank God, she's alive. I've been praying non-stop," Dom said, "are you alright?"

"I'm fine brother. I think a sprained ankle, no problem."

"Agnes was following the GPS on Belford's car, but we lost the signal. Does he know how we located him?"

"He must have figured it out and disconnected the GPS. Or, switched cars. Where was the last location Agnes saw his SUV?"

"Hang on a second," Dom replied, as I heard him ask Agnes. "He was on Canistear Road."

"Headed north of Wawayanda State Park?" I asked, glancing at Officer Cardenas.

"No, Agnes says he was headed south on Canistear. Does that help?"

"Immensely. There were helicopters ready to go up, and we were going to look north of us. So, he's headed south, huh? Where is he going?" I asked.

"You are asking me?" Dom inquired.

"No, brother, I was talking to myself. Listen, have Agnes continue to search for Gruntel. Anything she can find on him, let me know."

"Is this guy involved?" asked Dominic.

"No, but I think Belford is or was using his identity. I'll call you guys as soon as I have a working phone."

"We've called both of you a bunch of times. What happened to your phones?"

"Long story, brother. I'll call you. Oh, and Father, keep talking to the Man."

"You got it, Joey. Wouldn't hurt if you connected with Him your- self, right?"

"I hear you. Bye now."

Hanging up with brother Dom, I called Marcy's parents. It was very early in the morning. The sun was just beginning to rise. But they needed to know I had seen Marcy, and while I didn't want to share, we were not able to rescue her, at least, I had to tell them she was alive.

Her stepfather answered the call. After a quick good morning, he said, "Joey, tell me you have Marcy."

"Alberto, I'm sorry. I don't, but I did see her and she's still feisty as ever. We'll find her again."

He repeated what I said to Rosa, Marcy's mom. I could hear in the background, *'Ay, Dios mío,'* which I knew translated to 'Oh, my God.'

Alberto said, "Joey, we've canceled our annual trip to our condo in

Miami Beach. We're staying here until Marcy is safe."

"Hopefully, you'll be able to head down there real soon, Alberto. I forgot you guys have a place there."

Ignoring my comment, he asked, "Was she alright?" Not allowing me to answer, he followed immediately with, "So, what's your next step?"

I made sure that they both knew she looked fine. Of course, I didn't mention the attachment she had on her neck. I went on to explain what we were doing and that we had the New Jersey State Police and soon the FBI on the trail of Belford.

CHAPTER 28

Three helicopters were landing as Mr. Patrick was approaching me. He was dressed in bright orange overalls, which evidently the EMT crew had given him. "Mr. Pat, you look like 'Otto, the orange,' I said.

A few of the officers and the EMT crew members got the picture and laughed.

"I'm afraid I don't know who Otto is?" Patrick said.

"Otto, the orange. Mascot for Syracuse University. You don't follow college football?"

"I'm afraid not. But here. I've got one of these overalls for you, too," he said, handing me a pair of the brightly colored orange uniforms.

I walked over to Officer Cardenas. Handing him his phone back, I asked, "Who's in charge of coordinating the search?"

Cardenas took his phone back, and replied, "Lieutenant Phillips, with our state police. He's over there with the pilots. They're looking at a map."

"Thanks, Cardenas," I said. I gingerly put on my overalls, keeping on my tee shirt as an extra layer, and walked over to Phillips.

"Lieutenant Phillips, I'm Joey Mancuso," I said, extending a handshake.

"Mancuso, how's your ankle? He asked, looking at our uniforms. "It's sprained, but I'll survive. I have additional information on the possible location of Belford and Special Agent Martinez."

"We were just looking at the map," he replied.

I nodded toward the three pilots. "My office followed his GPS until it no longer transmitted a signal. He either disconnected it or switched cars."

"You said before he might be headed north and west?" Phillips asked.

"Yes. However, when my office lost the signal, he was on Canistear Road headed south."

Phillips exchanged glances with the pilots. "How long ago was that?" he asked.

"That must have been one hour ago, now."

"So, he's been gone almost two hours. And, one hour ago he was on Canistear?" He asked, unfolding the map on top of the hood of a car.

"Say he's traveling at sixty miles per hour at the most, he can't be over one hundred-twenty miles from us," I said.

"Shit," Phillips said, "I already had the state police north of us ready to go. Now, I must contact the states south of us. Are you sure, Mancuso?"

"Yes, Lieutenant, my office tracked him going south."

"Well, let's get these birds in the air. We'll fly over Canistear," he said, looking at the pilots. "Understand, that we'll need to hand this over, once we reach the state line.'

"I understand. What about the FBI? Are they bringing helicopters?"

"Yes, they are. They can cross state lines. I'll inform them of this additional information. You think this Belford switched cars, or just disconnected the GPS?"

I thought for a second, "I don't think he's going to risk stealing a car. My feeling is he switched license plates at the most and killed the GPS on his jeep."

"Okay, we'll go with that." He reached for his car radio and communicated the route he wanted the cars to take, and informed everyone, "The helos are going to be flying over Canistear Road."

Patrick was standing next to me. "What are we going to do?"

I replied, "I don't know, let me see." Turning to Phillips, I asked, "Can we go in the helos?"

Phillips turned to size up Patrick. Then he looked at me. "How about you each go on a different helo? But remember, we stop at the state line, then we go back to base. From there, we can get you a ride back to Manhattan. Is that okay?"

"Thank you, that will do just fine," I replied.

I turned to Mr. Pat, "You okay on a helicopter?"

"Really, lad? You know how many helos I have been in during the Viet Nam War? Remember, that war was like going to the office. Every day, they fly us over to the action and they picked us up at the end of the day. Screwed up war, that was."

"Mancuso," shouted Phillips, over the roar of the helos, "you can both jump in the third helo," he said, pointing to it, "you'll both be fine."

I gave Phillips thumbs up, and both Patrick and I ran to the helo. "Put these on, guys," said the second officer, as she handed us a pair of headsets, and motioned for us to put them on. Otherwise, the noise from the helicopter would have made our ride unbearable.

I had forgotten the feeling when a helo takes off. I had only been in one many years ago with the NYPD. The sudden thrust up is quite the surprise, and then you're feeling like you're floating on air. For Patrick, I imagined, perhaps he had some flashbacks to Nam that might be going through his mind.

"How many miles before we reach the border of Pennsylvania?" I asked.

The pilot replied, "About one hundred miles."

"Shit, then he may already be gone beyond your jurisdiction," I said, glancing at Patrick.

The second officer said, "He may have stopped for gas. Or, as you said, to get another license plate. We'll give it our best. How far south is he going, any clues?"

"No, mam, I have no clue," I replied.

The pilot said, "From Canistear Road, he'll get on the Jersey Turnpike. At that point, he can get on I-95, all the way down to Florida, if he wants."

Florida? I turned to Mr. Pat, and then a torrent of ideas began popping into my mind. 'Otto, Syracuse's Orange man, football, Orange Bowl in Miami, Marcy parent's condo in

Miami Beach.' "How far to Miami? Do you know?" I asked.

The pilot replied, "I drove it last year during the summer. We stopped, because of the kids. It's a twenty-hour drive."

"That's it," I exclaimed, "he's going to Miami Beach."

Patrick queried, "Why Miami Beach?"

Glancing at Mr. Pat, I replied, "Because Marcy's parents have a place there and it's empty. Perfect Plan B if he thinks we know about Whistler, British Columbia. That's why he went south."

Patrick retorted, "That's quite a stretch, don't you think?"

I shook my head, "Belford's been hanging with Marcy and her parents, and I'm sure they've been talking about their annual trip to Miami Beach. He assumes they aren't going, if she's missing. So, empty condo. No false identity required. It's ideal."

Patrick asked, "I guess it makes sense. You think he's using Gruntel's identity for gas, or, anything else?"

"Doubt it, now that he knows we're on to Gruntel. He'll use cash, or, another identity, if he has one," I replied.

"So, what do you want to do?" Mr. Pat asked.

I looked at my watch. Forty-one hours since Marcy's abduction. I glanced outside towards the east without responding to Pat's question. The sun was blinding me as we flew south. Turning to look back at Patrick, I replied, "I think we should fly to Miami to wait for this asshole."

"You're taking a big chance, Joey. What if they catch this guy before he reaches Miami?"

I replied, "Mr. Pat, the original plan was for you and me to catch him before the posse got involved. Now, we have the FBI, and state police involved in the chase. Not much we can do. We'll stick with these guys until they can go no further."

Patrick opened his massive arms and said, "Okay. Miami Beach, here we come."

CHAPTER 29

I wasted almost two hours flying over New Jersey until we could go no further. The Pennsylvania State Police and the FBI continued the search for Belford in the air, and on the ground. An all- points bulletin had been issued. But no one knew for sure if Belford was still driving south. Let alone if he was occupying his white Jeep SUV.

The New Jersey State Police helicopter that had taken us on this aerial search had asked and received permission to drop us off at the Manhattan Helicopter site on the East River just a few blocks from our pub. We landed, thanked the pilot, and the second officer. Mr. Pat and I, still dressed in our bright orange EMT uniforms, strolled the few blocks to Captain O'Brian's Pub and Cigar Bar.

Forty-five hours had gone by since Marcy's abduction. It was noon. Every time I looked at my stopwatch, my heart sank further in despair. 'Was Marcy drugged? Was she tied and bound? What could she possibly be thinking?' Those were the thoughts that occupied my every minute. I walked next to Patrick through New York's Financial District streets packed with people. Yellow cabs drove by every second. However, I did not see anything. Everything seemed out of focus for me at this point. It was like my first parachute jump before the chute opened. Falling at a million miles per hour with a knot in my stomach. The world was out of focus.

Patrick's thunderous voice and Irish brogue startled me, "We're here."

"What?" I replied, coming out of my nightmarish thoughts. "We are here. I'll knock on the door."

"Someone better be here. I used the second officer's phone to call Agnes an hour ago." The pub's door opened. Father Dom, Agnes, and Angela were standing by the entrance.

They all looked at our orange uniforms, but no one said a word. Quietly, we walked back into the pub, and across into our office. "Agnes, did you make reservations for Patrick and me?"

Agnes replied, "I did."

Angela added, "I'm coming with you guys."

I glanced at Angela with an inquisitive look.

Not giving me a chance to say anything, she said, "Joey, Miami is my town. I worked vice all over the city. You need my contacts there and my knowledge of the area."

I thought for a second, and asked, "Great, what time do we take off?"

"You're all on the three pm out of Kennedy to Miami International," Agnes replied.

I looked at my watch. My stomach turned. It was still on the stopwatch counter. I knew what time it was, but I asked again. "What time is it?"

Dom replied, "It's noon, Joey. I'll drive you to your place. You need a shower, and some packing to do. I suggest that you, Mr. Pat, have Angela drive you to your place, and do the same," he added, looking at Patrick.

"Very well," I said, "we'll meet at Kennedy at two o'clock. Agnes, did you make any reservations for us?"

"Done," Agnes replied, "I have all three of you staying at a little boutique hotel in Miami Beach near Marcy parent's condo. By the way, how's that ankle?"

"Much better, I had an ice pack on it during the wasted helicopter chase. It bothers me, that's all. I'll be fine."

Wasting no more time. Patrick and Angela left in her car for his place. Dom and I did the same.

"Nice Caddy brother, who's car is this?" I asked Dom, as we both sat in a brand-new Cadillac Deville.

"Is the Pastors' at Saint Helens. He let me borrow it."

"He's got bucks."

"It was a donation to our church from a local Cadillac dealer who's a member of our parish."

"Sweet," I replied, patting the leather seats.

"Joey, I think you're taking a big chance betting that Belford is on his way to Miami.?"

"Perhaps Dom, but I've given this a lot of thought. Marcy tried to tell us about Whistler, British Columbia. I think Belford picked up on that. Although, she was only able to partially shout out the name. Belford is too smart."

"So, because of that, you think he switched from there to Miami Beach?" He asked, as we were now on the Brooklyn Bridge driving to my place.

"If Belford will travel for three days to reach British Columbia with Marcy as a prisoner, his travel to Miami, which is about twenty hours, has to be much easier. Don't you think?"

"You're sure he knew about the condo?"

"I'm sure he knew. He's been hanging at Marcy's place almost twenty-four seven. The Rodriguez's go down there at the beginning of January until March. Marcy usually visits for a week, or two during that time. He knew. And, it's there empty and convenient to hide in."

"Then what? What's he going to do from there?" He asked, turning to look at me.

"That's four steps ahead, bro. I'm trying to be three steps ahead. If I can surprise Belford in Miami, his next move is not on his terms. It's on my terms."

Looking straight ahead, Dom said, "This fucking asshole, forgive my Spanish has been three steps ahead of us all the way. No more. What's your plan?"

"We'll be in Miami Beach before sundown. With Angela's help, we'll set up a surveillance of the condo. I hope to enlist one or two of her vice buddies."

"You're going to try and do this under the radar? No official police help?"

"If I can. I'm leery of a posse coming after this guy. He's well-armed. No telling what he'll do if he's cornered. He's got nothing to lose. You gotta agree?"

"I agree. He's demented. If he's killed all the ladies, we think he did plus his parents. We know he's unstable."

"Exactly. I don't want him committing suicide by cop with Marcy alongside him."

'Shit, you're right," Dom said, as we exited the bridge.

"If I'm right, and I need your prayers on that, Patrick, Angela, a couple of other guys, and I can handle the situation. The surprise is on our side."

"What made you think of Miami? I mean, that was quite a stretch."

"Funny you should ask that. It was a few minutes after I spoke to you. Remember, I said to you, *'keep talking to the Man'*? Well, suddenly, I looked at Mr. Pat, all six feet four inches of him with his red beard and hair wearing the bright orange overalls, and it happened."

"What happened? Miami just flashed in your mind?"

"It was more like a flurry of thoughts," I said, snapping my fingers as I recited the thoughts. "It went from looking at Patrick sitting in the helo to Otto, Syracuse's Orange man, football to the Orange Bowl in Miami to Marcy parent's condo in Miami Beach. Boom, I had it."

Father Dominic smiled, as if telling me the Man did put those thoughts in my head. "I think someone sent you a message."

We reached my humble abode. I was famished. I forgot when the last time was; I ate something. While I showered, shaved and packed, Dom made me a sandwich, which I inhaled in a few seconds. I packed my passport as a form of ID and other credit cards since my wallet was sitting, hopefully, in the back of Belford's Jeep.

On our way to Kennedy Airport, I called Angela to make sure she recruited only two of her past vice cops' associates. She was ahead of me and informed me that a Jote and a Tico were ready, willing and able to help.

Agnes had provided me the exact address of Marcy's parents' condo at Collins Avenue and 26th Street on Miami Beach, facing the Atlantic Ocean.

We were booked a few blocks south of the condo at the Raleigh Hotel that was an oceanfront, also. Except, I was not expecting to spend any time on the beach.

CHAPTER 30

Our flight arrived at Miami Airport on schedule at six- thirty in the evening. Miami welcomes you uniquely the moment you step out of the plane. It slaps you with a warm embrace of heat coupled with high humidity. Quite the change from New York's thirty plus degrees we left behind. One recognizable friendly scent was that of the cafecitos which are available everywhere in the airport. Angela led the way in search of her cohorts that were waiting for us outside the gate. She had spent six years with Miami police vice division before her husband's recent job transfer to New York City that led her to join the NYPD.

Angela smiled as we approached two characters that looked to have come out from the belly of the underworld. Or from the movie set for the next *'Pirates of the Caribbean'*. "Joey, Patrick, say hello to Jote and Tico," she said, embracing scary hombre numero uno.

Jote was a skinny little guy sporting gold earring in both ears and a Pancho Villa, a full mustache that hid his upper lip and dropped an inch on both sides. To add to the décor, he had sleeve tattoos on both arms. A closer look revealed a neck tattoo which was almost unrecognizable because of the very thick solid link gold chain that covered it. He wore gold President's Rolex that's known within the drug world as the confirmation of having done your first job or having been 'crowned.' Of course, there was a full gold wristband on his other arm. Tight jeans and a Grateful Dead colorful tee shirt completed the ensemble.

"Hi," I said to *numero uno* and asked, "how do you pronounce your name again?"

"Hah, always the same man. *Pero* think of Santa's laugh—ho, ho, ho, then add Te, like in Tennessee. Get it? Ho-te."

"Oh, like in a hotel without the L," I said.

"*Coño*, that's better, bro. I'll have to remember that one," said Jote.

I smiled, "I hear you guys speak and I think I'm back in Brooklyn or Jersey."

Jote said, "*Sí, pero*, one moment, man. In New York, you have a lot of New York-Ricans. Nothing against the brothers, but Cubans speak Spanglish. That is the art in one sentence to combine both English and Spanish words. We don't even think about it. It just happens."

"What do others do?" I asked, glancing at Patrick.

"*Bueno*, I don't want to be critical. *Pero*, others mesh an English word with a Spanish word together. We don't do that shit. *¿Entiendes?* See what I did there?"

"*Sí*, whatever you say, brother," I replied. We all laughed.

"You must be Tico," I said, turning to his partner. Other than one gold tooth, a scar under his right eye, a shaved head, and a Fu Manchu mustache, he looked reasonable compared to 'Ho-te.' I thought Johnny Dep was around the corner waiting for us.

Angela followed with introductions to Patrick who immediately became 'big red dude,' as Jote nicknamed him.

Walking out of the air-conditioned airport into a much warmer and humid atmosphere, Jote asked me, "Angela gave us the background story, man. We're sorry your lady is in such a predicament. But we'll nail this *hijo de puta*. Don't worry about that. What's your plan?"

Looking first at Jote, then at Tico, I replied, "I don't want the whole Miami PD to be involved in this. Did she make that clear?"

Jote smiled, glanced at Tico. Tico replied, "*Sí*, man, we're cool with that. Just the five of us. No one else. But are you sure this dude is coming to Miami?"

"I am now after speaking to my New York office. Normally, the parents of my fiancé call the condominium office ahead of time to have the hurricane shutters opened and rolled sideways on their windows. This way when they get here it's all done."

Jote asked, "Yeah, so what happened?"

"I had my office call the condo's office. We were playing a hunch, you see. The condo manager says Marcy called to have the shutters closed. She claimed the Rodriguez's weren't coming soon."

Tico inquired, "But that's true, no?"

I looked around the van, "The call from Marcy came in yesterday. That tells me Belford wants privacy. A place to hide."

Big red dude—Patrick said, "Finally, we are one step ahead of this guy."

I turned to face Patrick in the backseat, "I hope so, Mr. Pat. I hope so."

Jote asked, "*Bueno* Mancuso, what's the plan, *mano?*"

I shared my plan with the newly formed and mucho eclectic team.

My thoughts were on Marcy as I sat in the passenger seat. The ride in Tico's van was quiet. We made our way across Biscayne Bay headed to Miami Beach riding on what Jote told us was the Julia Tuttle Cause- way. Although, the signs read I-195. I had never been to Miami Beach before. A year ago, Marcy had invited me to visit her and her parents. But I had been busy with something or other. Riding east, with the sun setting on the west, made the colors of Biscayne Bay captivating. Biscayne Bay was enormously wide. As we reached the top of the bridge, blue, orange, and silver meshed together in the bay. It was as if an artist was delivering his craft in front of us. In the horizon, the buildings glimmered with the reflection of the sun striking their glass windows. Above them, the sky exploded with an abundance of ever-changing colors as we moved further east unto Miami Beach itself.

Reaching the end of the Causeway, Tico went straight on the street called Arthur Godfrey Way, still headed east. I asked, "How far are we from the condo?"

Tico turned to look at me and replied, "About three miles. This road will take us to Indian Creek Drive. We make a right and merge into Collins Avenue, and we're there."

From the back of the van, Jote said, "Joey, I've already scouted the location. The condo is facing the ocean on Collins Avenue. Indian Creek Canal parallels Collins at that location. We can park the van and surveil the entrance to the building with no obstructions."

Tico looked at me and asked, "What's your ETA for them?"

I thought for a minute, "If he drove straight here, stopping only for gas and bathroom, maybe the earliest about ten in the evening. So, maybe between ten and midnight."

Hearing that, Jote said, "You guys hungry? We have a couple of hours."

"Is there something close?" I asked. We now parked our van on Collins Avenue right across the entrance to the condominium building.

Tico pointed, "How close you want it? It's right there," he said, as we all glanced at a corner restaurant featuring Argentinian specialties. I needed sleep more than food, but both had been in short supply, lately. Sleeping was not an option right now. The couple of hours I got on the plane will have to do for a while. Hopefully, my calculations were correct, and Belford would show up tonight.

We ate and got to know Jote and Tico a lot better. Colorful characters who had been in vice way too long. Not anywhere like Detectives Crockett and Tubbs from the NBC hit series 'Miami Vice' of the late 80's. Jote and Tico were not going to set a trendy look. These guys were the real vice cops. Like I said before, I think they are into their characters way too deep.

As planned, we set up surveillance across the entrance at about ten. Jote and Angela in the van. Tico sat on the sidewalk by the door to the underground parking lot. Anyone paying attention to him would no doubt think he was a homeless person resting.

Mr. Pat and I had taken other positions from which to surveil. We did not want to be where Belford could see us. We sat and waited.

The phone Jote had given me was sitting on my chest as it rang and vibrated, waking me abruptly from a sound sleep. It was two in the morning. The ID caller read 305 something. I knew that to be Miami's area code. "This is Joey," I answered.

"Joey, this is Jote. A white Jeep SUV just went into the underground parking lot. Tico saw a man and a woman inside the van. Couldn't confirm it's them, but license plates are Pennsylvania's."

I replied, "Okay, Jote. That's got to be them. I knew he would change plates. We got this."

"What do you want us to do?" Jote asked.

"I'll let you know," I replied.

"Mancuso, you sure you don't want to call for backup? Or, the FBI man? I mean, your lady is FBI, right?"

"We have a plan. Let's stick to it. *¿Entiendes, amigo?*"

Jote replied, "Have it your way, bro."

Patrick and I sat inside the unit belonging to Marcy and her parents. As expected, the window's hurricane shutters were closed. Something the Rodriguez's would do every time they left the unit to go back to Jersey. There was not a speck of light inside the unit. I took a position to the left of the door, just inside the small kitchen. Patrick was about four feet ahead of me on the right side in a hallway leading to the bedrooms. The plan was to let both Marcy and Belford walk in. My assumption was Marcy would walk in first, followed by Belford. I would not expect Belford would hold a gun on her at this point. I was to let Marcy walk by me. Then, grab Belford while Patrick pulls Marcy into the hallway out of the way. Finally, I was going to be reunited with her and end her nightmare.

The front door opened. It was pitch black inside the unit. The hallway light made we could see it so that only a silhouette of the two figures walking in. I waited. A female figure walked by me, Marcy. Then, a male was upon me. He felt for the light switch to his left on the wall. Before he turned it on, I said, "Now!"

Immediately, Patrick pulled the female into the hallway as I pounded the male. I drive my shoulder, upper arm, hip, and elbow into the man. The definition of a check in hockey. As I did, Belford gasped from the pain and the surprise as his head hit the wall. Marcy screamed in fear from the hallway. The man slid, maybe unconscious, down the wall to the floor, as I hit the light switch.

"What are you doing?" the female asked screaming?

"Joey," Patrick said from the hallway location, "this is not Marcy."

"And this asshole is not Belford," I said, looking at a male figure who was knocked out in front of me on the floor. He looked like a Justin Bieber look-alike. Big teeth, skinny little punk, blonde bleached hair with streaks.

Patrick brought the female into the open area by the kitchen where the light was now on. "Who are you?" I asked.

She looked at the man on the floor, "Oh, my God, what have you done to him?" She exclaimed, running over to the man and kneeling beside him. "Did you kill him?" She asked.

"The lad will be fine in a few minutes," replied Mr. Pat, "Missy, answer the question. Who are you?"

She looked up as the man began shaking his head, trying to knock out the cobwebs. "I'm Joan, this is my boyfriend, Jack."

"Why are you here?" I asked, dumbfounded.

Jack, sitting on the floor with his back to the wall, looked towards me, closed his eyes and responded, "This man gave us five hundred dollars, and told us to drive here and enter the condo. He said we could stay here tonight. He wanted me to call him after we came in."

"Why would you do that?"

"Sir," he said, still recovering and on the floor, "Joan, and I are broke. Two guys stole all our money last night while we walked on the boardwalk. The five hundred was going to get us home tomorrow. We don't know—"

A phone rang, I looked at Patrick; he shrugged. We both looked around. Jack reached into a pocket of his Bermuda shorts and answered, "Yeah? Yes." Three seconds later he handed me the phone, "It's for you."

"This is Mancuso."

"Hell-oo, Man-cue-so."

CHAPTER 31

Belford, it's time to end this," I said.

"Why, my boy? You tired of chasing me? Always one step behind," he said, with deep sarcastic laughter.

F-'en asshole was, in fact, one step ahead all the time. I wanted to ask him how he knew we were here, but I didn't want to give him the satisfaction.

"Mancuso, Mancuso, you're probably wondering how I knew you were waiting for me, right?" He asked, and paused, expecting an answer from me. When he heard no reply, he added, "You see Mancuso, I've never underestimated you. I give you the credit you deserve as a thinker and observer. You, however, well, you've never seen my good side. You're unwilling to give me credit I deserve. That's why you are one step behind all the time."

"So, what do you want Belford?"

"What do I want? What do I want?" He repeated. "It seems the honeymoon and happy life ever after with Marcy are not in the cards. Although, we still have this moment together, she and I."

"I will kill you," I shouted into the phone. Immediately, Patrick moved Jack and Joan into a bedroom and closed the doors.

"Here's what we're going to do, Mancuso," Belford began, "I'm going to get out of town without any interruption on your part. I'm leaving the country, my boy."

"You're not going anywhere with Marcy," I said.

"You need to pay attention, Mancuso. I said, my future with Marcy is at an end. Perhaps in our next lives, Marcela and I we'll reunite in a lustful romantic relationship. So, as soon as I am safe, I will tell you where to find her."

I had no cards to play, "Belford, do what you need to do. No one is going to stop you. Just tell me where I can find Marcy. However, if something happens to her, there's no place on earth safe for you. Not a fucking solitary place. Understand?"

"I'm terrified. So much so that, let me see, oh, good, I thought I had crapped in my pants. But I didn't. Listen to me, in a little while I'm going to leave. Marcy will be fine for a few hours. After that, no telling what might happen to her. So, what I'm saying is if I'm somehow delayed or detained, well… that would not be good for her. Do you understand?"

Mr. Pat came out of the bedroom where he had been with Joan and Jack. He was motioning to his mouth and pointing at me. I interpreted that to mean he wanted to talk to me. I raised my index finger, asking him to wait a minute, realizing I had not responded to Belford.

"I need to talk to Marcy," I said.

He didn't reply for a moment. Then, I heard a muted sound on the other end. Before I could ask again, Marcy said, "Joey, I'm fine."

"Marcy?" I asked.

"She just told you she's fine. I will call you as soon as I'm safe, and tell you where she is," Belford said. He disconnected the call.

I looked at Patrick who was standing in front of me, "Fuck!" I expressed loudly.

Mr. Pat grabbed both my shoulders with his massive hands, "Listen, this fellow, Jack, may know where Belford and Marcy are."

"How so?" I said, raising my head and opening my eyes widely. Patrick went on, "They said they walked into a beer bar a few blocks away. Inside a boutique hotel lobby, and Belford was sitting there alone."

"How do they know it was Belford?" I asked without thinking. "Belford talked to them for a few minutes, bought them a beer.

They told him their sad story about being robbed, etcetera. That's when he offered them the cash, gave them the burner phone, and told them to drive here."

"So, where was this?"

Patrick went into the room to get Joan and Jack. As he did that, I called Jote on the phone he had provided me. "Jote, get ready. Belford is nearby. Maybe just a few blocks from here."

Jote asked, "What happened up there? We were just coming up."

"We're coming down. Get the van," I replied, disconnecting the call.

Jack came out of the room first with Patrick gently prodding him forward. Joan followed.

"So, where did you meet this man?" Quickly, I asked.

Jack pointed to the street, as if to show somewhere. "The Arlene on 29th and Indian Creek Drive."

"Was he alone?" I inquired. "Yes, he was," Jack said.

"Do you think he was staying there?" Jack glanced at Joan but didn't answer.

I shouted, "Was he?"

"He said he was not. That he had stopped in for a beer. But yes, he is or was. We have his room key," Jack replied, as he moved back and away from me.

"Let me have the fucking key," I said, turning to Joan putting my hand out.

Joan reached into her purse and pulled out a bright aqua colored plastic diamond key holder. The Arlene was written on one side, and 717, the room number, on the other side.

Mr. Pat's face took on an inquisitive look as he glanced at me. "These two aren't without funds or stranded in Miami, Mr. Pat. They're con artists preying on tourist and locals. They go from place to place pulling the same shit. I'm sure our gal here, Joan," I said, looking at her, "was ready to bait our guy at the bar, go up to his room and steal everything he had."

Jack said, "We—"

"Shut the fuck up. We are with Miami Vice. You're lucky we have bigger fish to fry. We're going downstairs now, and I want you to get lost. Understand? Lost. Both of you. If I see you in Miami, or New York City, I am throwing both your asses in jail."

We entered the elevator with both Jack and Joan looking down at the floor. As the door opened on the lobby area, Jack asked, "We can't go to New York City?"

"That's right, Justin. Stay the hell away from New York. Now, get the fuck out of here," I said, opening the building's massive double glass front door leading to Collins Avenue, and seeing Tico's van, parked in front of the apartment building.

I climbed into the passenger seat, as 'big red dude,' Mr. Pat, made his way to the side door of the van.

"Who were those two?" Tico asked,

"Not important. We need to go to The Arlene on Indian Creek and 29th," I said.

Jote said from the back, "Bro, that's three blocks from here." I asked, "Is that the street that's a one-way south?"

Tico replied, "Yeah, we were on it earlier today. Right there," he said, pointing with his left hand.

"Hang on a second. We have to go around the block to come back south, right?"

"Exactly," Tico replied.

"We may miss Belford if we go around. He was leaving now. Can you light it up?" I asked, referring to police blue and red lights.

Tico glanced at me and smiled, "We're vice, bro. We have no lights. But I can drive against traffic, if that's what you want me to do. It's just three blocks."

"Yeah, go slow. Let's inspect every car coming our way. Patrick, Angela, keep an eye out for Belford," I said, as Tico began a slow drive north into oncoming traffic.

Tico drove slowly, close to the curb on our right side. We only encountered three cars. After all, it was late and most everyone was sleeping. Those that were not were clubbing.

No one looked like Belford. A few minutes later, we were in front of The Arlene.

"Tico, drive around the side street. Does this hotel have under-ground parking?" I asked.

"No, bro," replied Tico. "This hotel has no parking. Everyone has to find a spot on the street."

"Good," I said, "so, no surprises. "Mr. Pat and I are going up to the room. Angela and you guys stay down here. Angela, you know what Belford looks like, right?"

Angela replied, "No, but you've described him. But Joey, you guys are not armed. You can't go up there like that."

"Here," Jote said, reaching down to his ankle. He pulled out a revolver from an ankle holster. "Tico, give yours to the 'big red dude.'"

"Nice one, Jote," I said, admiring the gun momentarily, "a K6S,.357 Magnum, Kimber. Beautiful small revolver. Thanks. Stay alert. We're on our way up."

"How do you know where to go?" Jote asked.

"We know, even have a key. Tell you later, not important now," I replied, entering the quaint lobby of the boutique hotel.

Mr. Pat asked, "Elevator, or stairs?"

I thought for a second. There was a night clerk behind a small counter by the front entrance. He was sitting working on a computer. He was looking at us with a concerned look on his face. Walking over to him, I asked, "Is there another elevator?"

The clerk remained seated, and asked nervously, "Who are you?"

"Look, we are with the vice squad. Is there another elevator?"

The clerk stood up. He was not much older than twenty, clean cut, wearing a white shirt and black tie. Probably working at nights while he went to school. "Yes, there's the cargo elevator all the way back in the hallway. What's going on?"

"How about stairs?"

"Just this one," he said, pointing to the stairs in the lobby.

"I want you to go outside. We have three associates there. See the lady. She's a cop, too. Stay out there for now."

"I can't leave the front desk, there's—"

Mr. Pat addressed the young man, "Son, do as you're told. This is for your safety."

"Before you go, tell me how many rooms are occupied on the seventh floor?" I asked.

"That's our top floor and most expensive rooms. They have a view—"

I interrupted, "How many rooms are occupied?"

"Just two rooms. 701 and 717," he replied.

"Okay, get out," I said, "Tell one of the pirates outside to come in here."

"What?' The kid asked.

"You'll see. Tell one to come in here. Pronto kid." Jote walked in the lobby, "What-sup?"

"Jote, we are going up. We are going to put both elevators out of commission. The only ingress and egress are going to be the stairs. If by chance Belford gets by us, he's yours when he reaches the lobby."

"I'll be here," Jote replied, holding another Kimber pistol. This one, a Micro Sapphire 380 automatic.

I turned to face Patrick, "Mr. Pat, I'm going back to the cargo elevator and hitting the 'Off' button. Do the same on this elevator. Then, we're going up the stairs."

"Couldn't we at least take one elevator to the sixth floor, then turned it off?"

I looked at Patrick, "Wait for me here a second. Let me deal with the other elevator. Then, I'll walk up the stairs. You take the elevator to the fifth floor and wait for me by the stairs. Is that better?"

"Much better, thank you," Patrick said, as he nodded and smiled.

I ran to the back and hit the 'Off' button on the cargo elevator. Belford was not coming down on that one. Then, running back to the lobby again, I sent Patrick to the fifth floor. I began walking up the stairs. If Belford were still here, the only way down would be the stairs.

CHAPTER 32

Holding the revolver with both hands in front of me, I walked up the stairs slowly. The only person I wanted to see on my way up was the 'big red dude.' Although in all honesty, if Belford were still here, an encounter in the hallway or stairs would be preferable than in the room with Marcy in it.

As I was reaching the landing of the fifth floor, I heard a door. I softly asked, "Red?"

"I'm here, Joey," Mr. Pat replied, almost in a whisper. "Okay, let's do this."

I led the way as we both walked up the final two floors. Room 717 was to the left of the stairs. Almost all the way to the back of the hallway near the cargo elevator. As I reached the door to the seventh floor, I stopped before opening it and said to Patrick, "If we both walk down the hallway and Belford steps out of the room, either we kill him quick, or we're sitting ducks if he still has his shotgun."

Patrick waved the Kimber revolver and said, "Our problem is, our guns will not be accurate at any distance. This two-inch barrel is great nearby. But if we're more than a few feet away, forget it."

I opened the door a smidgen, putting my right eye to the small opening. I started out, so I could see if Belford stepped out. I said, "Let me make a call," I said softly to Mr. Pat. I dialed Jote, "Can you have this kid, the night clerk, tell you how to turn off the hallway lights on the seventh floor?"

"Hang on. I'll ask him," replied Jote.

A minute later, Jote came back on the phone, "Joey, the kid says, the only way is to pull the fuse on the entire seventh floor. Both hallways and rooms are on the same circuit. Do you want to do that?"

"Shit," I said, "No, if Belford realizes the lights went out, he'll know something is going on."

"What do you want to do?" Jote asked.

"I don't want him in the room with Marcy as a hostage and all the weapons he has. I was hoping he was leaving like he told me on the phone."

"Man, maybe he has left already, and Marcy is there by herself," Jote said.

"Look, the kid said only two rooms were occupied on this floor. Find out from him if Room 717 connects to a room on either side of it. If so, we can enter it and listen."

"Okay, hang on," Jote replied.

"Joey, the kid says no one has come down in the last hour or two. So, if this is the place, Belford and Marcy are up there. Second, yes. Room 715 connects to 717. I'll bring the key up to you."

I kept a tiny slice of the door opened so that I could see if Belford stepped out. In the meantime, Angela brought the key to Room 715. Fortunately, she had a long firearm. A Remington 7615 Pump Action Patrol Rifle, which she had taken from Jote and Tico's stash in the van.

Angela asked, "Are we going into Room 715?"

I was still looking down the hallway. Without taking my eyes away from the door, I replied, "Yes, let's walk over. Angela be ready to shoot if Belford walks out of the room. Pat and I will lead, but we'll drop if Belford appears," I said, turning to Mr. Pat. He nodded in understanding.

We began our stealthy walk over, finally reaching the front door of Room 715. We entered the room, immediately locating the connecting door to 717. I put my ear to the door. Nothing. I motioned to both Angela and Mr. Pat by touching my right ear and then waving with my index finger, showing nothing.

Angela pulled out a thin cable from a small backpack she was wear- ing. I saw her attach the wire to her phone and open an application. Without saying a word, she pointed the cable at Mr. Pat, and showed me the image on her phone. The 'big red dude' was revealed on her phone's screen. I smiled as she handed me the phone and the attached cable.

Moving back to the connecting door, I slid the cable below a minuscule gap between the door and the tiled floor. I had Angela hold the phone so that I could maneuver the tiny camera in the cable's front.

A futuristic chrome lamp that was fastened to the headboard illuminated room 717. Very similar to the place we were in. It had a queen-size bed, a small desk, and a large modern recliner. In front of the bed, a flat screen television was attached to the wall. And there they were. Marcy laid sideways on the bed facing the wall opposite the recliner. Special Agent Belford's left leg and knee were the only visible part of his body. The recliner was very close to the connecting door. Thus, our tiny camera could only capture his partial image. However, right above his knee, we could see the butt of a rifle or shotgun that rested on his legs.

I slid the cable out. We all looked at each other, and, almost in unison, we sighed. Marcy was alive and here. So was Belford. No one said a word. Both Angela and Patrick were waiting for me to communicate my plan. I felt enthused knowing Marcy was safe and next to me, but as far as a plan, I had none. The fluidity of the moment called for spontaneity, albeit with maximum caution. Preferably, we could capture Belford alive so that he could answer for all his murders, and perhaps a few more we didn't know about. But frankly, all I wanted was Marcy alive. As far as Belford, I didn't give a shit whether he lived or died. It was going to be his call.

Moving very cautiously, I motioned to Angela and Patrick to join me in the bathroom. I closed the door, giving us some privacy. Whispering, I said, "We need to get Belford out of the room."

Patrick in a whisper asked, "Wasn't he supposed to be leaving? Isn't that what he told you?"

"Yeah," I replied, "I think that was bullshit. That's what he wanted us to believe. I don't think he has the plan to escape yet. He can't just go to the airport and fly out of here. He knows everyone is looking for him. He must think we have reported his whereabouts to the FBI and others."

Angela asked, "So, what's the plan?"

I looked at my watch. It was four in the morning. I didn't remember that last time I slept in a bed. Was it a day, two days, or more? Thank God for adrenaline. Otherwise, I would pass out somewhere. "The plan, yes. Call Jote. Ask him to ask the kid if Belford had ordered breakfast for anytime in the morning."

Angela looked surprised and retorted, "You think Belford is ordering room service ahead of time?"

"I don't know. But there was a sign on the desk at the entrance that read 'Complimentary continental breakfast is served in your room.' He's going to take advantage of that. Find out."

Angela called Jote while we were all still in the bathroom. It was a little crowded in here for the three of us. Mr. Patrick sat on a tiled bench inside a large opened shower. Angela sat on the seat cover of the toilet. I passed on the bidet so; I stood. After a few moments, she said, "You were right. Bagels, croissants, orange juice, and coffee are scheduled for delivery at six in the morning for Room 717."

I smiled, glanced at both and said, "That's when we take him down."

CHAPTER 33

Patrick and I shared the queen-size bed. We took a one-hour cat nap, fully dressed, of course, and on top of the sheets. Angela sat in the recliner. Angela's phone vibrated at five forty-five in the morning, and she woke us up.

"Get ready," she whispered, "fifteen minutes till six."

I jumped out of bed and swiftly walked into the bathroom. After taking care of number one, I splashed cold water on my face. Seconds later, I felt these enormous hands grab my shoulders and prodded me out of the bathroom. I guess Patrick felt the urge, too.

We had our plan, and we waited for breakfast to be served in Room 717.

Precisely at six in the morning, we heard the squeak of the wooden floors, and the wheels of a cart pass by our room. Miami Vice Squad Sergeant Jote, wearing a chef's long sleeve white coat to cover his tats, should knock on Room 717.

Angela had inserted the cable with the camera under the door. We were watching as the door knock would come from Jote. Marcy was awake. When the knock came, she sat on the edge of the bed. We heard Belford say, "do nothing stupid." We saw Belford get up, holding a shotgun with his left hand. He had a Glock 26, or what is called, a Baby Glock, on the small of his back. He placed the shotgun on the wall behind the front door and opened the door.

This was the cue for Patrick and me to open the connecting door. Patrick was to rush Belford from behind. Jote was to pull his gun and aim it at Belford's face, and I was to cover Marcy. Except, no one told Marcy the plan. As we opened the connecting door, Marcy was on her way, rushing into Belford from behind, driving him into Jote. Belford fell over the coffee cart and knocked Jote down at the same time. Marcy retreated into the room to grab the shotgun. Patrick and I found ourselves frozen amidst the action as we entered the room.

Two shots rang out in the hallway, as we saw Belford get off the floor holding the Baby Glock in his hand. Fuck. "Jote, are you alright?" I shouted. Belford reached for the room's door and closed it. Leaving him outside, and the rest of us inside the room. There was no response from Jote.

Marcy was startled and looked back at us. She realized for the first time what was happening. She had the shotgun in hand and without giving it a second thought; she pumped the gun, opened the door and went out into the hallway after Belford.

"Marcy, wait," I shouted, as I saw her look both ways, to see which way Belford had gone.

"I got this asshole," Marcy said, without looking back. With that, she stepped out of the room and strolled to her right, crouching down.

As I stepped out of the room, I saw Jote on the floor, bleeding from his arm. "Are you alright?" I asked.

"Dude, he hit me on the arm, I'll be fine, get his ass," Jote replied.

Angela and Patrick were next to Jote now. I followed Marcy down the hallway. Belford was on his way down and to the left of the hall. Neither Marcy, who was ahead of me about ten paces, nor I could see Belford. He had made the ninety-degree left turn in the hallway. But he headed to the cargo elevator, thinking he could escape that way. Except, we had disabled the elevator, and the stairs down, where opposite the elevator, behind us.

"Marcy, wait," I said, again.

"He's taking the elevator. I'm not waiting," she replied.

"No, wait. The elevator is disabled. He's trapped."

Marcy got to the turn in the hallway and stopped, raised the barrel of the shotgun, smiling at me, said, "What the fuck have you been doing for the last few days, Mancuso?"

"Are you alright?" I asked. She nodded. "Did he," I paused, "did he hurt you?"

"No, he hasn't touched me. I think I intimidate this asshole," she replied. "Did you say he's trapped?" she asked, as she peeked around the corner of the hallway.

"He has nowhere to go."

Two shots rang out from where Belford not aimed at anyone. More like warning shots.

"Any idea how long this hallway is to the cargo elevator?" she asked. "I ran it downstairs. From here to the elevator is about thirty yards to the end."

She looked at my right hand, "What are you holding there? A toy gun?"

"It's a.357 Magnum caliber," I replied, glancing at it.

"Two-inch barrel?" She asked.

"Well, yes. Short, but powerful," I said.

She smiled, "Are you still talking about the gun?" She raised the shotgun, and in a flash, turned into the hallway.

"Marcy, what are you doing?" I asked in desperation.

"Stay there, Mancuso."

I turned into the hallway behind her. We could both see Belford all the way down the end of the hall. He was desperately pushing the elevator's button. I shouted from behind Marcy, "Give it up, Belford. You're trapped!"

Marcy lowered the barrel and aimed at the floor, "Mancuso, go back. This is my fight."

Belford took a shot at us, missing us by a wide margin. His short three plus inch barrel was not accurate at thirty yards. He took a second shot. This one hit the wall in front of us.

Marcy raised the barrel towards the ceiling a few yards ahead of her and pulled the trigger. The sound of the shotgun resonated the entire floor.

"Marcy, we can bring this guy in. He needs to pay for what he's done," I said, still behind her a few steps.

"Oh, he's going to pay alright. As far as bringing him in," she paused, "we'll bring him in."

"Alive?" I asked.

"You ask too many questions, Joey."

Before I could answer that, two more shots came our way. This time, one hit the floor right in front of Marcy, and the other whisked by our heads.

I said to her, "I've never seen you like this."

"No, you've never seen me like this. Try abducting me, drugging me, holding me captive for three days, naked and afraid of being raped any minute. Joey, go back around the corner. I said, this is my fight."

"Marcy, how many rounds do you have in that shotgun?"

Again, maintaining her gaze forward towards Belford, she replied, "Four total. I have two left."

Belford took two more shots at us. He was desperate. Firing for the sake of firing. Hoping to hit us, but with little chance."

"Marcy, Belford just took his last shot."

Continuing her slow march forward, she asked, "You've been counting, Joey?"

"The Glock 26 has ten rounds. He's taken ten shots."

"Joey, I'm pleading with you. Go back around the corner. If you're right, then there's no more danger."

I dropped my head and agreed to her request. She was going to do what she was going to do. I walked back to the ninety-degree turn in the hallway. I listened.

"Marcy, we could have been the happiest couple ever," shouted Belford. "Don't kill me, please."

"How many women have you murdered, Belford?"

"What?" Belford asked.

"How many?" Marcy demanded, again.

"I don't know. Twenty, maybe," Belford replied.

"And your mother and father?" Marcy inquired.

I walked back into the hallway. I had to see what was going to happen. I remained at the turn. Belford had not replied when Marcy took her third shot, aiming right above Belford's head into the ceiling. Pieces of cement from the ceiling rained on Belford's head as he crouched from the shot. He sat on the floor, his knees up, almost covering his face, resting his back against the metal elevator door. Marcy was now right in front of Belford. Only three feet in front.

I began walking towards them. It was over. I took out my phone to call for Tico or anyone on the team downstairs to let them know we had Belford. Suddenly, a sonic boom went off in front of me. I dropped to the floor. Marcy had fired her last round. Right into Belford's face.

As I looked up, I could see brain matter and blood spattered on the metal elevator door all the way to the ceiling. Blood was still gushing from a headless body that quivered in front of the elevator. Marcy just stood there, looking at what was left of Belford.

I walked next to her, "Marcy, what have you done?"

"I said this was my fight, didn't I."

"Yes, but" I didn't want to finish the sentence.

She glanced at me. I could see she had this distant look in her eyes that I had never seen on her, "I told you to stay back. You did not need to see me do this," she said.

"You didn't need to do this," I told her.

"It had to be done," she said, as she dropped the shotgun she was still holding on the floor and began walking back.

I saw her walk away. I looked at Belford's body, now still, and back at Marcy, "He was out of bullets."

"Yeah? Look at his right hand under his right leg," she said,

as she continued to walk away without looking at me or back at the scene.

I stood there looking at her walk away. When she reached the corner of the hallway, she disappeared from my view. I walked over to Belford's body. Using my handkerchief, I pulled up his right leg up slightly. Underneath his leg, his right hand was grabbing a .38 caliber snub-nose hammerless revolver. The holster attached to his right ankle.

CHAPTER 34

My phone rang. It was Tico, "What's going on there, Mancuso?"

"Hey, Tico. How's Jote?"

"He's fine, a little embarrassed, but just fine. What's going on?" Tico asked again.

"Marcy is on her way down. Belford is dead," I said, with no more details.

"Did you kill him?"

I thought for a second, "No, Marcy did in self-defense."

"Joey, Miami Beach Homicide Detectives are here, as well as the Crime Scene Unit. FBI is on their way."

"Send the detectives and the CSU up. Don't use the cargo elevator. Have them come up the other elevator and keep the cargo one disabled until they're done. I'll stay up here to make a statement."

"Roger that, Joey."

The MBPD homicide guys and the CSU came up. I introduced myself and began a short version of the days happening, starting at Marcy's condo a few blocks away. I was ready to take the heat for keeping the whole thing a secret. I mean, shit, MBPD was going to be pissed that we had an operation going under their noses and they had no clue. The FBI, what can I say? They have been on Marcy's track for three days now nonstop. They had probably been all the way to British Columbia looking for Belford and Marcy, to no avail. They, too, were going to be ticked off.

Finally, I went downstairs to the lobby. They cordoned off the entire hotel as a crime scene. Marcy was sitting with Angela and Patrick off to a corner of the lobby. I looked around and, for the first time, I paid attention to the hotel's lobby. Lots of green plants every- where, white walls with white terrazzo floors. Very 1950s.

The furniture looked very retro styled from the animated television series 'The Jetsons', a futuristic view of a family. The lobby was a mix of cottage décor with a throwback to the 50s, and modern design. I guessed it all worked together.

I sat next to Marcy. She seemed to be still in a daze. She glanced at me. We embraced, and she started crying. For a few minutes, I held her tight while she cried. I could only imagine the stress she had been under. She needed to unwind and to realize the nightmare was over.

Two suits walked over to us, flashed creds and introduced themselves as Miami FBI, Special Agents. They asked to speak to Marcy. I stayed seated next to her. Angela and Patrick got up and walked away. The suits sat down. They remained quiet. I guess waiting for me to take a walk. Still, next to Marcy, I sat back, crossed my legs, and just said, "Guys, I ain't going anywhere. So, you might as well start doing whatever it is you came to do."

"We need to talk to Special Agent Martinez privately if you don't mind," said gray suit. While blue suit gave me a nasty look.

"Talk all you want. I ain't moving."

Blue suit, finally asked, "Are you Joe Mancuso?"

"That would be Joey Mancuso. Yes, I am."

"Mr. Mancuso," said gray suit, "You've made a bunch of people very unhappy. They have lots of questions for you, as well."

"Fucking A, that makes my day, Mr. Gray suit. Now, why don't you ask Miss Martinez your questions so that we can get out of here."

Gray and Blue went on for about an hour, asking and taking notes from what Marcy was relating as to the events of the abduction.

When they concluded with the questions to her, they realized from her answers that it was Giuseppe Mancuso who uncovered the Red Ribbon serial killer. Otherwise known as Special Agent Anthony Belford.

"Mr. Mancuso," said Blue suit, "since we have you here, we might as well ask you about your investigation, and how it led you to Belford."

"Of course, I'm happy to discuss that," I replied, smiling. "Except, I'm not doing it here, or with you," I said, widening my smile. "No, there're many people involved in this investigation, and I report to the NYPD. I'll do my report to my supervisor, Captain Alex Johnson, in New York. You know what I'm talking about?"

Blue glanced at Gray, or what is it the other way around. They grunted almost in unison, got up, shook hands with Marcy, avoided me altogether, and walked the hell out of my life.

Unfortunately, MBPD homicide detectives had waited their turn, and they, too, had questions for both of us. However, this hour-long session was much more pleasant. Especially since Mr. Pat had brought both Marcy and me two Cuban sandwiches, diet drinks and a large boiling café-con-leche for both of us.

Both the FBI and the MBPD heard from Marcy the entire story of the abduction and Belford's confession about killing his mother and stepdad. Marcy didn't have the details of the other serial killings. Although, Belford had admitted to killing about twenty women.

Marcy's shooting of Special Agent Belford was ruled justifiable. After all, he shot at Marcy and me ten times, and had a second gun at the ready. I think he expected Marcy to use up the four rounds on the shotgun she had taken from him. And then shoot her with his .38 Special. I don't think he expected Marcy to shoot him as she did. My questions were, did she know he had an ankle holster with a gun? He had pulled the gun out of the holster. But did she see that?

It was almost ten in the morning when we were free to go. Angela and Patrick headed back to New York on an afternoon flight to Newark. Marcy's mother, Rosa, and her husband, Alberto, were coming to Miami Beach tomorrow to be with Marcy. Bob Seger's song *'We've Got Tonight'* came to mind. But I wasn't sure what kind of mood Marcy was in. And, officially, we were still *'taking a break from each other,'* as she had wanted to do, what, a month or two ago? I had nothing to lose. I was turning to ask her, when the elevator door opened with two guys bringing out Belford, or most of him, in a body bag.

"Hang on a second," I said to Marcy, as the gurney with Belford's remains was wheeled right next to me. Standing up, I turned to the two men pushing the gurney. "Guys, can you stop for a second?"

They looked at me, surprised. The young man at the back of the gurney asked, "What do you need, sir?"

I moved closer, and said, "Do you mind if I open the bag and look at something?"

They glanced at each other, both raising their shoulders. "Be our guest, just touch nothing," said the other member of the coroner's team.

"Can I borrow a pair of gloves?" I asked.

"Who are you, sir?" One of them asked.

Angela and Tico were now standing next to me. "I'm MPD, open the bag, and give him a pair of gloves, please," said Tico.

They handed me a pair of latex gloves, as they unzipped the bag. Fortunately, the feet were the first to be exposed, I said, "You can stop, I don't need the entire bag open. Anyone have a measuring tape?" Everyone looked at each other. No tape was available from anyone.

"Tico, you got two bills?"

Tico took a step back, "I don't understand, Joey. You want two C-notes?"

"No, brother. I just need two bills, any denomination is fine."

Tico pulled out a five and a one-dollar bill handed them to me. He asked, "What are you going to do?"

"Tico come over. Give me a hand," I said, as I placed the two bills together, one after the other. "Hold the bag while I do this."

Tico asked again, "What is it you're doing, bro?"

I placed the bills under the sole of Belford's right shoe. "What do see, Tico?"

"What do I see?"

"Tico, is the sole of the shoe bigger or smaller than the two bills?"

Tico bent his head to inspect. "The bills are longer than the sole of the shoe. Is that what you're asking?"

"Exactly. That is the question. So, you agree sole is shorter than two bills?"

"Yeah, sure. What does that mean?"

By now I had a group gathered next to me. MBPD, FBI, and others involved in dealing with this scene. I spotted Mr. Pat and Angela standing next to Marcy.

"Sir, are you done?" The young guys responsible for the body asked. "Yes, yes. Sorry," I replied.

An MBPD detective approached me and asked, "Mr. Mancuso, what were you doing?"

I looked around and just replied, "Oh, I just wanted confirmation of something. We're good here."

The detective asked, "Anything we need to know?"

"No, we're good," I replied, taking off the latex gloves, and walking towards my team.

Mr. Pat knew I had something. As I got closer to him, he asked in a whisper, "What you got, Joey?"

I glanced at him, winked, and said, "Give it a few minutes. Let the lobby clear itself."

Marcy came over to me, "Let's get out of here," she said. "What do you want to do?" I asked, turning to face her.

"I don't know. Can we rent a convertible, and drive around?" she asked, excitedly.

"Of course, let's do it. What about—?" I paused.

"What about tonight?" She finished my sentence, "let's stay at The Four Seasons on the beach."

That would not be my question. However, I liked her answer. Looking at Mr. Pat and Angela, I replied, "Sounds good. I'll rent the car and book a couple of rooms," I said.

"A couple of rooms, why? Who else is staying with us?" she asked, smiling.

"So, we're not taking a break from each other anymore?"

"No, Mancuso. Is your offer still open?"

"What offer is that?"

"You and me, silly. You said it was open-ended. No expiration date. Right?"

"You mean my marriage proposal?"

"Mancuso, I'm waiting for an answer. My mom and stepdad are going to be in town tomorrow. Your mother is near here. How about we tie the knot tomorrow?"

Angela and Patrick were smiling next to us. Her proposal overwhelmed me. I've been waiting for this for over two years. "Marcy, I accept. But I want to do this back in New York. Father Dominic has been waiting for this moment for two years himself. He will be devastated if we don't do this at his church with him presiding. Besides, all our friends are back there."

"You're on Mancuso. But we start the honeymoon today."

I was ready. But was she? In the last three months she had killed a terrorist on a plane at the Newark airport, almost lost her life after being shot during the same incident. Just this morning, she stood in front of a man shooting at her, and she didn't flinch. Then, she killed the man that had abducted her, and held her captive for three days? She wasn't at fault for the killings in New York, but would she ever blame herself for the five horrific murders by Belford? A man she was friends with and visited her apartment for a few weeks. This was all happening a little too quick. I was concerned that she was reacting irrationally to so much stress in a short period.

But I was happy for us. Maybe I was playing a psychologist and worrying too much about nothing. This time, I would not miss the boat, as they say. Marcy and I were soul mates, and we were together.

I embraced her in the lobby, "Miss Martinez, you are on. Honeymoon now. Wedding next week."

Patrick said, "Congratulations you two. Finally, we have a wedding to plan."

Marcy turned to Pat, and replied, "Thank you, Patrick," hugging him.

I saw Marcy turn to Angela, whom she had not met and did a double take. "Marcy, this is detective Angela Asis. She was with Vice here in Miami and is hoping to join NYPD. She was helping us in your search."

"Hi Marcy," Angela said.

"Thank you for helping, Angela," Marcy said, as she moved in closer to exchange a kiss on the cheeks.

I added, "Angela's husband was transferred to New York, and Angela would like to continue working. She wants to join Captain Johnson's squad."

"Great, welcome to New York," Marcy said.

Patrick said, "Sorry to change the subject. Angela and I are headed back today. We're flying out at three this afternoon. I assume you guys are hanging around?"

"Pat, I'm staying with Marcy tonight. Her parents are coming in tomorrow. I'll be back tomorrow in New York."

My phone rang and vibrated, giving me a jolt. The ID caller read Captain Johnson. "Hello, this is Mancuso." I motioned to Patrick to come with me, as I moved away from the ladies.

"Joey," Alex Johnson said, a tad agitated. "Why haven't you called me back? I've left ten messages, at least."

"Captain, my phone was not working. Remember, Belford had taken it and he had removed the SIM card. I just got it to work."

"Well, listen. I need to meet with you before the mayor has his press conference tomorrow. He would like for you to be present for that."

"Captain, I didn't hear all of that, we have a poor connection," I said, although I heard him perfectly. "This case is not completely solved. I think we have another person involved in these killings."

"Joey, you're kidding, right?"

"No, Captain, I'm not at all. We don't know about the extent of the involvement, but for sure there's another person involved."

"Do you know who it is?"

"Sir, we think we do. But we have no proof. We're trying to put a plan together. My suggestion, Captain, is not to have a press conference."

"That will not be received very well by the brass," Johnson said.

"At least, cover your ass, Captain. I suggest they wait a day or two. Let us do our thing. Otherwise, Mr. Mayor is going to be embarrassed a second time. Not that I give a shit."

"I'll mention it, Joey. You're right. I'll CYA it. Stay in touch, please," said the captain.

"Another thing, sir."

"What is it, Joey?"

"We need to keep what happened here under wraps for a day, at least," I said, knowing it would be almost impossible.

"That's a mission impossible. Too many people involved. FBI, Miami Beach Police, and press. Then, there are you guys. How can we do that?"

"Can they report it as an abduction or a chase after a criminal? We need to keep Belford's name out of the news, and the fact we think he was the Red Ribbon Killer."

"Why Joey?"

"Like I said, Captain. There's an accomplice or a second person involved in these killings. If we tell the world we got the killer, we might not get the second person."

"MBPD and FBI are waiting for my call. They don't have all the facts from our end. Perhaps, I can ask them to stall for a few hours."

"I need forty-eight hours, sir."

"I don't know, Joey. Are you in New York now?"

"No, I'm still in Miami."

"Flying back today?"

"I was going to spend the night here with Marcy. Her parents are coming in tomorrow morning."

"You should be here if you're telling me there's a second person. We need to get this done."

"I understand, Captain. Here's the thing. In less than two months, Marcy has shot two people dead. They injured her in the first shooting. Then, she's facing losing her FBI job because of physical impairment from the damage to her shoulder. Add to that, the abduction at the hands of this animal and the fear and stress she must have felt. I'm not leaving her behind alone tonight."

There was silence for few seconds. "I'm sorry, Joey, you're right. Marcy has gone through more than anyone should. Stay there if you must. Let me work on the story and see how we can spin this."

"Remember what I said, the mayor does not want to be embarrassed twice. Let him know we need to wait. He'll spin it for you."

"We'll talk tomorrow, Joey."

I hung up with Johnson. Hopefully, we could hold off on naming Belford as the killer for a day or two."

Patrick stood next to me listening to the conversation, "Lad, can I ask you a question?"

We were still in the hotel lobby. "What is it, Pat?"

"You were going to share what you did with Belford's feet or shoes. What's up? I can see you were deep in thought."

"Patrick, the last victim," I paused and looked around.

Mr. Pat followed my gaze around the room. "What about the last victim?"

I whispered, "The person who went back in the room after the vic was dead. You know, the one who retrieved the Motorola Bluetooth gadget?"

"What about it?"

"The shoe prints on the carpet I found were measured to be thirteen inches from tip to heel."

"Yes, I remember that," he said.

"Okay, you saw me measuring Bedford's shoe. Each currency bill is six inches long. I placed two bills together. Therefore, that would measure twelve inches. However, Belford's shoe was smaller than the twelve inches. His shoe size is probably ten. Not thirteens."

Mr. Pat snapped his head back, "Are you saying Bedford is not the killer?"

"Belford admitted to killing twenty women. I just don't know if he killed the last one. At the very least, he was not the one who entered the room last."

Patrick grabbed the bottom of his red beard with his right hand, and asked, "Shit, lad. Are you saying the serial killer is still out there?"

CHAPTER 35

More coffee?" I asked.

We spent the night at the Miami Beach Four Seasons Hotel, and dined in their oceanfront restaurant, Le Sirenuse. Now, breakfast was served in our corner room that faced the Atlantic Ocean. The floor to ceiling glass walls allowed us to fully appreciate the orange sunrays that brightly shone on the sparkling and warm blue-green waters in front of us. The baby blue sky with puffy white clouds seemed to melt into the horizon.

"No, I'm good. Come back to bed and make love to me," Marcy said.

"Give me two minutes to get some nourishment, and I'll jump back in there with you," I said, as I swallowed a piece of hickory smoked southern bacon.

Marcy covered her entire body with the comforter, and pleaded from under it, "I'm lazy. I want to stay in bed all day with you."

"Love to stay, but I'm on my way back to New York. Plus, I have over forty messages on my phone, which I recovered from the back of Belford's car."

"Mancuso, are you passing up an opportunity to stay in bed with me all day?"

How do I answer that? I thought. After a few moments, I said, "Nothing would give more pleasure and satisfaction than being in bed with you all day." I'd probably die as a result of it, but no, I didn't say that. "However, this case is not over, and your parents are going to be here in an hour or two."

"Did you make reservations for them at the hotel?"

"Marcy, they have the condo in South Beach. You guys are going to be staying there."

"Shoot, but this hotel is so nice," she replied.

Nice and freaking expensive. "Yes, it is very nice. You and I will come back and spend more time here. I promise you."

"Okay," she said, as she yawned. "Get your ass in bed."

"By the way, we are all over the news. You're a hero again. I think you're going to need to wear a cape and come up with a hero's moniker and logo."

"Oh, no. I want no more press. Do they know we're here?"

"No, we're incognito. No one knows. And, fortunately, they're not aware of the connection between what we did and the Red Ribbon Killer. So far, they've kept Belford's name out of the news. I don't know how long that's going to last."

"Wonderful. Let's kept it that way."

An hour and a half later, I drove my red Mustang rental to the Miami Airport. Marcy parent's arrival coincided with my departure. She was to keep the car for the time she was to stay with her parents.

Everything came in bunches. Great food, comfortable sleep, and incredible sex. All three things eluded me in the past few days. The sex was longer than that since Marcy and I had been apart for almost two months. All I know is it felt like a year. But we made up for it.

No new killings took place in New York City since the last victim. I still knew that the person who was last in the room of our previous victim was not Belford. The other three suspects, the two uniforms first on the scene, and the apartment manager, well, we knew that none of them had a thirteen-inch shoe size. Who was it? And were they involved in the serial killings?

My flight lasted close to three hours. I took an Uber back to the pub in the Financial District of Manhattan. "Good morning, gents," I said, entering our office.

"Congrats, Joey. We heard you got engaged," Agnes said. "Thank you, we got engaged," I replied.

Patrick and Agnes were in the office. Father O'Brian was to join us in a few minutes. Also, I had asked Detective Lucy Roberts to come in. Our office was looking good. We had finally installed flooring, and what I thought was a smart squad room had taken shape. Our private detective agency had a comfortable feel to it.

"Have you picked a date yet?" Patrick asked.

"I'll let Marcy plan that part of it. Any day is good for me."

Agnes wanted details of what had happened in Miami Beach, and I gave her a short version of the events leading to Belford's death.

"How is Marcy doing?" Agnes asked.

Marcy needed counseling. Although no symptoms head been obvious. However, these things have a delayed reaction. And she may have been masking how she felt. Without giving too much information, I replied, "She seems fine. We spent a nice evening together. She's coming back in a few days."

Father O'Brian, followed by Lucy, walked into the office. We exchanged brotherly hugs and pleasantries for a few minutes while we sat around the conference table.

I explained to everyone what I had done with the dead Belford's shoe in the hotel's lobby.

Agnes spoke first, "Oh, my God. Do you think we still have a serial killer out there?"

I sat back, crossed my legs, and frowned as I replied to Agnes, "Belford admitted to killing twenty women. We didn't ask where. It is obvious that he was involved here because of the way he reacted and abducted Marcy. Marcy told me he said we forced him to act. He thought we might be on to him, and he counter surveilled us during our surveillance of Ernie's Bar. That's when he texted to cancel his blind date with Angela.

Lucy asked, "But the next day, he took Marcy to the range. Would he not think we would make our move and arrest him?"

"Since nothing happened that night, and we did not act against him, he was playing it by ear. However, he felt he was being watched. He told Marcy," I replied.

Patrick asked, "Why abduct Marcy?"

"In his mind, we had him cornered and under twenty-four-hour surveillance. He felt trapped. Belford himself told us when he was describing the characteristics of a narcissist. He said, *'a narcissist can become unpredictable when he's challenged.'* And, that's exactly what happened. He became more and more unpredictable. As for Marcy, he was obsessed with her. He planned on living with her as a couple. In his demented mind, he thought she would come around and fall in love with him."

Agnes observed, "Oh, my God. I don't want to even think of what Marcy went through."

Father Dom asked, "Do you think the serial killer is still out there. Or, was Belford, the serial killer?"

I turned to look at Father Dom, "Good question, brother. I'm not sure. I think Belford was the serial killer, but there's more, and I don't know what it is."

Dom asked, "What about Professor Gruntel?"

I moved up on my seat, grabbed the edge of the table and pulled myself in. "Something is bothering me about Belford," I said. "When I asked him if Gruntel was his partner, his first response was, *'Why? Did he tell you?'* Then, he said that he had no partners."

Dom asked, "Lucy, did they check if Gruntel had lived in any of the cities where we had unsolved serial killings?"

"Yes. Detectives Farnsworth and Charles checked that out. And, no Gruntel's homes did not correlate with those cities." I looked around the table, "Gents, I'm a little disappointed."

Patrick asked, "How so, Joey?"

I went on, "What was the question Belford asked, that I just told you? Come on, Pat. You were there."

Patrick replied, "When you asked him if Gruntel was a partner, he replied, *'Why? Did he tell you that?'* Is that the question you are referring to?"

I grinned, "Exactly. What does that tell you?"

Lucy responded, "It tells me they knew each other and must have collaborated. Why else would he make that statement?"

I pointed at Lucy and nodded, "Precisely," I replied, rotating my chair to face Agnes. I contemplated, "Besides the fact they may have known each other, one other angle we have not investigated is if there's a relationship between the victims and Professor Gruntel. After all, these ladies were in some form of the law profession. Gruntel is a law professor. Get my angle?"

Agnes fired up her computer as we spoke.

"You know, Gruntel's body language was all wrong when I questioned him in his home," I said to Lucy.

Lucy nodded and said, "I noticed that, yes. He was biting his lower lip when you asked if he knew Belford."

Patrick asked, "I bite my lower lip, occasionally. What does it mean?"

Lucy turned to face Mr. Pat, "When you do that, you are showing signs of stress, anxiety or worry."

"Now, I understand. I do it when paying my bills," Patrick replied with a chuckle.

I said, "Gruntel did it when I questioned him. I bet his shoe size is thirteen."

"Guys, listen up," Agnes said. "Guess who was a guest speaker last month at Gruntel's class?"

I shook my head as Father Dom replied, "Special Agent Tony Belford?"

"Exactly," Agnes rejoined.

"Why didn't we see that before?" I probed.

Lucy replied, "There was no reason to connect these two. None."

Turning to Agnes, I said, "Agnes, see if you can tie these two before New York."

"Joey," announced Agnes, "I found a connection between Belford and Gruntel going back to Chicago. It seems Agent Tony had Gruntle speak at an FBI meeting in Chicago. Plus, one time, Belford took Gruntel to the Academy at Quantico to address the newbies."

Lucy questioned, "Hon, where are you getting this information?" Agnes lowered her reading glasses and looked at Lucy smiling, "This information is from NYU's blogs. It's a couple of press releases. Nothing nefarious here, Detective Roberts."

"Check the dates of the killings with his visits in those two cities. Let's see if they correlate."

Mr. Pat asked Lucy, "Can Gruntel be arrested?"

Lucy replied, "We have nothing to hold him on. We can arrest him, but we will not hold him."

Pat added, "He lied about knowing Belford."

Lucy uttered, "He can always say he forgot about that."

I sat there looking at Lucy and Patrick, "Damn it. Lucy, let's arrest this guy. We'll worry about holding him later. I have an idea."

CHAPTER 36

A familiar face was sitting in with our new suspect in one of the precinct's interrogation rooms. All two-hundred and, say, about sixty pounds of him. Stevan Kopzoff, Attorney at Law.

"Well, Mr. Mancuso, we meet again," Kopzoff said with a smirk, as I entered the room with Captain Johnson.

I replied, before sitting down, "Good to see you again, Mr. K. Sorry about the last time we met. I think all your clients are serving time, right?"

Peter Gruntel, sitting to the left of Kopzoff, immediately turned to look at him. His facial expression became one of disquietude. Some- thing like being in line to buy the last remaining Super Bowl tickets and getting the feeling you must take a shit, now!

Kopzoff ignored Gruntel's stare. I turned to Gruntel, and pointing my finger at him, said, "But I think he got them good accommodations. So, you're in excellent hands." I expressed, cupping my hands like the insurance commercial, 'Is it Allstate, or State Farm?'

Kopzoff barked, "Mr. Gruntel has been inconvenienced a lot so far. What is it you all want from him?"

"Mr. Gruntel lied to us when we questioned him regarding Special Agent Tony Belford," explained Captain Johnson.

"How did he do that?" Mr. Kopzoff inquired.

Johnson glanced at me and Kopzoff and replied, "He was asked if he knew Mr. Belford, and he replied, *'No, I do not.'* He lied to Mr. Mancuso and my detective, Ms. Roberts."

"Perhaps," Mr. K began, "You should have Detective Roberts and Mr. Mancuso check their notes. Captain, at no point did anyone ask Mr. Gruntel if he knew Mr. Belford."

It surprised Johnson as he heard that and turned quickly to me with an inquisitive look. I shrugged.

"I believe the question was if he had heard the name of Anthony, or Tony Belford. Mr. Gruntel admitted to me he was nervous at the time thinking someone was in his home and he misunderstood the question. Obviously, it was not his intent to lie, since he knew of Agent Belford. Mr. K went on, "The question was asked of Mrs. Gruntel. And, she replied truthfully. She does not know Belford."

Johnson smirked and inquired, "Shouldn't your client have informed us he knew Mr. Belford?"

Mr. K. smiled, turned to look at Mr. Gruntel who returned the smile, then Kopzoff replied, "Captain, Mr. Gruntel is a law professor. He's happy to answer questions directed at him to his best knowledge. But he will not volunteer answers when nothing has been asked of him."

"Very well, Mr. Kopzoff. We have direct questions for him, now. So, can we get started?" Johnson inquired.

"Ask away, gentlemen," responded Kopzoff.

Johnson glanced at me to see if I wanted to start. I motioned with my hand for him to begin. After all, he had the prelim q's that needed to be asked.

"I have many nights and times to which I will need to find out where Mr. Gruntel was. May I begin with—"

Kopzoff interrupted, "Captain, if it is over one night, I'm going to ask you to write these down and we can get back to you on them. You can't expect my client to have an immediate recollection of various nights right now, do you?"

The captain shook his head, "Very well, I'll write them down."

"Thank you, sir. We'll get them right back to you," announced Mr. K, glancing at Gruntel who nodded in agreement.

I inquired, "How long have you known Agent Belford?"

"At the moment," advanced Mr. K "my client will admit that he met with Agent Belford three times. One recently, when the agent addressed his class at NYU. And two before, when Belford invited Professor Gruntel to speak in Chicago at the FBI's office and in Quantico addressing the new group of agents."

"They didn't meet any other times?" I pressed.

"My client will have to think back and see if he recollects having been with Belford other times. Right now, he has no recollection. May I ask you, fellows, a few questions?"

The Captain replied, "Please, do."

"What is the crime here? So far, I have heard no accusations or a crime. The fact your detective and consultant didn't ask the right questions a few days ago of my client is their mistake. But surely, not a crime on my client's part. Further, these dates you want and other information when they met, that is Belford and my client, unquestionably, you have that from Mr. Belford. So, I'm truly baffled by these questions. Sounds like a test. Is Mr. Belford using my client to alibi out of something?"

Either Kopzoff was bluffing, or indeed, they were not aware Agent Tony was deceased, and that we knew of the killings, and his involvement in them.

The captain looked at me.

I took the cue and proceeded, "No, Agent Belford is not using your client as an alibi. It turns out Belford is the subject of a criminal investigation, and what he has done," I glanced at Mr. Gruntel, who had blinked rapidly, showing to me a little distress, or discomfort on his part.

"Mr. Mancuso, go on," requested Mr. K.

"Yes, Agent Belford has implicated your client," I revealed, while I continued to look at Gruntel, whose eyes dilated. He looked as nervous as a long-tailed cat in a room full of rocking chairs.

Kopzoff sat back in his chair. "Oh, I see. You are playing twenty questions. You're like mice chasing cheese, except you don't have any cheese. Evidently, the implications are not severe enough. Otherwise, you would have arrested my client on some charges. Is Mr. Belford under arrest?

"Agent Belford has admitted to a series of crimes already. We still have more questions." I replied. I didn't lie.

Mr. K. stood up, padded lanky and skinny Gruntel on the shoulder to follow suit, and expressed, "If you have any charges against my client, we'll be happy to return, voluntarily. Just notify me. In the meantime, we have nothing else to discuss. Have a pleasant afternoon, gentlemen."

I stood opposite these two. Gruntel was one third the width of Kopzoff. Both were over six feet tall. I was pissed, frustrated, looking at a probable serial killer. The other was a professor of law at NYU. No, just kidding. It implicated Gruntel for sure.

The captain advised, "Make sure your client stays in town until we're done with this investigation."

Both men walked out of the interrogation room.

"Fuck. Captain, I have work to do. It involved Gruntel in these murders, sure as death and taxes. How to prove it, is becoming a challenge."

"Joey, I feel like a ship lost at sea. We have nothing to throw at this guy. And by tomorrow, the story about Belford's death will be out. Gruntel will know he's in the clear after that."

"I'm going back to the pub. Agnes is working hard to find some angle we can use. I'll keep you posted."

"At least the murders have stopped."

"Let's hope it stays that way."

CHAPTER 37

We batted zero yesterday in our quest to solve this crime," I stated to our gathered team in our private squad room. Father Dom, Patrick, and Agnes sat around the conference table, as we observed Agnes' artwork on our whiteboard. Agnes had posted everything we had on Gruntel.

Agnes added, "I think I have additional information that may help us."

I turned to face her. She was smiling and had this facial expression as if she had found Al Capone's secret vault. "What is it, Agnes?"

"All five of our victims have either taken a direct course from Professor Gruntel or have attended one of his lectures at NYU."

Patrick observed, "So, he knew the victims. Gruntel, that is."

I replied, "Not necessarily. But that's too much coincidence, right?"

Father Dom asked, "Are you saying that the Facebook idea we came up with where we thought Belford was using it as a menu to select victims is wrong?"

Agnes responded, "No, I don't think so. I think that was part of the mix. I suspect Gruntel was the one researching Belford."

Patrick quizzed, "What about our theory of Marcy look-alike?"

I replied, "Easy. Belford gives Gruntel a picture of Marcy. Gruntel then seeks look-alike. Both these guys have sick minds. Gruntel was acting like a sommelier, but instead of selecting a fine wine, he was selecting victims."

Agnes added, "There are more, guys. I found the porn pictures that Gruntel has collected. Remember Belford told you guys about Gruntel's porn?"

Patrick beamed and replied, "Yes, he did."

I shut my eyes and inquired, "Do I want to know how you got those?"

"Suffice it to say," Agnes began, "that what I found will not be admissible in a court of law."

I affirmed, "Will deal with that later. Show us what you found? Wait!" I exclaimed, turning to Dom, "Brother, I think what Agnes will show on the screen are pornographic photos. You want to stay?" Dom thought for a second, "May I remind you all that I was twenty- one when I entered the seminary. We priests don't live in a bubble. Now, the way you phrased the question 'do I want to stay?' The answer is no. However, I'm involved in a murder investigation, so, I should stay. Proceed, please."

Agnes flashed on our large television monitor a series of pornographic pictures that made Dom, Patrick and I blush. She was stoic throughout the presentation. "Now, for the pièce de résistance, ready?"

I replied, "Yes, ready."

Agnes had grouped four different pictures of a man and woman having sex. But not just sex. No, the sex was in the style of the murders in New York City.

We sat there staring at the photos. Four different couples, all in the same positions.

I inquired, "By any chance, Agnes, are there any photos of our victims?"

"No, not in the cache of pictures in his computer."

Dom asked, "Is that where these came from?"

Agnes turned to look at me before answering, I nodded. "Yes, Father. I hacked into Gruntel's computer."

Patrick queried, "Isn't there some cloud, or something, where he can file other pictures?"

"Yes, the iCloud account he has. But no, there are no photos of our victims there," Agnes replied.

"We need the captain to get a warrant for this guy's home. I'm certain, just like we'll have fireworks on the fourth of July, that Gruntel has pictures of the murder scenes, and maybe even, in the act in his home somewhere."

Dom asked, "Do we have enough for a warrant?"

Shaking my head, I replied, "No, we have nothing to warrant a warrant, pun intended. However, Agnes, find out if Professor Gruntel is at NYU. If so, call Mrs. Gruntel and see if she's at home, but don't talk to her, just hang up."

Patrick said, "Here, I'll call Mrs. Gruntel at her home."

Both Agnes and Patrick made their calls. The professor was at NYU teaching a class, and Mrs. Gruntel was at her home.

"Father Dom, you and I are going to visit Mrs. Gruntel. I have an idea."

"When? Now?" Dom asked.

Replying, I said, "Yes, now. Why? You have something else to do?"

"No, let me change," Dom said.

"No, Father. You are visiting Mrs. Gruntel in full uniform."

"Joey, you know I don't like to mix things. I don't wear my collar when I work the pub or interview people on our cases."

"Today, you will. I'll tell why on our way."

"Agnes, print a few of those pictures. Maybe two or three." "You mean the porn scenes?" She inquired.

"Yes, the same."

"Joey, remember the doctrine of the 'fruit from the poisonous tree?' Make sure we don't screw this up with those.

"Thank you, Agnes. I'm aware we can't use these illegally obtained photos in our case. If so, we could blow the entire case. But I know what I'm doing. Just print two of them. Any two."

I picked up my phone from the conference table and dialed Lucy at the precinct. "I love Lucy," I said, as she answered.

"What's up Joey?"

"We need to go to visit Mrs. Gruntel. Can you pick Dom and me up at the pub?"

"Now, you want to go?"

"Yes, I want to question her before her husband comes back. I have a plan."

"Oh, oh. One of your plans? Do I want to be there? Keep in mind, honey. I only have one year before I hang it up. Don't screw it up for me."

"When was the last time I led you wrong?"

"See you in twenty minutes. Be outside the pub," she said disconnecting the call.

My phone went off and immediately rang. I was happy to see a smiling picture of Marcy. I answered, "Hey, love, *que pasa?*"

Marcy replied, "I'm in town. Just got back a few minutes ago."

"So, how you doing?"

"Feeling great, Joey. I spoke to Victoria Stewart, my boss. I'm taking the firearms test tomorrow. I can't wait to get back to work."

I hesitated a moment. I didn't think she was mentally ready. Perhaps physically, she was. But her demeanor after shooting Belford dead was as if nothing had happened. She did not react to killing someone.

"Joey, did you hear me?"

"Yes, I did. I'm excited for you. I know you'll do great. Anything I can do to help?"

"No, just come over tonight. Can you?"

"I'm wrapping this case up. I'll call you and let you know. Your parents in town?'

"No, they stayed in Miami Beach. It's that time of the year when they hang there."

"Good, good. I'll call you later. Did you pick a date yet?"

"About that, let's talk when we get together."

"Will do," I responded. Was that a good thing, or a bad thing? Did she have a date picked out, or was she having second thoughts again?

CHAPTER 38

We arrived at the Gruntel home in Paramus, New Jersey. As we had done before, Lucy knocked on the door and flashed her creds. After Lucy asked if we could come in, Mrs. Gruntel ushered us inside.

"I'm afraid my husband is not here. He's still at NYU teaching a class," she said, seeing Father Dom for the first time.

I said, "That's quite alright, Mrs. Gruntel. We wanted to talk to you."

"Oh, okay. Please, call me Harriet," she requested, as she smiled at Father Dominic.

"Harriet, this is Father Dominic. He's the Associate Pastor at Saint Helens in Brooklyn."

"Oh, what a captivating and enchanting church that is. Happy to meet you, Father," she said, bowing her head.

Dom glanced at me, and I motioned with my head towards the larger-than-life crucifix on the wall. Dom's eyes opened wide, as he saw it.

"May I get you some tea or freshly made lemonade?" Harriet asked, with her eyes fixed on Dominic.

I replied, "We are fine Harriet, thank you. Father Dominic was admiring your crucifix. Weren't you, Father?"

"Indeed, I was, it's very nice," Dom let out.

"Oh, thank you, Father. It belonged to my mother. God bless her heart."

"Mrs. Gruntel, Harriet, as you know," I began, "we are still involved in the investigation of this man who somehow was using the identity of your husband. And, using your mother's cabin in Wawayanda Park."

"Oh, my God, yes. Was he captured?" She inquired, turning to look at me.

"It's all working out," I replied. My cell phone and that of Lucy's both chirped at the same time.

A news app had just posted a 'breaking news' story. The headline which was the only two lines visible on the texted message read, 'FBI Agent killed in Miami Beach two days ago linked to the Manhattan Red Ribbon Killer.'

Lucy glanced at me as we both read the same message.

'Shit, we either get this guy now, or we're SOL.'

Seeing the lull in the conversation, Father Dominic asked, "Harriet, which church do you and Mr. Gruntel attend?"

"Father, we go to Saint Philip here in Paramus. Are you familiar with the church?"

"I'm afraid I have not visited Saint Philip," he answered.

Time was of the essence, and I needed to get down to business. "Harriet, may we ask you some questions?"

"Please, go right ahead," she replied.

I would not play games, "Harriet, the man was in your mother's cabin was hiding there because he abducted a young woman."

"Oh, my," she said, as she made the sign of the cross.

"The man told us when questioned that he knew your husband. He further told us that your husband kept pornographic photographs."

Harriet sat back on the sofa, rapidly covered her face with both hands and started weeping. I sat next to her on the couch with Dom and Lucy across from us in two chairs. I said, "Father, sit here, please."

I got up and Dominic sat next to Harriet. Then, I took the seat vacated by Dom. "Harriet, do you know where these photos are?"

She put her hands down, took out her rosary and tissue from a small bag that was on the coffee table. Turned to Dominic and with her hand quivering; she grabbed his right hand and held it tight.

Her breathing became erratic. I was getting a little concerned for her and felt horrible for pushing her.

"Harriet," I started again, "There are five dead young ladies who were victims and died horrible deaths."

She began crying, but held onto Dom's one hand, and attempted to dry the tears with her other hand and the tissue.

"Harriet, we believe your husband has pictures of these victims amongst his collection of other dirty ones."

She wept uncontrollably and was seemingly out of breath. She reached for an asthma inhaler from her small bag and took a hit.

I nodded to Dom, and he got the cue.

He took both his hands and held on to hers, "Harriet, do you know where your husband kept these pictures?"

Her green eyes fluttered and inundated with tears, opened wide and she nodded in the affirmative.

Dom added, "Harriet, trust me. As soon as you tell us, you'll feel a lot better."

Putting her head down in embarrassment, I assumed, she whispered, "In the attic," as she pointed up with her index finger. She let out a sigh. "Peter doesn't know I know about those photos. They are horrible. Father, he needs to confess to you."

"Thank you, Harriet," Lucy said, then inquired, "may we look in the attic and retrieve those photos?"

She nodded.

"Harriet, I need you to verbalize your answer. May we—"

Harriet interrupted, "Yes, you can take all those pictures. They're in a box labeled 'Student Pictures'.

I retrieved the box from the attic while Lucy stood below the stairs leading up to it. Dom was still consoling Mrs. Gruntel.

I asked, "Harriet, may we sit in your dining room?"

She got up from the sofa, "I meant Detective Roberts and me. You and Father Dominic stay there. Is that alright?"

She waved us off and remained quiet next to Dom, still holding her rosary.

Lucy and I opened the box. It was a file box full of letter-sized envelopes. But it did not take us long to find what we were hoping to see. The top five envelopes were the pièce de résistance, as Agnes had said. Each envelope had photos of our naked victims during sex. As we looked closer to all the pictures in each envelope, we could tell two different naked men had been with each victim. Photos from a side shot showed both Belford and Gruntel having anal sex with our victims at different times while the other photographed the event. They showed both holding the red satin ribbon around the vic's neck. The last photo in each deck was a shot of the dead victim from behind.

I got up from the dining room table, horrified. This was not my first rodeo. After sixteen years in the force and ten years in homicide, I had seen my share of horrific murders. But to think I was seeing the victims alive minutes before their death was revolting.

I came back to the living room. I had to solve another minor mystery. "Harriet, may I see your husband's bathroom?"

She replied in a slow cadence, "We have but the one upstairs. Yes, you may."

Going upstairs, I took two steps at a time, anticipating the results. Once in the small bathroom, I opened the medicine cabinet, and there, I could smell it. The intense fragrance of the cologne scent I had picked up at the last murder scene.

Using my handkerchief, I brought the bottle with me. I wanted the ME, Doctor Frankie, to confirm the cologne. But that was immaterial. We had these two with the incriminating photos. I walked downstairs when I heard the front door opening.

CHAPTER 39

"What do you think you people are doing here?" Inquired an indignant Peter Gruntel.

Lucy waited for him to enter his home.

She got up from her chair, went behind him and said, "Mr. Gruntel you are under arrest for multiple murders. You may remain silent. Anything you say, may and can be used against you. You have the right to an attorney. If you cannot afford—"

He exclaimed loudly, "Blah, blah, blah. I'm a law professor. I know my rights. Where is your warrant to enter my home?"

"Your wife invited us in, sir," replied Lucy, as she finished cuffing him.

He turned to look at his wife. In a demanding fashion, Gruntel shouted, "I want to call my lawyer, now."

I said, "Just as soon as you're booked for multiple murders, we'll notify your attorney. In the meantime, perhaps, you want to cooperate."

"You've entered my home illegally. You've violated my fourth amendment right. I have no reason to cooperate with..." his voice trailed off, as he saw the file box labeled 'Student Pictures' on top of the dining room table. He shouted, "Why is that box there?"

"Mrs. Gruntel told us where to find it. She permitted us to retrieve it from the attic."

He again turned to look at Mrs. Gruntel, whose head was down, unable to look at her husband. "Harriet, what have you done?"

Harriet looked up, her eyes were full of fury now, "You're a despicable and a sick person. All these years, I've put up with your dirty pictures. But now, now, you went too far. You're doomed for eternity. May God forgive you."

Peter Gruntel's legs went wobbly. He stumbled backward as I grabbed and held on to him.

"Can I sit," he asked.

Holding on to his right arm, I helped him sit on a chair in front of the sofa. "You want to talk about it, Peter," I asked.

"I'll talk, but not in front of my wife.'

I nodded to Father Dom, as he got up and said, "Harriet, let's make some tea in the kitchen."

Catatonically, she replied, "Chamomile is the best. With lemon."

Lucy sat on the sofa with me, both of us in front of Gruntel. She opened the 'Recorder App' on her phone, and asked, "Mr. Gruntel, do you wave your rights to an attorney?"

"I do," he responded.

We moved to the dining room table. I sat at the head, while Peter sat to my right, with Lucy following him. The oval table was a six-top. We removed the doylies from the top of the glass cover. Lucy recorded the time, the date, location and those present at this interrogation. Then, told me to conduct the questioning.

Gruntel sat there with his hands cuffed in front of him. He became introspective. His head was looking down, but it didn't seem he was focusing on anything. "Did you kill my brother?" He inquired in a somber tone.

Lucy looked at me. She was as surprised as I was to hear that question. "Excuse me?" I replied.

"My brother, was it you that killed him?" He asked, without raising his gaze.

"Are you referring to Special Agent Tony Belford?" I asked.

Still without looking up, but excited and raging, he asked, "Did you kill him?"

"No, Peter. I did not kill Tony Belford."

His body relaxed, he took a deep breath, keeping his gaze down. "You and Peter were brothers?"

He whispered, "Yes."

"Was your father Reverend Thomas Stiles? Peter's stepfather?"

"No, I'm the firstborn of Richard Belford."

"So, you and Peter had the same father?" "And, the same mother, Annamarie Belford."

"Your father died when Tony was one-year-old, correct?"

Still looking down, he grinned and said, "My father was poisoned and died, yes. Tony was one, and I was nine."

Lucy's eyes were about to pop out as we exchanged glances. "You said, he was poisoned?" I inquired.

"Rat poison."

"Did you," I paused, "did you kill him?"

He raised his gaze and looked at me. His eyes were hollow, "Our mother had a knack for marrying perverts. He started molesting me when I was five. Four years I took it until I could no longer contain my hate. Yes, I killed him. Only wish I could've had done it sooner."

"How old were you when your mother divorced him?"

"My mother was screwing with Reverend Thomas, and my father found out. So, he used that to make me part of the settlement when they divorced, and he agreed to keep it quiet so that the Reverend wouldn't be embarrassed. I was six years old."

"Where are you guys from?'

"Bethlehem, New York, just south of Albany."

"What happened after the death of your father?"

"The Gruntels, Alicia and Robert adopted me."

"How did that work out?"

"Very nice people. God-fearing family. Raised me correctly and put me through law school."

"When did you and Tony meet?"

"Tony left his home when he was sixteen, I think. He moved in with our maternal grandparents. They told him about my existence, and he looked me up. I was twenty-four, or five."

"Did you know he killed your mother and his stepfather?" Peter chuckled, "I told him what to do, and how to do it."

"You were present when he did it?"

He glanced at me. "Wouldn't miss it for anything in the world. How did you know?"

"You guys took what your mother did personal. Blamed her for what happened to you both."

"And you wouldn't? She stood by, allowing both her husbands to abuse her sons while she fucked around town."

"The shot to the face signified an emotional reaction," I said.

"I wished we had had two guns. Believe me, I would have shot her myself."

"Peter, tell me about the serial killings. How were you involved?"

He sighed, shook his head, and replied, "Might as well. Can I have some water?"

After a few moments, we reconvene in the dining room. Lucy took a minute to call Captain Johnson. He would come over with Detectives Farnsworth and Charles.

Lucy had the recorder going again.

I asked, "Peter, tell us about the serial killings."

"Tony confessed to me his obsession with the extreme sex. He also confessed to the satisfaction of killing these women. He said it felt like killing our mother repeatedly."

"When did you start?"

"Chicago."

"How did you select your victims?"

"We both did it. He did in Chicago since he lived there. Once he had chosen the lady, he followed her to make sure they lived alone, and that there were few cameras or potential for witnesses."

"Then what?"

"He would entice them with the extreme sex idea, and if they agreed, they would go back to her place."

"And they didn't have a problem with you showing up?"

He moved uncomfortably in the chair. "Mancuso, I know I don't look handsome. I'm skinny like a rail, big ears, my big rim glasses don't help," he paused, glanced at Lucy, looked back at me, smiled and continued, "but I'm extremely well endowed. Believe me, extremely."

I glanced at Lucy and while she was an African American; she was turning beet red, *rosso come un peperone.* I rolled my eyes.

He noticed the roll of my eyes, "You doubt me? You want to see?"

Lucy had been quiet, but she snapped, "Keep it zipped."

I held back from laughing, "So, what you're saying, the ladies had second thoughts, but once they saw your Super Johnson, they acquiesced?"

"Exactly, they could see it would be like a once in a lifetime experience."

I was thinking of Harriet outside. Was she having a once in a life- time experience regularly?

"Why kill them?"

"It was killing our mother over and over."

"That's what Tony felt, and that's what he told you. You, I think you are simply a psychopath. And you're going away for the rest of your life."

"I didn't kill anyone."

"Really. So, you're going with Tony did it. What? You watched?"

"I didn't kill anyone."

"Fine. I have one more question," I hesitated. "What about."

"Marcy, why abduct her?"

"Your Marcy? It obsessed my brother with her. Frankly, if she had returned the attention to him, I think he would have been done with the killings."

"That's bullshit. You're saying Marcy was the antidote to his personality disorders. All that hate and rage you both have inside of you would be over? Sorry, I don't buy that. You're both psychopaths and murderers. Marcy was simply an excuse to continue the killings."

We packed Peter Gruntel in the detective's car and had them take him back to New York City.

Now, I felt it solved the Manhattan Red Ribbon murders for real. What a screwed-up pair of brothers these were. Unfortunately, they suffered as children, and yes that experience influenced their behavior. But becoming serial killers was a choice they made.

Captain Johnson was on the phone with the NYPD Chief, who would report to the NYPD Commissioner, and then the New York City Mayor could have his press conference.

Father Dominic had spoken to Patrick, Agnes, and Angela, bringing them up to date.

I called Marcy. "*Marcela, ¿mi amor, que pasa?* How are you?"

"Doing good, feeling good. Are you coming over?"

"I can if you want me to?"

"You want me to beg?"

"I wouldn't want you to take over my role. No begging required. I'm over in Paramus, so give me a little to get there."

"I'll get some food. Hungry?"

"You're getting Cuban?"

"No, I had plenty of that in Miami. How about Italian from Vinnie?"

"I'm in. Say hello to Vinnie."

"See you soon. Oh, and Mancuso."

"Yes?"

"I picked the rings, and I spoke to Father Dom. We have our date all set."

I got euphoric, palpitations followed. Two years in the making, and I was finally going to marry my soulmate?"

"Mancuso, are you still there?" Marcy asked. "That's significant news.

I'm on my way. Love you."

CHAPTER 40

Two weeks had gone by, and I had moved back in with Marcy. Preparations were on their way to the wedding. I was living the dream. Two more days, and we would be Mr. and Mrs. Mancuso.

My only concern was that she was having nightmares and had become, on occasions, very irritable. Furthermore, her angry outburst in my estimation, were uncalled for.

Marcy had lost interest and postponed the FBI's firearms test until after our honeymoon. After seeing her pump, the shotgun in Miami, I had no concerns that she could pass the test with no issues.

Finally, I approached her and air my concerns after dinner one evening in her apartment.

"How are you feeling?" I asked, enjoying an after-dinner drink together.

"I feel great, Baby. Why do you ask?"

"Your nightmares, occasional outburst of anger. And, I think you've lost interest in getting your job back."

She looked at me with a somber look. "I'm suffering from the stress of the wedding. I'll be fine after we both say, '*I do.*' You'll see. Think about it, we have tried to tie the knot twice, and what has happened? Both times something terrible happened to one of us. So, it's anxiety, my love."

"I can see that. I just want you to feel great and happy about what we're doing."

"Thank you, but there's nothing I'm looking more forward to than our wedding. Hang in there, Giuseppe, let's do this."

—THE END—

EPILOGUE

St. Helen's Church looked beautiful the day of our wedding. Associate Pastor Father Dominic O'Brian was smiling from ear to ear.

Marcy was beaming with excitement. Her wedding dress was magnificent. Alberto, her stepdad, was to walk her down the aisle.

We had thought of having our reception at The Plaza, but at the last minute, we opted for Captain O'Brian's Pub. A little tacky perhaps, but it was a place we loved to be. And a hell of a lot cheaper.

After our first night at The Plaza, we were heading to the Cheeca Lodge at mile marker 81, in Islamorada, Florida Keys.

I had never felt happier than after I said, "I do."

A NOTE FROM OWEN

Thank you for taking the time to read the first three novels of the Joey Mancuso Crime Mysteries. I trust you enjoyed it.

My thanks:

The many experts, attorneys, and law enforcement personnel that assisted me with the research. As I always say, despite the research, I may have taken some liberties, and any mistakes, or inconsistencies are my own.

All authors appreciate reviews on their works, and I would appreciate yours on Amazon.com. Thank you again.

Please visit my website at www.owenparr.com, or

Amazon.com/author/owenparr, for my other titles, and the next Mancuso, O'Brian Crime Mystery Novel.

We welcome your comments and suggestions. Please write to us at: owen@owenparr.com and be sure to visit our website: www.owenparr.com

I donated partial proceeds from all my books on a monthly basis to Wounded Warrior Project

(https://www.woundedwarriorproject.org/) and The Gary Sinise Foundation (https://www.garysinisefoundation.org/).

We would appreciate your support to these two and other charities in helping our soldiers, first responders, and their families. Thank you.

Other titles by Owen Parr

Operation Due Diligence. An Alpha Team Spy Thriller -Vol 1
Operation Black Swan. An Alpha Team Spy Thriller -Vol 2
Operation Raven— The Dead Have Secrets - An Alpha Team Spy Thriller -Vol 3

A Murder on Wall Street —A Joey Mancuso, Father O'Brian Crime Mystery –Vol 1
A Murder on Long Island —A Joey Mancuso, Father O'Brian Crime Mystery –Vol 2
The Manhattan Red Ribbon Killer —A Joey Mancuso, Father O'Brian Crime Mystery -Vol 3
The Case of the Antiquities Collector —A Joey Mancuso, Father O'Brian Crime Mystery -Vol   4
The Murder of Paolo Mancuso —A Joey Mancuso, Father O'Brian Crime Mystery —Vol 5
The Abduction of Patient Zero—A Joey Mancuso, Father O'Brian Crime Mystery —Vol 6
The UNSUB —A Joey Mancuso, Father O'Brian Crime Mystery — Vol 7
THE LABYRINTH —A Joey Mancuso, Father O'Brian Crime Mystery — Vol 8.

Jack Ryder Crime Mystery -Novellas 1, 2 & 3. The Case of the Dead Russian Spy, Murder Aboard a Cruise to Nowhere, Murder at the Beach Cove Hotel.
How to Sell, Manage Your Time, Overcome Fear of Rejection —A non-fiction, Self-Improvement Book

All titles are available at Amazon.com, BarnesandNoble.com, and other online retailers and on as audiobooks at Audible.com

Made in the USA
Coppell, TX
09 October 2021